FOR EVERYTHING A REASON

PAUL CAVE

2QT Limited (Publishing)

First edition published 2010

2QT Limited (Publishing)

Burton In Kendal

Cumbria LA6 1NJ

www.2qt.co.uk

Cover design Hilary Pitt

Images sourced by iStockphoto.com

Printed in Great Britain by Lightning Source UK Ltd

A CIP catalogue record for this book is
available from the British Library

ISBN 978-0-9562368-9-0

In loving memory of mum . . .

Chapter One

Madison Square Garden was packed to the rafters with thousands of spectators baying for blood. Some were standing out of their seats, tossing abuse or empty soda cups towards the centre of the arena. Others remained seated, though their wish to see pain and suffering was just as burning. A small contingent sat near the centre of the arena, with shoulders hunched and nervous eyes watching as the large crowd headed towards lunacy. The whole stadium felt as if it was about to ignite, hatred and hostility fashioning themselves into real chemical components, the combination of the two forming a deadly explosive cocktail. A dozen or so stewards watched on anxiously, positioning themselves among the frenzied mob, praying the aggression would end soon.

Joseph Ruebins stood in the heart of the maelstrom, sweat dripping from his brow, lungs filling themselves to capacity. Across the boxing ring another tower of a man ambled his way over to a corner, and then sat heavily on an undersized stool. Instantly he was swamped by three of his corner-men: a trainer, a cut-man, and an unfortunate soul there to catch mouthfuls of spit in a small bucket.

"What are you waiting for, Kid? A written invitation?" a grizzled voice snarled.

Joseph Ruebins turned towards the speaker. His coach, Eugene Profit, a small old ex-pro, shoved all of Joseph's 200 pounds down onto his stool with surprising ease.

"What the hell are you doing out there? Sleeping?" Profit asked.

"Huh?" Joseph gasped, barely able to draw breath. His mouth was full of stringy spittle and thick plastic. Profit reached up and ripped the plastic gumshield free, almost taking the top row of Joseph's teeth with it.

"Water!" Profit demanded.

A spray bottle appeared between them. Profit took it and began to pump. Now both sweat and water covered Joseph's face, turning his features into a spotted mask of ebony. He dropped his head to allow the water to cascade over his head. A peppering of black and greying hair dotted his shaven scalp. He leaned back against the padded corner and reigned in his breathing.

"The guy's got a slab of granite for a chin," Joseph said. For such an imposing size his voice was barely above a whisper.

Profit snapped, "You're fighting like a goddamn amateur."

Joseph shook his head defensively. "No. He's really tough."

"Bullshit!"

"Hey, there are four rounds left. Why don't *you* give it a try?" He held out his gloved hands and pushed them into the old coach's chest, leaving two red smears of his opponent's blood. Joseph himself was untouched – not a single bruise or cut, nor even the slightest graze, marked his dark skin.

Profit snarled out a rosary of expletives and pushed Joseph's gloves away. "Listen, Kid. I ain't a fool. Something's happening here that you ain't telling me."

Joseph opened his mouth to tell him all was fine, but closed it again without saying a single word. What could he say? That he was done fighting? At thirty-eight he was well past his best. His waistline had lost some of its shape, degenerating from an impressive six-pack of muscle into a soft roll of flesh. The flamboyant shorts he wore, with the embroidered words: *Joe 'The Jaw-Breaker' Ruebins,* were three inches too high, and almost touched his nipples when he sat down. He was still a formidable size, but the once youthful body of lean muscle had been replaced by a tired middle-aged physique that had seen better years. His biceps were the only remnants of his earlier days, two solid lumps of steel, which endowed him with the strength of a crazed bull.

In truth he could have ended this fight within the first two rounds. But for what reason? A shot at the title? To become World Champion!

Joseph Ruebins had already decided that tonight he would retire. This was his last fight. His swan song. He'd been fighting since he was eighteen – six years as an amateur, fourteen as a pro. Twenty long years of pain and sacrifice were more than enough for any one man to suffer through. Now, the only thing that drove Joseph on was the thought of his family. His wife Marianna and their son Jake sat at the ringside, enduring it with him.

Joseph chanced a look over at the boy, tipped forwards on his chair, focused totally on his father. One of his small hands clasped his mother's, as much for her sake as for his, the other clenched into a tight fist. The tirade of foul language seemed to wash off him, unable to stick, so close to the protection of his father. Jake grinned as he caught his father's gaze: A huge toothy grin. He was small for his age, barely over four feet and already seven years old. He was handsome to be sure; his smile, a brilliant burst of sunshine, which never failed to warm Joseph's heart – even now, when it seemed the entire world was baying for his blood.

Jake's grin widened. He shook his fist and then jabbed it upwards above his head. "Man of Steel," he mouthed.

Joseph nodded.

Four weeks earlier, he and Jake were shooting hoops at the side of the house. Jake had been beside himself, already three baskets up on his father, and more to come. It was the middle of winter and they'd first had to shovel all the snow away. They were dressed in hats, scarves and thick overcoats. Joseph was lunging and sliding about like a demented fool, giving Jake all the advantage.

Halfway through the game, Marianna returned home, parking their modest Sedan in front of the garage. She beeped the horn and offered them a wave. Joseph paused to wave back, while his son scooted around him to score yet another basket. Five-one. Marianna laughed, and Joseph made a huge show of disappointment. Activating the garage door, Marianna found the winter tools piled untidily at the entrance. She climbed out of the car, asking Joseph to park it in the garage and reminding them both to clean up.

"Okay, sweetheart," Joseph said.

They returned to their game, working up large appetites and enjoying the afternoon sun. Just before Jake scored the winning basket, the ball slipped from his small fingers and bounced over by the car. Joseph dashed after it, swinging his arms about like a crazed bear. Then, unexpectedly, his foot slipped on a patch of ice. The swinging of his arms was now for real as he windmilled towards the hood of the Sedan. What stopped him was the edge of the open garage door. He clattered into it head-on, shaking the whole structure down to its foundations.

"Dad! Dad!" Jake called, finding his father stunned.

"I'm okay," Joseph reassured him, his head spinning.

Seeing that his father was okay, Jake then burst into a fit of laughter. "Silly Dad!"

Joseph prodded the egg that had begun to grow from his forehead. Just a heck of a swelling, nothing too serious.

"Stupid! Stupid!" Jake teased.

Joseph laughed, too, relieved it was only a bump, embarrassed by the fall, yet amused by his son's enjoyment.

Jake fell quiet. His gaze turned upwards. The garage door had not only taken the full impact of his father's head, but it had also bent right down the middle. A distinctive crease ran from front to back. The door had come off second best. Jake looked at his father through astounded eyes. Then he tore off, yelling, "Mom! Mom! Dad's really Superman!"

Now, remembering the battered door, Joseph and Jake stared at each other, the unfriendly world around them instantly gone. Once again, Jake punched his fist upwards, as if the gesture could launch him up to the roof of the Garden.

"Man of Steel," Jake mouthed again.

"Listen, kid, if you don't do something soon, then we'll both have us a new ass to crap out of," Profit warned, bringing Joseph back to the moment and the crowd reaching fever-pitch, just as the ninth round readied to begin. "They'll tear us a new one for sure."

Joseph nodded. If only for the sake of his wife and Jake, he couldn't allow this to go on much longer. He opened his mouth and allowed a long spray of water to quench his thirst.

"Okay," Joseph said, "what do you suggest?"

Profit grinned maliciously. "Knock his block off!"

Joseph shook his head in slight amusement. Profit would be getting twenty-five percent of his purse. Not a bad payday for someone of such limited instruction.

"Guess I'll do just that," he said, climbing off his stool.

The timekeeper bellowed, "Corners, ten seconds!"

Profit stepped through the ropes. He snatched the gumshield from one of the other corner-men and jammed it in Joseph's mouth. "Remember the plan. Knock his block off!"

Joseph began to shake the stiffness from his legs, kicking them out, readying himself for the next three minutes. At the opposite side of the ring, his opponent stood on unsteady legs. His face was bloodied and swollen, a result of Joseph's sticking left jab. A deep cut had opened up just above the right eyebrow. Now that his corner-men had applied adrenaline, the wound had stopped bleeding, leaving instead an open, raw tear.

Eddie Wolfe – The Warrior from Queens – looked as if someone had beaten him with a baseball bat. The curly, once-auburn hair on his chest was now a deep shade of crimson. His previously white shorts had turned pink, blood and sweat mixing to form a blossoming stain. His arms looked too heavy to carry, as if the padding in his gloves had been replaced by iron or lead. And now, such an advantage as horseshoe-lined gloves would be the only realistic way of Eddie Wolfe dispatching his opponent. The last thing keeping him upright, Joseph figured, was the baying of the crowd and the fear of failure. In all, he looked like a man who'd just collided with a Mack truck.

"Seconds out. Round nine!" called the timekeeper.

Joseph moved away from his corner, raising his arms high in a defensive position. Eddie Wolfe reluctantly stepped forward, looking like a man heading towards the gallows. They met in the centre of the ring, two mythological Titans doomed to do battle.

Joseph circled to his left. Even though his opponent had offered little to worry about, Joseph was still wary of the Warrior's left hook – a single punch that had served Eddie Wolfe throughout his long career, but had had little effect so far tonight. A shrewd and seasoned fighter, Joseph was the master craftsman, able to dictate the natural flow of the fight to his advantage. Like a lumbering giant, Eddie Wolfe followed Joseph around the ring.

Joseph threw a left jab. The punch knocked the Warrior's head back and a gout of fresh blood burst from his flattened nose. A collective gasp rolled in from the back of the stands to the front. Joseph leaned in, jabbing his opponent in the stomach. In an almost comical display, Eddie Wolfe folded in on himself, his arms shooting out together and the air exploding from his lungs with an audible *whoosh*. Sensing that his opponent had weakened, Joseph stepped forward, intent on delivering a crushing right cross to the chin. However, as he moved in for the kill, the unthinkable happened.

Joseph blinked and the huge arena went dark. He paused, his arm pulled back, waiting to be released. Then his gloved right hand began to drop. His right leg went instantly numb, as if it had been cut off just below the hip. He staggered, still in darkness, and then fell to his knees.

Eddie Wolfe looked up, drawing air into his lungs, as a deep and sickening ache spread across his bruised solar plexus. He shook his head in an attempt to clear the fog. Through his swollen eyes, he looked upon his opponent's fist, about to land the killer punch. In a sudden shifting of fates, Joe *'The Jaw-breaker'* Ruebins stopped. The right side of his face collapsed, turning his mouth into a macabre slash. Then, as if an invisible punch had landed against the left side of his head, he fell sideways, tottered for a second and collapsed to his knees. Seizing the moment, the Warrior from Queens sent a crashing left hook to the side of Joseph's head.

Eddie watched, as in a twitching helpless heap, Joseph fell to the canvas. And, in the next second, the crowd around him launched itself into a savage frenzy.

Chapter Two

Silence engulfed Joseph Ruebins. He lay motionless, arms draped across his chest, in a funeral pose. The right side of his face hung slack, a symptom of the debilitating stroke he'd suffered. In contrast to his right side, his left cheek had swelled into a dark ball of agony, and the eye was almost sealed shut, now just a tight slit. A white shaft of sunlight cut through the room, dousing Joseph's misshapen face in a harsh glow.

"You should get some rest," a grizzled old voice advised.

Marianna looked up, her face tired and drawn. "I'll stay," she said. Her attention returned to Joseph. Her dark fingers continued to run across the smooth skin of his brow.

Eugene Profit shuffled uneasily. "What about the boy?"

Marianna's gaze shifted to the small boy, curled up alongside the still form of her husband. Jake snored softly. The events of the previous evening had worn him out, and now he slept peacefully in the close comfort of his father. "We should let him sleep," she said.

Profit glanced from the boy to the face of the silent giant and sighed. What the hell had happened last night?

The promise of victory had quickly turned to defeat. Profit had been on his feet, both hands gripped tightly onto the ropes of the boxing ring, when Joseph collapsed.

"Knock his block off!" he cried.

Joseph pulled his arm back, ready to deliver the finishing blow. Then he paused, blinking uncontrollably, before falling onto one knee. The Warrior from Queens had seized his chance, landing a vicious left hook on his opponent's head. And, as Joseph slammed to the canvas in a twitching heap, the crowd had launched itself into a triumphant rage. Two minutes later, however, they'd been stunned into silence.

"Hurry!" Profit called, as the ringside doctor finally made his way into the ring.

Marianna was kneeling beside the old coach, Joseph's head cradled gently in her lap. Jake stayed just inside the ring, one of the other trainers holding the boy back.

It had taken almost twenty agonising minutes for the paramedics to arrive and a further ten to securely tether Joseph to a stretcher. The once-hostile crowd had now become a mass of concerned faces, but offered nothing but hindrance as they gathered in front of the small group, who were eager to rush Joseph to the nearest hospital. With a single bark of annoyance, Marianna had sent them scattering for the four exits, clearing a path for the gurney.

Now Marianna continued to caress her husband's face, the nightmare of last night a jumbled mess of confused thoughts.

"Maybe I should see what's keeping that doctor," Profit said.

She nodded. "Okay." In truth, she wasn't too sure if she wanted to hear what the neurosurgeon had to say. Uncertainty had begun to gnaw away at hope, little by little, leaving only fear and frustration. The old coach backed quietly out of the room in search of the doctor.

Marianna's attention returned to her husband's face. His eyes twitched slightly under their lids, and she felt her hope swell, restored by this tiny indication of life. If his thoughts still ran, even in darkness, then at least that in itself was an indication of brain activity. She'd had many nightmares over the years involving Joseph receiving a cerebral injury, and now that fear was real.

***

9

The darkness before Joseph's eyes had become impenetrable, so much so that he thought for a moment his soul had been launched into space, forced to roam for all eternity, lonely and lost. He felt as if he'd been trapped in this bleak universe for what seemed like an aeon, and had now started to wonder if he'd actually entered the Great Beyond, only to find it lifeless and empty.

***

Struggling to breathe, Marianna stood and moved towards the window. She parted the drapes further, which allowed a magnificent burst of sunlight to fill the room. She looked down at the passers-by and wondered how many of them were at the mercy of their own burden of grief. She slid the window open as far as the track allowed. Cold air billowed in, turning her dark hair into a living black scarf. The coolness helped to dispel some of the unwanted tension.

***

Something brushed past Joseph's face: A breath. He inhaled deeply, surprised and excited by the unexpected sensation. How could it be? Trapped in this dark void, another equally surprising sensation stirred his consciousness.
The sounds of music.

***

Marianna turned away from the window, the faintest hint of song drifting in from some workman's distant radio. She returned to her husband's side and found him motionless. Not even his eyes moved. Now a solid ebony statue, only the rise and fall of his chest gave any indication he was still alive.

***

Joseph focused his attention on the noise. It came from far away, barely discernable in the rushing cacophony of silence. The darkness that surrounded him split, tearing open in front and behind. Two blinding lights exploded, one on each side of him. Multiple white lines, running in parallel to each other, appeared from one of these lights, snaking towards the other. The music increased, now clear and distinct, and Joseph recognised the clash of guitars and bass. A chain of shapes broke through the farthest tear, seemingly linked together, rushing in the same direction as the white lines. At first they posed a mystery, strange symbols and complicated swirls, but then Joseph realised they were the components of written music. Making up one continuous chain, treble and bass clefs, quavers and semi-quavers, rests and crotchets, careered towards Joseph, riding the lines of the stave like a never-ending freight train. As the combination of notes and signs drew closer, the once melodic sound became a rushing boom of thunder.

The lines snaked towards Joseph, and for one terrible second he thought they were about to rip into him. But no, they twisted away and continued towards the second open rift. Joseph became aware of his own substance. On impulse, he reached out towards the musical notes, and felt unexpectedly pulled towards them. A double quaver raced past him, sending a pulse of energy through his spirit-like body. More signs and notes rushed by in a dizzying blur. With startling clarity, he knew this magical ride had been sent to collect him. He reached out again, this time snagging a semi-quaver, and felt himself pulled along.

The note he rode turned brittle. It began to crumble, pieces breaking away, disappearing into darkness. Joseph began to panic. At this speed, he knew that if he lost his grip, he would be sent spinning into oblivion. He chanced a look behind and spotted the twists and turns of a treble clef. Leaping away from the disintegrating note, he landed awkwardly on the hurtling sign. He slipped and almost fell clear, but with grim determination held on. Soon, though, the clef too began to fragment.

***

Marianna looked up from her husband's face. The noise outside had changed in pitch and amplitude. A grating noise, rasping like the lungs of an asthmatic, drowned out the music and shook the open window. Marianna stood up, intent on shutting out the dreadful noise.

***

Now hanging from the top of a double quaver, Joseph leapt across the void and landed on a vibrating crotchet. Without warning, the notes and signs had become an explosion of movement, not only travelling forwards at breakneck speed, but also vibrating up and down violently, as if the lines they rode had been plucked like the strings of a guitar. Joseph chanced a look ahead. What he saw made him whimper like a terrified child. The rift had begun to shrink. Notes struck the sides, shattering instantly in a shower of gleaming white ceramic. Joseph knew now that if he didn't make it to the opening, he would become trapped in this abyss forever.

***

The window opened out an inch, just enough to allow the clatter of music to filter through. The door swung shut, turning Marianna's thoughts away from the troublesome noise outside. A young, pretty nurse had entered, carrying a clipboard and chart underneath her arm.

***

*****

The nurse stepped back from the foot of the bed, her initial job completed. She frowned slightly, something clearly beginning to bother her. "What's that god-awful racket?" she asked, her attention drawn to the window. She stepped past Marianna and reached out, intent on shutting out the annoying sound.

"Wait!" Marianna said, stopping the nurse's arm short.

"What is it?" she asked, concern written across her face.

Marianna stepped closer to the hospital bed. "I-I thought I saw something."

"What?" the nurse asked eagerly.

Marianna bent over her husband. A faint exhalation of air was the only real sign of life. Then, just as it had happened moments earlier, Joseph's eyebrow ticked upwards. "There!" she said, pointing towards his face. The nurse joined her at the bedside, and the noise outside was momentarily forgotten.

"I don't see anything."

"Wait," Marianna said.

Together they stood silently. For the third time Joseph's eyebrow jumped, causing the smooth skin of his forehead to crease.

"Did you see it?"

"Yes," the nurse replied. "But it may not mean anything, just a reaction, possibly from a dream or something else."

"Something else?" Marianna parroted.

"Okay, I'll inform the doctor," she said on her retreat to the door.

***

The light was so close now that Joseph could actually feel heat radiating from it. The sign he held onto had disintegrated to little more than a fist-sized rock. With only feet remaining, he watched as the three central lines pulled together, contracting sharply to fit through the tiny gap. He threw away the white rock and gripped the two outer lines. Laying his head tightly against the line in the middle, he closed his eyes and then held his breath. His clenched hands were pulled together, until barely inches apart. One final look upwards revealed that the light had dwindled to the size of a mailbox. Joseph had one terrifying moment to think he'd never fit through, especially his ample gut, before fire burnt at his knuckles.

"OOOhhhh shit..!" he cried, as the rest of his body caught fire.

In the next instant he was through.

***

And once again, silence.

Pain stabbed at his eyes. He squinted, surprised by the sensation, the light source harsher than the one he'd just witnessed. Something shifted above him, a dark silhouette, and unexpectedly, he was confronted by his wife's beautiful face. She looked tired, dark circles under her eyes. Two clear rivers of tears sprang from them, which ran down the fine contours of her face, before coming together at the tip of her

14

elegant chin.

She watched as his mouth opened slightly, just the left side under his control, and a thick stream of saliva pooled out onto his shoulder. He grinned sheepishly. With his swollen left side and his slack right, he could have put Quasimodo to shame. Yet, as Marianna looked down at his battered and distorted face, she thought it was by far the most beautiful she had ever seen.

Chapter Three

Ice-cold wind bit into exposed flesh with the same conviction as cruel fangs. This, the coldest day of the month, had sprouted vicious teeth and nails, which would have given any beast from the Jurassic Age a run for its money. Winter held on with unsympathetic malevolence. The branches of the trees that lined the streets and avenues were burdened with frost – stark white limbs reaching desperately towards the washed-out February sun. In some places, patches of grey snow lingered on colourless swathes of frozen land, out of reach of the sun and children alike.

The remnants of snowmen lurked along sidewalks; obese sentinels watching the hub of New York City go about its business. Like a superhuman heart, Manhattan Island pumped people into its core – millions of corpuscles, each charged with enthusiasm – held them there momentarily, and then sent them home, worn-out and defused. Wrapped in long scarves, thick overcoats and insulated boots, the city's inhabitants rushed home in the early-evening twilight, eager to take refuge from the biting wind.

In stark contrast to the freezing horrors of outside, indoors was a warm haven, which offered sanctuary to both saints and sinners, irrespective of whether their hearts were filled with innocence or murderous intent.

The aroma of the bowl of stew beneath Thomas Carter's nose barely registered. Small, unidentifiable pieces of god-knows-what floated on the surface and seemed to avoid Carter's spoon, no matter how hard he tried to scoop them up. A crusty bread roll lay untouched beside the bowl. Carter eyed it with uncertainty. The roll looked stale enough to have come from some recently unearthed Egyptian tomb. Dark crumbs dotted the bread intermittently, reminding him of sand. He'd read somewhere that ancient Egyptians had mixed fine sand with dough in an attempt to make supplies of flour go further, before offering it to unsuspecting slaves.

"Are you gonna eat that?" someone at his side asked.

A dreadful stench wafted towards Carter. He turned to his right and found a wrinkled old face looking at him expectantly. The old man's head bobbed towards the crust, his hooked nose almost close enough to peck at it.

"Gonna eat it, or what?" the man asked. Blackened gums barely retained one or two yellowed teeth, and the choking stench of rotten breath assaulted Carter's nose.

"Take it," Carter said.

Fingers that hadn't seen soap or water in a long time scooped up the roll and then began to tear it into more manageable pieces.

Sandwiched between two ragged tramps, Carter turned back to the bowl of stew in front of him. He continued to trawl for the few lumpy bits on the surface half-heartedly, his belly still full from the meal he'd eaten in the comfort of his uptown apartment. Consciously aware that he had not started eating, he raised a spoonful of the watery stew to his lips.

Fire erupted inside his mouth. Tongue, gums and throat screamed with the unexpected bite of the clear liquid. It was then he realised that the dish before him was basically hydrated pepper. He looked around the table, expecting others to be fanning open mouths or grabbing for the jugs of cloudy water dotted around the table. Everyone else was spooning mouthful after mouthful of this fiery broth into gaping mouths without complaint. Carter shook his head, understanding why. Most of the people in the room had the desperate look of chronic alcoholics. Bright red bulbous noses, eyes that seemed incapable of focusing, no matter how hard they tried, and that slight nervous tic that accompanied most hardened drinkers, reminded him that his fellow diners were the unwanted, unseen community of New York City's homeless. People who lived day-by-day on a diet of small handouts, neat whisky and narcotics.

A feeling of pity washed over him. Not a condescending demonstration of fake compassion, but the honest sincerity of someone who was witness to the lowest depravations of man.

"Not hungry?" the tramp at Carter's right asked. The guy's bowl had been licked clean, and all that was left of the bread roll were the few crumbs sticking in his tangled beard.

Carter looked down at his bowl. He had barely touched his stew. For a second, he battled between an uneasy feeling of looking out of place and a sense of guilt.

The tramp's clothes looked about ready to split at the seams, just dirt and grime holding them together, and his eyes were deep and hollow. Those eyes contained a desperate yearning that would not be satisfied by the offer of a thousand bowls of stew.

Unwilling to give the tramp his meal, Carter grumbled a warning then hunched over his bowl. He cringed slightly, expecting the guy to launch into an uncontrollable rage. Ten seconds passed; nothing happened. An eagerness to get out of this desperate place drew Carter's thoughts away from the bowl before him, and his eyes towards the door marked 'EXIT'. His gaze settled on a small doorway leading to the only washroom. As if he was suddenly in danger of fouling himself, he offered a surprised look of agony, stood clutching at the seat of his pants, and then quickly tottered towards the doorway.

He'd barely taken three steps before the homeless guy reached over to take the bowl of stew. A black man opposite him chuckled, revealing a mouthful of pink gums. He muttered, "Crazy asshole," then returned to the half-empty bowl in front of him.

In the washroom, Carter breathed a long sigh of relief.

Now was not the time for mistakes. He'd only get one shot at this. And he needed to be sure his target stayed oblivious to his presence.

Presley Perkins had been a hard man to find – not at all surprising, considering the amount of shit he'd gotten himself into. A two-bit loser, with barely the sense that God had given him, Perkins had somehow managed to remain out of sight for almost three months now. He'd seemed to have left town, leaving behind him the aftermath of a despicable act of violence.

Carter knew better. Perkins was still here in the city, somewhere.

The guy didn't have the smarts to leave. Stupid to the nth degree, Presley Perkins should have been born with the word 'Loser' tattooed on his forehead. Son of a slumlord, the sad fuck had never travelled farther than the Eastside Express could take him. While the real estate boom of the 1980s had given the family a somewhat classier cachet — bad habits die hard. Old Man Perkins, called Don 'Dolly' Perkins, had a taste for greasy food, good booze, dumb cheap hookers and strippers with big chests and gold-digging ambitions, and, most of all, high stakes gambling. The moniker 'Dolly' was added to his name by his gangster buddies because he went through women like he did cocktail napkins. He also paid protection money to established Italian crime bosses to keep himself out of trouble. Black and Latino gangs and certain Eastern Bloc syndicates were constantly trying to expand their borders into Dolly's turf. Despite his substantial real estate earnings, his string of easy women and his big player lifestyle, running with the mob always tapped Dolly's cash-flow.

Presley Perkins possessed the additional bad luck of being named after his father's favourite musician and getting his mother's less than room temperature IQ. Dolly learned early on that Presley needed to be kept away from any of the Perkins money if there was going to be anything left at all.

That all changed the night Dolly moved on to the next world. His considerably high cholesterol count finally pushed his heart too far. He died in spectacular fashion, in the embrace of one of his paramours. Presley inherited his late father's wealth, and within just eighteen months had lost all of it. Slave to the roulette wheel, he'd gambled Dolly's fortune away, and had also found himself in debt to a Russian mafia boss to the tune of twenty-five grand. Now in serious trouble, he'd taken the only option left available to him.

These were the events that led to Presley standing at the counter of a convenience store, arm outstretched and pistol in hand. Head clad in a ski-mask, he was in the process of demanding a register full of cash, when, in a terrible stroke of bad luck, the door opened and a uniformed cop walked in. Cop and robber froze, both rooted to the spot, the unexpected presence of the other freezing each of them solid. Then, instinct taking over, the cop reached for his sidearm. Already at an advantage with his gun drawn, Presley squeezed off a shot first. The bullet caught the cop across his throat, nicking the carotid artery and sending a bright red spray of blood across the aisle.

It was the first time Presley had ever fired a gun.

He fled the scene empty-handed, with the stench of blood thick in his nostrils. Taking to the back alleyways, he stopped abruptly, the magnitude of what had just happened overwhelmingly apparent, and dropped the contents of his bowels, along with the firearm, which he hid unimaginatively in a half-filled dumpster. In simplest terms, Presley Perkins had sealed his fate by leaving behind him a big pile of steaming DNA for all to see.

Now, three months after the shooting, Thomas Carter lay in waiting, the moment of Presley's reckoning fast approaching. In an attempt to disappear, Presley had done the most obvious thing – hidden amongst the homeless. Not a bad plan in itself, but somewhat compromised by Perkins's occasional use of ATM machines. Six weeks after the shooting, small amounts had been withdrawn from Perkins' small savings account. Just enough for someone who was living on the streets to survive with the tiniest measure of comfort. It had been a simple case of triangulating the cash withdrawals and locating the nearest soup kitchen. What had been harder for Carter were the weeks trawling the underbelly of society in the hope of catching his quarry.

He took a deep breath, the stench in this windowless room almost overpowering. He moved towards the single cracked basin and drew water from the one remaining tap. Cold water snapped at his fingers with an icy bite. He cupped his hand and then ran the water over his forehead.

"Almost time," he said, taking another long breath, using the ice-cold water to help focus his thoughts.

Raising his head, he caught his reflection in the dirty mirror, which hung crookedly before him. His heavy jowls had a peppering of brown and white whiskers, a symptom of not having shaved for the last three days, and his naturally curly hair looked grey and unruly. His eyes were red-rimmed and tired – and if they were to be considered the windows to his soul, then Thomas Carter was a haunted man. He looked ten years older than his actual forty-four, and his air of wild desperation made him seem anything but out of place among the bedraggled mob eating outside.

He stepped away from the mirror and cracked open the door. The chaotic noise from the room beyond flooded in, a clamour of scraping bowls and unsatisfied stomachs. Carter scanned the crowd. Amid the hollowed-out and desperate faces, one stood out. Presley Perkins sat less than twelve feet away, his newly grown beard dripping with soup, his once manicured fingernails now blackened and chipped.

Thomas Carter drew his weapon, a small Smith & Wesson snub nose revolver. He opened the cylindrical loader to count the brass shells. Without actually looking, he knew that five remained. He'd counted them many times over these last three months. He snapped the loader home, then flicked the safety off with his thumb. The gun felt familiar to him, even though it had been found abandoned only months earlier. Tonight there would be no peaceful arrest or reading of rights, just a brutal finale to Presley Perkins's life. For tonight, Thomas Carter wasn't here on police business. No, tonight he had come as a grieving father, here to avenge the death of his son: a rookie police cadet who'd been shot and left bleeding to death.

Detective Thomas Carter pulled open the door and stepped back into the pandemonium of noise and clatter. Raising his arm, he took aim. Then, just as he was about to pull the trigger, all hell broke loose.

Chapter Four

Chairs scattered in all directions. The two tramps caught in the centre of this chaotic scene launched themselves towards each other, fists flying and teeth visible. This sudden and unexpected act of unrehearsed violence temporarily locked Carter's finger in place. He found himself unable to apply the pressure required to fire his weapon.

Rage burst from one of the tramp's lips. The other homeless guy backed away. His act of theft now seemed foolhardy and reckless. Still, the mouldy old bread roll stayed clasped between his grime-coated fingers, clutched protectively against his chest.

Carter maintained his position, his arm rigid, and the weapon's target fixed firmly within its sights. He felt an all-consuming hatred boil to the surface of his being, rage twisting his face into a ghastly contortion. His arm began to tremble uncontrollably and the weapon in his hand felt too heavy. He wrapped his other hand around it, forcing the short barrel to steady, channelling all of his pain and grief into an unbreakable chain of concentration. A deep, bestial whine rose from his gut, which was both agonising to hear and awful.

***

Presley Perkins sat just a few yards away, watching the bizarre confrontation before him, unaware of an even greater threat. Then, as one of the tramps moved forward, he spotted the detective. His blood turned cold. The worn-out face looked familiar, even though they had never met. It was a face that visited him every night, albeit younger, which haunted him from the darkest recesses of his mind.

As Perkins jumped to his feet, his chair fell backwards with a clatter. What he now faced made the two tramps fighting over a crust of bread seem almost comical.

Perkins' once expensive Italian shoes, now scuffed and torn, tangled within the overturned legs of his chair. He landed in a pathetic heap, scrambled up, and lurched toward the exit. From behind he heard a cough – barely audible over the ruckus. Just above his shoulder, a crater appeared in a puff of exploding masonry. He ducked instinctively as a second bullet slammed into the doorframe, launching a hail of splinters.

In the next instant he was outside. In contrast to the sombre interior of the soup kitchen the near-blinding brightness of the street was disorienting. Neon signs streaked the dark canvas of night in an ultraviolet splash of brilliant colours. Perkins heard the door behind him bang into place, and his brief paralysis broke. He tore down Southern Boulevard as if the hounds of hell themselves were snapping at his heels.

***

Carter pushed his way through the doorway and then skidded to a halt. To the left and right of him, a sea of multiracial faces expressed shock at the sudden appearance of a homeless gun-wielding lunatic. A scream drew his attention to the right. A young couple had been knocked to the pavement. Carter caught a flash of movement beyond them, and pursued.

***

The street took Presley Perkins in a wide arc, away from the busy sidewalk and towards the dark corridor of Tremont Avenue. The lights from a civilised world dwindled, and instead, Perkins found himself racing through a tight canopy of trees. Up ahead, two solid barriers blocked any further progress. In large letters, formed from moulded iron, were four words stencilled on a plaque, which sat at the top of the two gates.

Bronx Zoo: Asia Gate.

At this time of night the gates were sealed tight. A chain threaded itself through adjacent bars to keep out unwanted visitors. Perkins turned, his chest labouring under the exertion, and watched as a shadow not far behind him took shape. He whined hysterically. Then, belying his size and bulk, he began to climb the gates.

Fear pushed Perkins over the top. He landed on the other side and soon regained his footing, then ran deeper into the attraction that was *'Jungle World'*. Sounds that belonged to another land, not the heart of Manhattan Island, met him as he raced through the tangle of trees.

***

Carter hit the pavement. He scanned the way ahead in time to see Perkins disappear into the darkness farther up the trail. His hand tightened around the grip of his gun, he found comfort in its weight.

The trail funnelled towards an ominous black hole. It took Carter another few seconds to realise he was peering into an overturned and hollowed-out tree. Some unaffected part of his mind was impressed by the authenticity of the attraction. He entered the mouth of the tunnel and hurried through. Glimmers of light ignited at the periphery of his vision – bioluminescence? The earthy smell of his next breath told him the giant tree was not a clever plastic fake, but the actual remains of an uprooted forest tree. A thick clogging stench of mould filled his nostrils, and the sparkles of light revealed themselves to be glow-in-the-dark mushrooms.

Something else moved within the gloom, and the detective grimaced as a foot-long centipede marched along the curve of the inner wall, matching Carter step-for-step. He broke through the tunnel to find himself in the depths of a rain forest. Somewhere out of sight, the sounds of running water could be heard, possibly masking the sounds of other things that ran: feet. Carter stood still and strained against these strange noises. Up ahead came the slap of footfalls navigating a trail leading deeper into the thick undergrowth. The detective began to follow the path through the manmade jungle, home to an unknown number of possible nightmares.

***

Perkins' laboured breath reminded him of the wheeze of a rusty old steam pipe in one of his late father's old slums. His shoes slipped continuously on the small stones shifting under his feet. Next, a face broke through the trees to his right. A pair of luminous eyes locked onto him. Perkins threw his arms up instinctively, expecting the whip-crack of pistol fire. Instead, the small black and white face rocked to one side, and the creature clapped its furry hands together. Perkins remained rooted to the spot for another second. The little bastard swung out of the branches and dropped to the ground in front of him. Were monkeys carnivorous? Probably not, but that didn't stop his imagination from flashing terrible pictures of the flesh being torn off his bones.

He let out a nervous laugh and hurried along before the idea could be tested. The path opened out into a mock setting of a safari encampment. The bleat and hoot of recorded animal noises filled the night, and over that, a counterpoint of radios, speaking to each other in a hiss of metallic voices.

Footsteps echoed towards him. They were heavy and coming fast, and definitely not those made by a monkey.

Presley's chest tightened, his beating heart aware once more of real danger. He ran over to a table littered with binoculars, water canteen, radio, and mercifully – with the screech of animals growing louder - a rifle. He grabbed hold of the stock, but the rifle refused to budge. The fucking thing was glued to the table. A desperate whine burst from Perkins' lips. His attention turned instantly to the radio. That, too, was fixed firmly to the surface. The only movable parts were a large dial to change settings and a sliding volume control. Perkins fumbled with the latter, and the wild noises around him grew to a deafening pitch. Covering his ears, he spun on his heels and headed toward a nearby field tent, its entrance an open flap, like that of a hungry, gaping mouth.

***

The fine hairs at the nape of Carter's neck bristled. He froze at the sound of a ferocious roar. The guttural noise came again - close enough this time to hold him rigid on the spot. By the next repetition, he recognised the hollow, metallic quality to the roar – it was a recording, not one of nature's fiercest predators stalking him through the fake jungle.

The pathway gave way to an encampment. The only visible and hungry beast was the open maw of a tent.

"Perkins, you son of a bitch!" Carter yelled into the darkness, levelling his weapon towards the flap. Marshalling his resolve, he crossed the distance and stepped inside.

The tent was surprisingly bright thanks to a pair of lights at the rear, each casting a shine of electric blue. The entrance itself sat steeped in shadow. As Carter inched deeper inside, his feet crunched over glass. He chanced a glance down to see a pattern of sharp diamonds and white powder. More broken glass lay several feet away, directly beneath the remains of a light bulb still fixed within its socket.

"You in here?" he called.

A few bare tables and chairs loomed on the inside of the

tent; this part of the attraction possibly out of bounds to the public. Carter banged his thigh against the side of a table. Metal legs screeched out a warning. He halted his advance.

"Show yourself, you coward!"

Still no response came. Carter resumed his press forward. Then the sound of a laboured breath reached beyond the cadence of his racing heart. He faced its source and fired. The bullet tore through one of the tables, splitting it in two halves. As the table collapsed, the source of the noise revealed itself: four stumpy legs ending in a short snout. "Christ," Carter huffed.

The spotted pig tottered over to the detective and eagerly sniffed at his shoes. In the broken light, he saw that the animal's coat looked almost two sizes too big, the folds of brown and white flesh hanging off its body giving it the appearance of a walking concertina. The pig waddled to the rear of the tent, where it disappeared through a tear in the canvas. Carter followed it through.

He almost lost his footing as he emerged from the tent. The ground on the other side sloped away abruptly as it ran towards the edge of a concrete wall. Below him was an open enclosure, filled in places with a dark body of glistening water. The rest of the area was dotted with islands. On this side of the tent the air felt easily ten degrees cooler, as though winter had been bottled up in this one specific place.

Sprawled out on the ground in front of him in a foot or so of water, with arms and legs akimbo and surrounded by a flock of agitated penguins, was the object of Carter's search. Perkins took a backwards swipe at one of the short-winged birds; the penguin hopped effortlessly out of the way. Another stepped forward, its white chest puffed out in a show of angry defiance. Perkins scrambled to his feet before kicking at the little birds and scattering them to the edge of the pool.

Carter took aim and yelled, "Perkins!"

Perkins turned his attention from the penguins to his

pursuer, and slowly raised his arms in surrender.

Fresh anger surged through Carter's blood. "You killed my son!"

Perkins shifted from one leg to the other, as if they threatened to give out on him at any moment. "It was an accident," he said. Even to his own ears, the response sounded pathetic, pointless.

"Accident?" Carter parroted.

"Wait…" Perkins begged. "You don't understand."

"Understand what," Carter closed on his prey. "That you cold-bloodedly killed my son?"

"It was an accident. I didn't mean for it to happen."

Carter opened his mouth, intending to speak, but no words emerged. He heard the hammer of the gun click in that terrible, mute moment.

Now faced with the real possibility of death, Perkins began to ramble. "The Russians. They were going to make me pay. You don't understand. They're animals! I had to get them their money – or they'd have killed me."

Carter found his voice and asked, "And I'm supposed to care?"

"If I could take it back…"

"It's too late." Hand shaking, Carter readied to fire.

Perkins looked around desperately for any hope of rescue. To his surprise, salvation came in the form of an almost recognisable dark blue uniform.

Chapter Five

Joseph opened his eyes. The right eye peeled open, tearing a thick crust of sleep apart. The left eye was a tight slit, little more than a cut in the centre of a swollen mass of tissue. His entire left side looked blackened and sore, and a drop of blood had dried into a red jewel along his cheek.

The hospital room was dark now. All day he'd slipped in and out of awareness, occasionally hearing a snippet of conversation, either from an anxious sounding Marianna or the snap and snarl of his coach, or the hushed, measured tones of hospital staff. At first he thought they were speaking in an alien language. Perhaps his sudden illness had rendered him stupid, he thought worriedly, but then even the most brilliant of minds would have struggled with some of what he'd heard.

Cerebral infraction, ischaemic stroke, hypertension, atrial fibrillation, and a confusing monologue of fantastic sounding words had momentarily forced Joseph to believe he'd either awoken in a foreign land, surrounded by imposturous doppelgangers, or that he'd lost his mind. Only when Marianna returned to his side to tell him she loved him did he realise that they had just been speaking words that were simply beyond his understanding.

Now, at this late hour, Joseph found himself alone. His thoughts turned to the previous night: the night that should have seen him retire, financially comfortable, a long career behind him, ready to spend all his time with his family, and also in good health. *Yeah, right.*

Without actually having been told, Joseph knew that he must have either suffered an almost fatal blow – maybe The Warrior from Queens had finally found his range – or he'd had a stroke. It really didn't matter; either scenario had led to him laying here, immobilised and fearful.

He forced his head to one side, the muscles on his right side offering little help, and focused on the window on that side. Darkness pressed against the glass.

Where were Marianna and his son? Were they elsewhere in the hospital or back at home, huddled in bed together in an attempt to keep both the cold winter's night and darkest despair at bay? A teardrop slipped down Joseph's cheek. He should be at home with them, their protector.

A slight noise pulled him away from his own bleak thoughts, to the second bed in the room. The top sheet had fallen down to reveal a single bony white leg. The leg twitched spasmodically, which caused the sheet to slip even more. Another leg appeared, as white as ivory, and this one too did a short tap-dance, before going slack. Now the sheet had practically worked its way onto the floor, and the patient's hospital gown had gathered around his waist, exposing the shrivelled stump of his penis.

Joseph turned away, embarrassed by the man's nakedness. A wheeze from constricted lungs drew his gaze back. The privacy curtain that separated them stood partway open, but a short section hung in place, blocking the upper-half of the other bed. Joseph tried to lift his head in an attempt to get a better look. The muscles in his neck screamed out in protest and his head sagged into the soft embrace of his pillow.

Joseph licked at his dry lips. He spoke, but the word he'd formed in his head sounded nothing like the one that escaped from cracked lips. He tried again; what emerged was guttural, alien. He traced the outline of his face, only to recoil as a jolt of pain arced across his left cheek. Delicately now, he lightly brushed his fingers over the swollen contours of his face. His heartbeat quickened as they walked over to the numb right side. Nothing. He prodded harder. His right arm fared no better; it was just an impotent lump of flesh and bone, incapable of feeling movement.

"Shit," he moaned, only what came out was more the hiss of a snake than the curse of a man.

His arm slumped to his side, the examination over, for now. The man in the other bed wheezed again, and a macabre picture formed unwanted in Joseph's mind. He imagined that the stick-thin legs and shrivelled penis gave way not to the torso of a human being but to the scaly body of a huge fish. And, instead of a deeply lined, wizened old face, the head of a trout would lay on that pillow, its gills gulping for air.

Joseph forced these bizarre images out of his mind. They were replaced instead with a burst of annoyance. Where the hell were the old man's caregivers? And more to the point, where the hell were *Joseph's*? What if he needed to use the bathroom? Infuriated now, both by the indignity of the old man's exposure and by the lack of any compassion towards himself, Joseph scanned for either a call button or other means of drawing attention. Apart from the two beds, there was little else in the room. A couple of straight-backed chairs sat empty by each bed. A simple nightstand each – Joseph's with a vase of flowers on top and the old man's bare – stood on either side of their beds. The window on Joseph's side was the only indication of an outside world and adjacent to that, a single doorway, tightly shut.

Unable to find a call button, Joseph reached out, intent on pulling the curtain further back. He managed to grab a handful of material, which felt cold and slimy under his touch, like that of a mouldy shower curtain, and tugged.

Nothing as hideous as a man-fish lay dying in the other bed, just an old guy with a crown of tufted white hair. An oxygen mask was fitted tightly around his face. An IV bottle hung from a stand; clear liquid dripped silently from it, into a long tube, which entered the man's brachial vein via a steel needle. The slight hiss of released oxygen could be heard over the man's laboured breath. His narrow chest heaved with the effort of liquid-filled lungs. Pneumonia gripped him in a parasitic embrace. A couple of twisted wires ran from under the old man's blanket to disappear somewhere inside the wall, reappearing at a nursing station, where the beat of his heart ran in green lines across a monitor screen.

"Hey," Joseph whispered, trying to get the old man's attention. The noise that left his lips could quite easily have come from a leaky oxygen tank. Still, Joseph called over again, not wanting his roommate to be found by a relative, or worse, a young nurse, in his present condition.

"Hey, old man."

The tuft of white hair shifted slightly, and the old man's grey-yellow eyes opened and then fixed themselves to Joseph's. The eyes appeared fearful before turning away.

"Light…" he wheezed from behind the mask.

"Huh," asked Joseph; this noise actually forming as it should.

"The light…" the man said again.

It was then when it became apparent that the room's light source came from directly above and behind Joseph. He forced his head back and caught the full glare of the lamp above. Bright spots burst across his eyes. He squeezed them shut and watched as phantom colours washed across the insides of his lids. Blindly, he reached up, fumbled around for a moment, and then found the light switch. The light clicked off and darkness filled the room in a heartbeat. Words from years long past flashed through Joseph's mind.

Muhammad Ali had once said: *"I'm so fast that last night I turned off the light switch in my hotel room and was in bed before the room was dark."*

Joseph chuckled quietly; once he'd believed he was capable of similar feats. Not now. Seemed like both Joseph and Ali had fallen victim to fate and illness, and would now have only memories and past triumphs to boast about.

He lay in darkness for a while, the old guy at his side unwilling or unable to speak. Eventually the silence was broken with a wheeze of breath, and then the man began to talk.

"They'll never find what they're looking for…" he rasped from behind the mask.

Joseph turned towards the darkness. Now, the old man's form was little more than an outline, barely darker than the gloom that surrounded it.

"Huh?" Joseph asked.

"My secret. My *insurance,*" the man said with a hint of both slyness and contempt.

For a second Joseph thought the guy was boasting about himself. About some astronomically sized savings account or life insurance policy. But then the guy chuckled slightly and said, "They wouldn't dare touch me now. Not with what I know."

Had Joseph's brow been capable of expression, he'd have offered the guy a frown. *"Insurance?"*

The guy paused. He took a few agonisingly liquid-filled breaths before speaking. "Who are you, some sort of foreigner?"

"Huh..?"

"Never mind," he said, dismissing Joseph's inability to communicate clearly as either ignorance or misapprehension. "Let me tell you, they think they run the whole show. But not now. Hah! I'll have the last laugh – now that I've secured my insurance."

What the hell was this guy talking about? A parasitic family member ready to claim the guy's inheritance? Or some sort of bloodsucking financial body waiting in the wings to recoup monies owed to them?

The old man rambled on for a while, muttering incoherently, Joseph catching just a few words at best. He kicked out with his stick-thin legs, hooking the hem of the fallen sheet with one calloused foot, and then succeeded in drawing the blanket over himself.

The room fell silent, and Joseph drifted into a fitful sleep.

***

A deep, gnawing chill woke Joseph some time later. Frost had covered the window with a white crystallised layer, which had formed the outlines of macabre faces into it. Joseph pulled the single sheet tightly around him, and again felt an abrupt gutful of anger towards the absent hospital staff. This time, though, an ample serving of self-pity was mixed into it.

Where the hell were the nurses? Why would they just leave them to freeze like this? He looked over at his roommate and found the old man shivering uncontrollably. A cold sweat broke out across Joseph's body. His teeth started to chatter.

To hell with this!

He reached up, intent on hitting the light switch, ready to find assistance, even if it meant lying here bellowing or gibbering or slapping the side of his bed until he got somebody's attention. However, before he connected with the switch, a sudden burst of pain ripped through his skull. *God... no.* Not again. The shadows engulfed him and, before he knew it, the fragile ship that was his consciousness became swamped with darkness, and then quickly sank towards oblivion.

***

Not long after the door opened. Light flooded into the room, a burst of false dawn. The thin membranes that were the old man's eyelids scrunched tightly, hypersensitive to brightness. Someone entered. The figure moved over to the old man's side, ignoring Joseph completely – for now. A hand clad in latex reached out and the hiss of oxygen died slowly as the flow to the patient's mask dropped.

The old man's eyes shot open and filled with terror.

"Can't breathe…" he wheezed. Underneath the mask his nostrils flared and then clamped tightly shut as he desperately tried to draw breath.

The face above him smiled. The valve on the oxygen tank stopped turning, now fully closed. The visitor's hand moved away from the tank and gently traced the line of morphine, which ran from an intravenous drip to the old man's arm. A button was pressed: once, twice, three times, increasing the flow of morphine to the patient's brachial vein. Instantly, his pupils dilated, and his initial panic seemed to flow away, diluted by the increase in opiates.

The old man felt himself drifting on a calm sea, as if the water from his lungs had flooded out from his every pore. He managed to stay afloat for a short while, but then his frail body lost its buoyancy and, quickly, he began to sink. Skeletal hands shot from under the blanket, gripping tightly onto the rails of his bed, desperately trying to keep him afloat. However, his ragged and weakened body was unable to resist, and soon he felt the current pull him under. In one final attempt at survival, his brain released a burst of adrenaline. His head cleared and a flow of energy flooded his veins. He kicked hard, using both feet to propel him towards the dark surface above. He reached out, ready to punch his way through the surface. His hand hit something solid. The water above had iced over. Winter had somehow found its way inside this room, trapping all inside in its icy embrace. The old man kicked again and his hands slapped feebly against the ice. The air in his lungs turned suddenly caustic. He opened his mouth to inhale and filled his lungs with ice-cold water.

The latex glove stayed clamped over the old man's mouth for a little while longer, thumb and forefinger pinching both nostrils closed. Eventually, the pale feet stopped kicking. The blanket had gathered around two bony kneecaps to reveal stick-thin legs and skin like parchment.

The room fell quiet.

The visitor lingered at the bedside, head bowed and shoulders hunched. Then the gloved hand traced out the sign of the cross, from head to navel, from shoulder to shoulder. Finally, two fingertips drew the old man's eyelids down. Something metallic glinted. A few minutes passed as the visitor worked on the patient. Next, the morphine drip was returned to its correct setting and the oxygen valve reopened. A faint hiss of compressed air filled the room.

The figure walked to the other hospital bed. In contrast to the feeble, ancient in the first, this bed was filled from top to bottom and from side to side with a giant of a man. His dark ebony skin glistened slightly, a fine film of sweat catching the meagre light available like moonlight on a pond. This patient's chest rose and fell steadily, rhythmically, and with strength.

The visitor smiled. "Don't worry, you'll soon be joining him…" the voice said, devoid of any compassion or warmth. Eyes filled with cold contempt traced over the second patient's face, mapping every curve, feature and characteristic to mind, with the same attention to detail as would an expert cartographer. Then, silently, the visitor disappeared back through the doorway, leaving the old man and this silent witness alone.

Chapter Six

What sounded like the roar of a mating walrus drew their attention. Even the penguins surrounding Presley's feet flinched at the sound. The jarring bark came again, only this time it took on a human quality.

"What the hell's going on here?" a voice demanded.

Carter dropped the gun to his side.

"The park's closed, you shouldn't be in here," the security guard said, stepping out of the shadows.

A heap of blubber stepped out of the darkness, wrapped in a dark blue uniform with *'Bronx Zoo Security Enforcement Officer'* stitched across its chest pocket. The man's undersized shirt covered swollen breasts that any teenage girl would have died for. A large, bushy moustache wandered across the lower half of the ruddy face at an odd angle; he barked again, his voice breaking with a bronchial dry rasp.

"What the hell are you doing here?" the guard asked.

What seemed like a hundred different questions and answers raced through Carter's head, all within a second. Was he prepared to shoot Perkins in front of a witness, possibly endangering an innocent bystander? Would he be able to convince the security guard that he was indeed a cop, tracking down a cop-killer? Possibly. But the guard would probably want in on the action, offering to assist – no doubt. No, Carter thought, he couldn't allow someone else to intervene. Perkins was not, under any circumstances, heading towards a prison cell this night – or any other night.

None of these things mattered in the end, because it was something else entirely that stopped Carter from blowing away the figure before him.

Hate.

Surprisingly, this hate was to be Presley's saviour – for now.

Was Carter ready, willing, *able* to relinquish this hate? Hate: an emotion that had driven him like an obsessive and tormented drug addict for the last three months. If he did, what would be left? Grief?

Grief was too potent an emotion for Carter to handle. The detective knew now, unquestionably, that if he was to kill Perkins then all that would be left for him to do was grieve. And he also knew that that would tear him apart, piece-by-piece. What he needed was a reason for being. Only Perkins offered that now, and incredibly, only if he continued to live.

His mind reached this conclusion before the guard had a chance to either draw his weapon or activate his flashlight. And, before his identity had been compromised, Carter turned his back on them both.

In a show of bravado, the guard took a few faltering steps, demanding for Carter to freeze. But Carter was back through the torn tent flap, returning the way he'd come, before being forced to explain or identify himself.

The guard's attention returned to Perkins. "What the hell is this?" he questioned, now unbuttoning his holster. "You'd better not be some goddamn animal activist. We had us a few of those earlier. Idiots opened up a load of cages, chanting a load of crap about equal rights and love to all God's creatures. We had to kick their butts all the way back to suburbia first thing this morning."

Surprised to be alive, Presley uttered a nervous laugh.

"What the fuck's so funny, wiseass?" the guard asked.

"Nothing," Perkins replied. "Just thankful to be alive on such a wonderful night."

"Really?"

"Yeah – really."

The guard grunted something under his breath. This wasn't how things should have gone. This asshole and his disappearing friend should have pleaded for forgiveness, regretful for their intrusion, and followed him heads bowed and in tow until they'd been escorted – permanently - out of the main gate.

Not knowing what else to say, the guard said, "Get the fuck out of my pool."

Perkins dutifully obliged, leaving his captivated audience behind him. He stepped out of the shallow water, quickly forming a small pool of his own around his scuffed shoes.

"I should arrest you for trespassin'," the guard said.

Thinking on his feet, Perkins replied, "Listen, buddy, I ain't got anywhere to go and I was just hungry."

"What?" his captor gawped. "Wait... You weren't gonna eat one of... those, were you?" One fat finger pointed towards the group of assembled penguins.

Presley almost laughed at the absurdity of the remark, but then realising he was in the presence of an intellect even more inferior than his own, a rare occasion indeed, he decided to play out the situation. "I'm real hungry, haven't eaten in weeks."

The guard eyed him with indecision. "My Mary's gonna kill me if she finds out, but I've got a few sandwiches left over in my lunch. She always packs a few too many," he said, patting his ample gut. "Okay, I can let this minor incident go – this time. You'd best come this way," he directed, tipping his double chin.

Presley took the lead, with the guard trailing a few paces behind.

***

As they made their way towards the security station, the guard felt his initial anxiety surprisingly lifted. Just a homeless guy in search of food was all that had transpired, nothing he couldn't handle. In all honesty, the guard actually felt relieved at having company, no matter how unsavoury the source. All this darkness and hootin', hollerin' and squawkin' had started to get the better of him. And, although the morning's clean-up had gone well, just a few native pigs and monkeys to round up, he couldn't shake the feeling that something far more malevolent had been released and, was out there, somewhere, licking its lips hungrily, and just waiting for a tasty bit of prey to cross its path. At least now there'd be two of them to tackle, and the guard had already decided a shot in the homeless guy's leg would give him the advantage to get away. Afterwards, he could simply say he'd accidentally shot the tramp while trying to save him. There could even be a medal awarded if such a thing happened.

The guard followed the hobo, happily oblivious to the fact that the only thing free to kill a man tonight was walking a few feet in front of him.

Chapter Seven

Eugene Profit's gnarled hand punched the vending machine. A female orderly passing by witnessed the confrontation; she sucked air through clamped teeth in a show of disdain, and unwittingly brought herself within striking distance of the old coach's venom.

"They did what?" he said again, his hand banging out another hollow boom.

Marianna reached out to take the old guy's arm. "They posted Joseph in the wrong unit. He spent the night in geriatrics, instead of intensive care."

"Ridiculous!" Profit barked, turning his anger away from the drinks machine.

"I know," Marianna agreed. "Anything could have happened to him." She looked tired. Her hair was scraped into a tight ponytail, and although she only occasionally wore make-up – her skin naturally healthy and flawless – today two dark rings had fixed themselves around russet eyes. Her cheeks were drawn, making her normally radiant face look gaunt.

"How did this happen?" Profit asked.

Marianna shrugged her shoulders. "Some sort of mix-up with names… I'm not sure."

"So where is he now?"

"Back in intensive care."

"C'mon," Marianna said, "Jake's already with him."

"You thought about suing this goddamn hospital?" Profit snarled.

"That can wait. Joseph's our only concern, for now."

They left the battered vending machine behind them and, after a short elevator ride, arrived on Joseph's level. Marianna led them towards his room.

"Mrs. Ruebins," a voice called.

Marianna spun on her heels to find Joseph's doctor heading quickly towards them. She sensed Profit tense, as if he was readying himself for a much wanted – and needed – confrontation. Having already endured a torrent of apologies regarding last night's blunder, Marianna decided that diplomacy, rather than dispute, would be more helpful towards Joseph's immediate future.

"Doctor," she greeted, forcing a weak smile.

The man caught up to them, his necktie askew slightly and lungs breathing heavily. Feeling he hadn't apologised nearly enough, he began to offer another string of apologies, hands raised in submission.

Profit took an unconscious step forward, and Marianna watched as his gnarled fingers formed into tight fists.

"Eugene," she said, bringing herself between the two men. "Why don't you see if either Joseph or Jake needs anything? Both must be getting hungry by now."

The doctor started to speak – something about Joseph needing to follow a restrictive diet – but, then seeing the hostility written across the old man's features, apparently decided to let protocol slip on this one occasion.

Profit grumbled an expletive under his breath before turning to disappear through the door.

The doctor too looked as if he hadn't slept well the previous night. Twin bags, large enough to take away on vacation, hung around the bottom of bloodshot eyes. His face had a hint of stubble and a dishevelled necktie completed his frazzled look.

"We had a major incident last night," he began. "Tanker truck jack-knifed out on Highway 97, killed three instantly and brought another six seriously injured here just before dayshift was ready to handover to nights. One of the nurses in emergency made a stupid mistake: she sent Joseph to our geriatrics care floor and a 'Rueben Jackson' to intensive care. She got the notes mixed up. Things got really intense for a while last night. I'm so sorry."

Marianna nodded, having already endured two similar explanations and apologies. "Okay, I accept that, but what about last night? You said Joseph suffered a second attack?"

"Not an attack as such." He led Marianna a few paces away from the closed door.

"Tell me," Marianna pushed.

"Okay, Joseph's condition is stable now. We've given him a small combination of antiplatelet and anticoagulant drugs, to help stop any further blood clots."

"Blood clots?" Marianna asked nervously.

"It's a precautionary measure. Our CAT scan didn't reveal any abnormalities with Joseph's brain. But until we can follow that up with a full MRI scan then we can't be one-hundred percent sure."

"Wait, I thought CAT and MRI scans were the same?"

The doctor shook his head. "Common misconception. A CAT scan is very similar to your standard X-Ray. Only difference is, we sometimes inject dye into the patient's veins to enable a clearer picture. Still, it's only good for picking out the most severe of clots, tumours and haemorrhagic bleeds. Where the MRI, Magnetic Resonance Imaging, scan differs is that it uses magnetic waves to build up a three-dimensional picture of the entire brain tissue. From this, we can detect even the slightest of aberrations."

"So when is Joseph scheduled for this MRI scan? Today?"

"Yes, later this afternoon. Then we'll have a greater understanding of what we're dealing with."

"Right," Marianna acknowledged. "But what do we know now?"

"That your husband's most likely suffered a stroke."

There it was: the word Marianna had been dreading to

hear. *Stroke.*

"Are you okay, Mrs. Ruebins? This is a lot to take in all at once. Maybe we should wait until all our tests have been carried out."

"No, please, continue," Marianna said, taking a deep breath.

"Okay, I need to explain that there are three different types of strokes. The first is the ischaemic stroke. This is the most common. This type of stroke can occur when a blood clot forms in the brain - a cerebral embolism, or, when a clot is formed somewhere else in the body and is then carried to the brain via the blood supply. The second most common stroke is called a lacunar stroke, which is a blockage in the tiny blood vessels deep within the brain."

"So which one has Joseph suffered with?" Marianna asked.

"The MRI scan may reveal he's had a lacunar stroke, but I think that's unlikely. We could be looking at the third type of stroke, though."

"Which is?"

"This is what we call the – haemorrhagic stroke, or bleed. In other words, when a blood vessel bursts, this causes haemorrhaging into the brain. This can come in two different forms. An intracerebral haemorrhage, which is when a blood vessel bursts within the brain, or, a subarachnoid haemorrhage, a bleed between the brain and the skull."

Marianna felt herself go faint. All this talk about clots and blood and strokes was making her feel nauseous. She leaned heavily against the hospital wall. "Okay, so what type of stroke has Joseph had? In simple terms, please."

"That's just it, I honestly don't know. Until we perform the MRI, we'll just have to make him as comfortable as possible and monitor him at all times."

"But what about last night, you said Joseph had suffered another attack, or something."

"Yes, I did."

Marianna's throat clicked as she tried to force herself to swallow, her mouth suddenly completely dry. "Go on."

"Okay, there is an uncommon fourth type of stroke – a mini-stroke – if you would. This is called a Transient Ischaemic Attack, or TIA for short. This happens when the blood supply to the brain is interrupted for a very brief time. The symptoms are very similar to a full stroke, i.e. weakness on one side of the body, loss of sight and slurred speech. This is temporary and usually passes within no more than twenty-four hours."

Marianna's face flushed with hope. "So that's good, right?"

"As far as the stroke is concerned, yes. These next twenty-four hours will be crucial. If Joseph starts to recover during this time we can rule out a full stroke and start looking at a TIA."

Marianna sensed the doctor had more to say. "And?"

"The more worrying thing is the fact that Joseph has had at least two of these 'incidents', which suggests that there may be something more malevolent at work here."

"What?" she asked, the colour draining from her face.

"We can't at this point rule out that this condition is an indicator to something far more serious."

"Like what?"

"Like heart disease – for one."

***

By the time Marianna entered the room, Jake was busy explaining how Captain Jean Luc Picard had thwarted yet another attack on the Starship *Enterprise*, thus saving his crew heroically. The old coach had seated himself in a chair and was splitting his time between, watching Jake's animated face flip from emotion to emotion as he drew his tale to a conclusion, and the dog-eared magazine, which was opened out across his lap.

"Hey, you," Marianna said, flashing Joseph a smile.

"Honey," Joseph replied.

Jake stopped abruptly, his father's almost incomprehensible reply sending an obvious beat of fear through him. Marianna stepped forward to place her hand on Jake's head. "Maybe you should finish your tale later, when Pop's feeling less tired?"

"Okay Mom," Jake agreed. The young boy hopped off the side of the bed and ran the short distance to Profit. "What's that?" he asked, now interested in the magazine.

"This?" Profit said. "This is the August ninety-six edition of Ringside Magazine – the one with your father on the cover. You remember, from when he stopped Jonnie Tucker inside of three rounds."

Years ago, Joseph had already been on the brink of international success. Admittedly, the title belt he'd taken from Jonnie Tucker had been one of the less prestigious of them, awarded by the IBO, International Boxing Organisation, which was a governing body based outside of the US; thus bestowing its titleholder with only a small measure of moderate success.

Still, as a stepping-stone to greater achievements, this had launched Joseph into the top ten ranked fighters in the world, and had surely been the beginning of something special. Until, that is, his untimely accident. Nothing too spectacular, either, just a slight bump while pulling out of the driveway one morning as Joseph was heading towards training. The resultant collision had jarred his neck severe enough for him to miss three months of solid training, during which he'd missed a mandatory defence of his title.

By the time he'd made a full recovery, his world ranking had slipped, along with any immediate chance of another title fight. The next few years had proven difficult. A young street fighter had exploded onto the scene, rising quickly to the top, unifying all major belts, and totally dominating the heavyweight division. That left the lesser belts to contend for. Most of the top ten fighters had competed for these, pushing Joseph out of contention. Only Joseph's grim determination had offered him his second shot. Something that in Joseph's mind, and heart, had simply come too late.

Now, as Jake stood on tiptoes in an attempt to peek over the magazine, the old coach chanced a glance over the young boy's shoulder to see how Joseph was doing. He felt a stab of pain and anger in his chest, and cursed himself for not seeing this potential life-threatening event before it had happened. Then as he looked over at Marianna, anger turned to deepest regret as he saw in her face both pain and fear.

Profit climbed to his feet, intent on offering her his support, but before he'd taken two steps, the door opened with a mighty bang.

The doctor stood in the doorway, his face a mask of worry. He took a deep breath and, speaking directly to Joseph, said, "We've got a problem. A real emergency!"

Chapter Eight

The homicide division took on a sombre, subdued air the moment Carter entered the room. The usual morbid and juvenile banter was replaced with hushed tones and attempts at working that looked over-exaggerated. Carter instantly sensed the change in atmosphere. He concentrated on looking down at his scuffed brown shoes during the short time it took him to reach his desk, open a desk drawer, and place his shield and holster inside. Closing it, he turned towards the single piece of paper in the 'IN' part of his work tray. He reached out to take it.

My office, as soon as you get in. C.M.

Carter read it again, the handwriting unmistakable, and then looked over to the closed office door, which bore the name: *Captain Mendoza*. He crossed over to the door and rapped on it twice. Captain Mendoza's coarse voice barked for him to come in from the other side.

"You want to see me?"

Mendoza looked up from the stack of paperwork spread across his desk. "You look like shit."

"Yeah," Carter agreed. "I feel like it, too."

Captain Mendoza gestured towards the single seat that faced his desk. "Sit."

Carter did as ordered and silently braced himself for what was about to follow.

"I phoned your house again last night," Mendoza stated.

"I know."

"You weren't in – again."

"I know."

"Thomas," Mendoza began, "you can't do this all alone."

Carter met the captain's eyes and held them steady. "Yes I can."

Mendoza shook his head. "You're an idiot."

"Can't argue there."

Mendoza shook his head again, but his dark brown eyes held only affection within them. "I don't mean that asshole Perkins. I mean you can't get through this grief – Billy's loss – all by yourself."

"I know what you meant. And you're wrong."

"How long have we been friends?" the captain asked.

"A long time."

"Right," Mendoza said. "And I'm not gonna let some asshole punk allow you to throw your life away."

"What life?"

"This one!" Mendoza said, now infuriated with his friend's beaten manner. "What about Billy? Would he have wanted you to throw your whole life away, because of what happened?"

"I guess we'll never know, will we?"

Mendoza stood, his squat body taking up most of the room on his side of the desk. He moved around to sit on the edge, next to Carter. "If you find him, and kill him, you'll go to prison – you know that, don't you?"

"Yeah."

"So quit this bullshit, and return to the real world, will you!"

Carter just stared down at his feet, his captain and friend's concern having little effect on him. "What else would you have me do?"

Mendoza exhaled heavily. He reached up to rub tiredness or frustration from his eyes. "Leave Perkins to the cops in charge. They'll bring him in, and then the fucker will spend the rest of his life rotting in some stinking prison cell."

"How many leads have they got?"

"Enough to keep them busy. I'm serious, Thomas, let it go, or I'll have you arrested for interfering with police business."

The warning had been weak and lacking in substance. Mendoza would love nothing more than to wake up, to find the newspaper headlines stating that Officer William Carter's killer had been found floating face-down in the Hudson River; but not at the expense of his lifelong friend. The captain had watched Carter slip deeper towards despair over the last three months, and had been unable to do anything about it.

"Look," he began, "give us another forty-eight hours, and if we still haven't caught the bastard, I'll help you myself. And then we'll both spend the rest of our lives eating cold slop and making number-plates."

Carter glanced up, his friend's final comment registering somewhat. "And what would you have me do until then? I ain't taking any leave – you can't force me to."

Mendoza nodded. Indeed, the last thing the captain wanted was for Carter to have even more time on his hands. No, that would be bad, very bad. "I've got something for you."

"What?"

Mendoza reached behind him. He took up a single sheet of paper. "This just came in."

"What's that?"

"I'm not sure – yet. A patient at St Mary's Hospital died this morning."

"So?"

"So, the hospital staff suspect foul play."

"Isn't there anyone else out there," he said, with a gesture at the door, "that can follow this up?"

"Yeah, Tyler is available."

"Then send her."

"I am," Mendoza said. "I'm assigning the pair of you, together."

"Like hell, you are," Carter announced.

"Either take this graciously or you can take time off –

alone. Your choice."

Carter clenched his jaw and wavered for a second, his mind trying to figure out which of the two scenarios would be worse: trapped in his apartment with nothing but silence to keep him company, or fathering a wet-nosed female detective on a complete no-brainer? In the end, fear of being alone won. He snatched the crime-report out of Mendoza's hand and mumbled a curse under his breath.

Carter left the office and was met once again with a hush of conversation.

"Tyler!" he yelled.

A young, shorthaired brunette stood up from her desk. The sea of faces that turned to her relaxed as one, and an almost palpable sense of relief filled the room.

***

Detective Tyler picked up her shield and holster as she rounded her desk. And, as she made the short trip to Carter, she shot a look towards Captain Mendoza's office and damned the captain for assigning her to this duty – duties that involved keeping Carter out of trouble for at least the next 48 hours.

Chapter Nine

By the time the two detectives arrived at St Mary's, Joseph and Marianna had been informed about some of what had happened. The doctor had revealed some of the worrying details, but not all or the most important one.

Marianna sat close by her husband as the doctor returned with two strangers in tow, a man and a woman. Mercifully, Eugene had taken Jake back home, on the pretence that Joseph was in need of clean clothes and toiletries.

As the three entered, Marianna's back straightened, subconsciously preparing herself for the possibility of conflict.

"This is Joseph Ruebins and his wife, Marianna," the doctor announced, tension clear in his voice.

The male newcomer nodded and said, "Thanks Doc, we'll be a few minutes."

Detective Tyler led the doctor out of the room. She returned and offered her partner a simple nod.

"Okay, Joseph," Carter began. "We understand you had something of an eventful night last night?"

Joseph looked first to Marianna and then back to the detective. "I guess so," he said, slurring the words.

"Wait," Marianna began, "we've already said we aren't discussing legal action right now."

A puzzled look crossed Carter's face. "Sorry?"

"Over the mess up. Last night," Marianna said.

The detective nodded, now finally understanding. "Yes, Joseph's physician has already explained the mix-up. But we're not here for that," he replied.

"Oh?" Marianna said, her back straightening even further.

"Maybe we should introduce ourselves," Tyler said, stepping forwards. She extended her arm across Joseph's midriff and said, "I'm Detective Tyler, and this is Detective Carter." She shook Marianna's hand, and then after an awkward moment waiting for Joseph to take it, she patted his shoulder instead.

"Detectives?" Marianna asked.

"Yeah, we're from Fourteenth Precinct, downtown," Carter announced, withdrawing his ID from his breast pocket. "There was an incident last night, in the same room Joseph occupied during the hospital's screw-up. We need to ask you a few questions."

"Like what?" Joseph slurred.

"Come again?" Carter asked.

Marianna took hold of her husband's arm. "He's had a stroke and is having trouble communicating clearly."

"I'm very sorry to hear that," Carter said. "But he does understand us, right?"

"Speak to him," Marianna demanded. "He isn't a dim-wit."

The reprimand caught Carter off guard. "Right, sorry. So – Joseph, last night, did you see anything suspicious?"

"Like what?"

Carter looked on blankly.

"He said: like what?" she explained.

"Oh," Carter said. "How did you…?"

"We've been together a long time, Detective, and endured more than one beer fest. The way he's speaking now, it isn't a million miles away from when he's had a drink."

Joseph squirmed slightly, embarrassed by his wife's confession. Marianna read his distress. She patted his arm gently and said, "Don't worry sweetheart, a hard working man deserves the occasional minor indiscretion."

Now understanding that at least he had some sort of three-way communication system, Carter pressed on. "So, once again, Joseph, did you witness anything unusual?"

Joseph shrugged with just the one working shoulder. "No."

Carter raised his hand to Marianna – no need to translate such an obvious response. "Did either of you have a late visitor, or treatment by any of the hospital staff?"

Joseph barked with laughter.

"What's so funny?" Carter asked.

Marianna said, "Funny? No. Negligent – yes. That's the thing, Detective. Nobody checked in on either of them all night. Not even an orderly with a bedpan or to bring them something to eat."

The word *'shambolic'* entered Joseph's head, but he didn't even attempt to vocalise such a word – even Marianna would have been hard pushed to translate that one.

Carter turned briefly to Detective Tyler, but she was busy jotting down their conversation. "Okay, but what did you and he talk about?" he asked.

"Insurance."

It took a moment for Marianna to understand what her husband had just said. Joseph repeated it for her, slower this time.

"He says 'insurance'."

"Which means?" pushed Carter.

Another shrug from Joseph.

"Take your time Mr. Ruebins, this is important."

Joseph sighed. What was this all about? Had something happened to the old man, and if so, why weren't they telling him? Understanding that things would be quicker if he was to write a reply – one that required more detail, Joseph used his left hand to phantom write against the bed sheet.

Detective Tyler understood instantly. She stepped forwards and tore off a sheet from the rear of her notepad. She handed it over to him and then offered him her pen.

"Thanks."

"Joseph," Carter said, "I need you to be as clear as

possible about what was said between the two of you."

Joseph paused for a moment to gather his thoughts. Then he simply wrote what he could remember from the previous night. It took him a while, Marianna first needing to find something hard enough for him to write on – they made use of the hospital chart at the foot of the bed. Using both sides of the paper, he eventually handed pen and paper back to Detective Tyler. She passed the paper to Carter instantly, curiously using only the very tips of her fingers. Likewise, Carter held the sheet in an almost reverent fashion.

He said something about, his insurance: His secret... And that, 'They' – he didn't elaborate – that 'they' wouldn't dare touch him now. He added also, that 'they' thought they ran the whole show? And about him having 'the last laugh'.

Carter flipped the sheet of paper over. On this side, Joseph had added his own thoughts about their exchange.

The guy was really old, barely able to breathe. He had some sort of clear liquid dripping into his arm, probably morphine, or some other painkiller. And the reason I called out to him was because his bed sheet had slipped, and that he was showing the whole world his business.

This last bit of information seemed to interest Carter. "How could you have seen that?" he asked.

Joseph frowned. Granted, the old man's member had been tiny - but not *that* tiny. Joseph shook his head. "What?"

"How could you have seen that the sheet had slipped?" Carter asked.

"The curtain was open – between beds."

Marianna opened her mouth, but Carter stopped her short. "It's okay, I think me and Joseph are now starting to understand each other."

Tyler nodded to herself. Yes, Joseph Ruebins' speech had improved remarkably in just the few minutes that they had been here.

"Let me get this straight," Carter said. "The privacy curtain was open and you had full vision of the other guy?"

Joseph nodded.

"Did you get out of bed at anytime and touch him?"

"No," Joseph said, now clear enough for all to hear.

"You sure of that?"

"Hey," Marianna said, standing now, her protective instincts at their greatest. "Detective, Joseph is seriously ill. He can barely move, never mind walk or sit. Now what's this all about? Is he in trouble?"

Carter spread his hands. "No, Mrs. Ruebins, he's not. We just need to try and establish what happened last night."

"Happened?" she echoed.

Carter stood quiet for a second. "The hospital hasn't told you?"

"Told us what?" Marianna asked.

"About Joseph's roommate. He was found dead this morning. Murdered."

Chapter Ten

The alleyway Presley Perkins found himself in looked like it had come directly out of a bad 70s TV cop show. At any moment, he expected the red and white Gran Torino from *Starsky and Hutch* to come tearing around the corner in hot pursuit of some greasy perp, sending boxes and debris high into the air.

Cardboard boxes littered one side almost entirely, those broken up only by rusting dumpsters heaped full of trash and home to the city's rat population. Tall buildings stretched toward the grey sky like ancient pagan monoliths, offering prayer and sanctuary to the underbelly of New York's inhabitants: the homeless.

Presley's scuffed shoe caught an empty glass bottle, and it skipped away from him with a clink and a clatter, breaking his train of thought. He continued along, until coming to a solid-looking doorway. His hand formed into a fist, but he hesitated before rapping heavily against it.

A few seconds later, a view hole scraped open. Dark eyes peered out.

"Yeah?"

"I need to speak to Moses," Perkins said.

"You do, do you?"

Perkins nodded.

"Hold on."

Presley stepped back from the door and anxiously scanned both sides of the alleyway. Nothing had changed in the last few seconds. No worries, Presley thought, Starsky was probably too busy knitting turtleneck jumpers, and Hutch composing his next love song. The moment dragged on, the distant noise of sirens howling over the city like the wail of the damned.

The eyes soon returned. "You got enough to open up an account?"

"Yeah," Perkins replied.

"Let me see."

He dug into his pants pockets with both hands, retrieving a handful of bills. "I got enough, see."

"Wait there." The eyes disappeared for a second time. This time, though, it took a good few minutes before they returned.

"Well?" Perkins asked.

The eyes roamed over Presley's face, as though attempting to commit every detail to memory.

"Wait there."

Oh, for the love of God!

The muddy-brown eyes became just a dark slot in the doorway for a third time. Another couple of minutes passed by before the sound of a heavy-duty bolt sliding back came from the other side. The slab of steel slowly cracked open. A dark corridor stretched out before him.

Muddy eyes gave way to a burly lump of muscle. The doorman stepped away from the door, his firearm drawn and a look of menace etched across his face.

"Moses will see you now," the heavy said. A hand big enough to crush Presley's face pushed the door shut before sliding the bolt back into place, sealing them both within this tight corridor.

"That way," the heavy ordered, waving his gun towards the opposite end of the passageway.

Perkins took the lead. The hallway was littered with empty food wrappers and drinks bottles. A few used syringes – dark-brown liquid staining their dirty barrels – lay scattered about, along with hundreds of scraps of tinfoil, wrapped into small balls, enough to cover the floor like a glittering carpet of stolen dreams.

Several doorways lay open to reveal empty rooms, each cold and bleak. Impossible to believe that they had once held warmth and happiness, at a time when the building had sheltered hard-working families.

"Stop," the heavy demanded.

Presley halted.

"Up against the wall."

"What?"

"Against the wall, *now*."

Presley turned, "Is that necessary, considering what I'm here to buy?"

"Just do it."

"Okay," he huffed, turning towards the decaying, bare wall. He laid his hands out, palm-flat, and then spread his legs. A moment later, the heavy's shovel-like hand began to pat him down.

"Okay, you're clean," the man said. "Follow me."

The heavy led the way up a short flight of steps and along another barren passageway. He stopped outside the only room to have a door still hanging from its hinges and rapped on it twice.

A thin, reedy voice screeched from the other side. "What now?"

The heavy cringed slightly, as if the voice had shattered his eardrums. He pushed the door open to reveal a small office beyond. Stretching out before them was a table that almost spanned the entire room from wall to wall. An assortment of firearms, ranging from small homemade zipguns to larger, polished assault rifles, were laid out across the table's surface. And a skinny balding man sat behind them, grinning foolishly, Presley thought, like a man displaying his prize-winning home-grown vegetables.

"Who we got here?" he asked, in a voice straight out of a Bugs Bunny cartoon.

"Fella looking to open up an account," the heavy answered.

"Really, Timothy?"

Perkins turned towards the heavy – Timothy – and shook his head in slight bemusement. The guy looked like a Brutus, or Butch or Bulldog, not a *Timothy*.

"An account, hey?" echoed the skinny guy. He hopped off his oversized chair and walked around the table, barely squeezing past one of its wide edges. He stood in front of Timothy with his hands clasped together tightly, his face almost serene in its poise. Then, his hands parted and one opened out to slap Timothy hard across his face.

"Are you totally fucking stupid?"

"Gee, Moses, what did I do wrong?" Timothy asked, tears welling in his eyes.

Moses brushed past the heavy and stopped in front of Perkins. "You a cop?" he asked, scrutinising the unfamiliar face of his mysterious visitor.

"No," Perkins replied. "I'm not a cop."

"You wearin' a wire?" Moses asked, leaning his face to within inches of Presley's, but tipping a look toward Timothy's. "You check him for a wire?" Moses asked over his shoulder.

"Yeah boss, he's clean," Timothy said.

The scraggy face hovered in front of Presley's for a moment longer. Despite the man's name, there was nothing remarkably wise or divine about the weapons-dealer's face. He was skinny to the point of emaciated, with hollowed-out eyes that were little more than empty craters. He had a beakish nose covered by angry red pimples, and the slash of his mouth lay home to a paltry few intact teeth. Most were black stumps, crooked and broken, and embedded in blackened gums that oozed rot like the pores of the dead.

Moses stepped away from Perkins, his sly eyes finally satisfied with their inspection. "Nah, you're no cop. Not even a real cop smells like an actual pig."

Moses returned to the other side of the table. He spread his arms wide as if ready to engage in a bit of holy preaching. "So, what can I get you?" he asked, crooked teeth and blackened gums visible.

Presley moved to the table and scanned its contents. An elaborate assortment of weapons lay there, some shiny and new, other pitted and scarred, a few quite possibly genuine relics from battles past. Handguns covered one side of the table entirely, Magnums, Smith and Wessons, Colts, and designs he couldn't identify. Knowing that his limited amount of cash would not afford him a rifle or mini-machine gun, Presley paid particular attention to the lower end of the arsenal.

"How much you got?" Moses asked, rubbing his hands together.

Presley showed him.

Moses sighed. "Not gonna get you much."

"Then what will it get me?" Perkins asked.

Moses scratched at his pointy chin for a second with dirty fingernails. His spider-like hand reached out to take a small handgun from the table. He held it up, barely able to contain his humour. "What about this one?"

"What the hell's that?" Perkins asked.

Between Moses' thumb and forefinger hung possibly the smallest weapon he had ever seen. It was comprised of two very short barrels and a handgrip that would have been smothered in a child's grasp.

"Is this a joke?" Perkins asked.

"What?" Moses mocked.

"There has to be something better than that?"

Moses cocked the pistol and the small hammer clicked back. "Do you know what this is?"

"A fuckin' ladies gun, that's what," Perkins cursed.

"True," Moses agreed. "But for fifty bucks, you ain't gonna get anything bigger."

"Yeah?" Perkins said. "I could get the whole lady for

less."

Moses nodded. "Yeah, maybe, but she ain't gonna save your hide like this baby can."

"What. *That?*"

Moses smiled his rancid smile. "This is a DA 38 Double Action Derringer. The World's smallest and lightest .357 Magnum."

"Really?"

"Yeah."

"How many shots it hold?" Perkins asked.

"Two."

"Two? What the hell am I supposed to do with just two shots?"

"Hit your target the first time," Moses elaborated.

"Jeez."

The compact gun disappeared inside Moses' hand. "Look, if you can find something better, somewhere else?"

"No – no. I'll take it. What other option do I have?"

Moses shrugged.

"Okay, how much?" Perkins asked.

"How much you got exactly?"

Perkins spread his money out on the table. It took just a few moments to count it out. "Fifty-two bucks."

Moses scrunched up one side of his face. "Sorry, Pal. This baby costs fifty-three bucks at least."

"What?"

"Yeah, she's a real nice piece. Can't just give her away.

Presley stood there and soaked up the indignity of his situation like an obedient child.

"Okay," Moses began, "I got us a solution."

"What?" Perkins asked.

The weapons-dealer clicked the small loader open and, with dirty fingers, retracted both bullets. "Okay, you can take the pistol, but the shots'll cost you another buck." He placed the two surprisingly large-looking casings on the table.

"This is stupid," Perkins stated. "What am I supposed to

do with that?”

Timothy spoke from behind. “You could use it to pistol-whip someone.”

Moses laughed louder, now unable to contain himself. “Yeah, you could use it for that. Or, you could improvise and get yourself another wad of cash.” The lines at his eyes abruptly disappeared as his face became serious. “Now, either take the fucking thing, or get the fuck out of my sight. I ain’t got time for two-bit losers.”

Chapter Eleven

Detectives Tyler and Carter arrived at the crime scene. Three white jumpsuits moved around the tiny room, each completing their tasks, before moving out, arms laden with sealed bags and plastic cartons. The forensics investigators vacated the room, the last bidding the detectives to enter. Carter moved over to the dead man's bed. Tyler joined him on the opposite side.

Carter looked down at the old man's body. "So who've we got?"

Tyler took a pair of latex gloves from her pocket, slipped them on and then reached out to take the chart from the foot of the bed. The clipboard was covered in white powdery swirls, some large, others small, but all the potential signature of a killer.

"Mr. Henry Jones," Tyler said. "Aged eighty-six. Suffering from chronic pneumonia, which had become untreatable - according to this, and the hospital were simply doing their best to make him *feel comfortable.*"

"Right," Carter nodded. "So they must have had him on a steady drip of morphine?"

Tyler took a moment. "Yes, here it is. He was being administered 10cc's every hour, automatically." She turned her head to examine the pump at her side. It was nothing special, just a cream-coloured plastic box, which had a clear tube running into it at the top, and a similar tube out the bottom. A small dial at one side had a range of measurements and speeds, which would invariably feed the morphine at the desired rate required. Again, forensics had been busy powdering down the instrument. The bag of morphine that must have been hanging from the stand behind the pump had gone, and she guessed that forensics had bagged and tagged it.

Carter took a clear bag from his pocket. The short note that Joseph had written earlier was held inside. "According to Ruebins, the old man said, 'they wouldn't dare touch him now'?"

"Maybe he meant the hospital staff?" Tyler offered.

"Meaning?"

"Meaning, they may have manhandled him a little – you know, a nurse having a bad day, consulting physician too busy wondering how he was going to explain to his wife the presence of an unknown receipt for a hotel they hadn't stayed in, or a relative who couldn't wait to be rid of the old man."

"Okay, that almost fits his next comment. 'That 'they' thought they ran the whole show'."

"See, he's probably referring to the staff. Hospital's can be somewhat abrupt, especially the expensive type – types that run to the tune of profits and turnover."

"So you think he means a doctor or nurse? Maybe they wanted their bed back, sooner rather than later. For another paying customer?"

Tyler shrugged. "Can't be too certain about anything. Too early to say."

"Yeah," Carter agreed. "But what about his comment about 'insurance' or 'his secret'?"

"The guy was at death's door. Who knows what he meant? He was so high on morphine. Would we be as concerned if he'd expressed a wish to fly away with the pixies?"

Carter's lips almost curled into a smile – almost.

Tyler said, "When we're done, I'll get a full list of all his visitors since he arrived, and see if anything stands out. You know, a distant relative, here watching over their favourite uncle or grandfather, eagerly awaiting their cut of his or her inheritance.”

“Hang on.” Carter returned his attention to Joseph’s note. “Says here, he did make a couple of references to his ‘inheritance’.”

“Exactly,” Tyler agreed. “We’ve both seen the *Jerry Springer Show*, right? And how many times have some family of hicks been duped out of their inheritance – only to find out that their recently deceased loved one willed all of it to their favourite charity?”

“Fair point,” Carter said. “Perhaps that’s what he meant by ‘his secret’?”

“I’ll also check for recently changed insurance policies, see if one of those relatives had been in line for a sudden jackpot, or discovered they were about to miss out on a small fortune.”

“Good idea.” Carter turned away from the corpse on the bed. He slipped his hands into his pockets and drew a set of latex gloves out. Simply holding one glove, he began to draw open the curtain that separated the beds. The curtain slid easily, held on the rail above by large hoops similar to a shower-curtain’s. “Look here,” he said, drawing Tyler’s attention away from the body.

“What’ve you got?” she asked.

“Look,” Carter said, indicating a white pattern halfway along the length of material. The white powder from forensics formed a cauliflower shape, clearly that of a hand – a large hand. The detective frowned.

“What is it?” Tyler asked.

“Wait a minute.” Carter moved closer to the second unoccupied bed, the one Joseph Ruebins had occupied. He slipped onto the cot and then laid himself flat, allowing his head to rest against the soft pillow. Then, reaching out, he tried to touch the curtain. His outstretched fingers missed it by a good six inches. He shuffled his body closer, jabbing straight fingers as far as he could.

"What are you doing?" Tyler wanted to know.

He responded with a question of his own. "I'm about the average size for a guy, right?"

"If you say so."

"And look, I'm still a good half-dozen inches away from even brushing against this with my fingertips."

"So?"

"So, how long would a person's arm have to be, to reach close enough to actually grasp a handful of material?"

Tyler did a quick mental calculation. "Not even someone the size of Joseph Ruebins could have reached it."

Carter's eyebrows rose. "You think our would-be champ is a liar, and he did get out of bed?"

"But even if he could, for what purpose?"

"I'm not sure – yet," Carter said, climbing off the bed.

He returned to the corpse. He bent to take a closer look. In an attempt to offer a measure of dignity, the old man's eyes had been forcibly shut, but the lids had begun to creep back, showing the detective a hint of sickly yellow-whites. Two indents cut along the man's cheeks, deep lines coming together at the corner of his grey lips. Elastic, Carter realised, to keep the oxygen mask in place. The bed sheet had been folded neatly just below his collarbone, and both his arms were laid outside of it, palms in an upward fashion. His skin was a combination of yellow pallor on top, and a mottled scarlet on the lower half. A couple of pinpricks were visible against the paleness of his skin – the calling card of a hypodermic needle. The body underneath the sheet was insubstantial, its feet the most prominent part, pushing the spotless white sheet up into twin mountains.

"Wait a minute," Carter said.

"What is it?"

Carter pointed to the sheet. "That."

"What about it?"

"Look how clean it is."

"So?"

"So, how come there isn't any blood?"

"Why would there be any blood?"

Carter looked back blankly for a second, before reaching into his back pocket. "You didn't get chance to read the original crime report?"

"No. Why?"

"I think you'd better take a look." He handed it over.

Tyler quickly scanned the document. Her expression tightened. "Good God."

"I know," Carter said. "Sick or what?"

She handed the report back. Carter tucked it into his pocket, and then bent over the old man's face. Using the latex glove for a second time, he gripped the man's pointed chin and carefully opened his mouth. And even though he'd read what to expect, he still took a startled step back.

"Christ…" he cursed.

Tyler pushed her own nausea to one side, allowing her professional curiosity take over, and bent to examine what lay inside.

An open cavity revealed itself to her. The gums had no teeth present. They were coated in dry blood, angry and red, and full of disease – or so Tyler thought. However, on closer inspection, she found that it was a coating of thick congealed blood that gave them their gory appearance. The source of bleeding was more than obvious. For the most part, the old man's tongue was missing, just a bloody stump remaining, severed veins exposed like worms boring through something rotten.

"What the hell have we got here?" Tyler asked.

"Not sure," Carter said. "But I can tell you what we don't have."

"What's that?"

"A complete no-brainer," he announced, with a shudder.

Chapter Twelve

Joseph lay still – very still. However, he found the more that he tried to remain motionless, the more difficult it became. About an hour earlier his right arm had begun to tingle, just a slight sensation at first, and not too unpleasant. Now, though, that arm felt as if it were being held within the flames of baptism, his flesh, muscles and sinews screaming out for contemplation.

Although it wasn't completely dark inside, he still felt like he'd been sealed within a casket, all his senses devoid of their required input. The machinery's knock reminded Joseph that he was indeed still in the land of the living and hadn't as yet entered into the Great Beyond.

An hour earlier, his doctor had announced that his MRI scan was ready to begin. Two orderlies had arrived and they'd quickly wheeled him out of his room and towards the elevator. He'd taken a short trip downwards and had then found himself in something that reminded him of the Starship *Enterprise*'s transporter room.

The huge machine dominated the centre of the room, tubular in shape, and as thick as the hull of a nuclear submarine. In fact, Joseph had first thought that the object was most similar to a small diving vessel, like the one he'd seen recently on a Discovery Channel programme. On the other side of the room, separated by thick glass, was another smaller room with multiple computer screens and keyboards inside. Joseph wondered if that was where Scotty punched in complicated coordinates to teleport patients to distant worlds. Something even more spectacular was about to happen, though. The hospital was about to map the secrets of Joseph's brain, which was far more worrying to him than being separated into a zillion atoms and reassembled halfway across the cosmos.

He tried not to think too much about what he'd been told, something about magnetic waves, that were 30,000 times more powerful than the earth's magnetic field, distorting and shifting every single nucleus in his body, enough for each cell to generate its own magnetic wave, thus allowing the complicated machinery to catalogue his innards. The thought of this internal shift worried him and, as he lay there, his mind began to wander. Seth Brundle from *The Fly* took shape in the forefront of his thoughts, a hideous contortion of a human being, stretched and warped, and offered back to the world as a nightmare creature forced to roam the streets and alleyways under the cover of darkness.

Joseph took the deepest breath he could without inflating his lungs too much and tried to guide his mind toward more pleasant subjects.

Marianna's face came to him, tired looking but beautiful nevertheless. How long had they been together, he wondered, counting the years – not as simple numbers, but as events, happy events, that had gone by? He remembered the first time they'd met. It had been complete luck; he, away at training camp; she, attending an interview for a job that didn't exist; and both a hell of a long way away from home.

Joseph should have been 1500 miles away, on the west coast, readying himself for his first real test as a pro. Instead, his opponent – a bruiser named Freddy Tonk – had had his jaw broken in a bar fight, and Joseph had been forced to take another fight in Las Vegas, on short notice.

Marianna was visiting Vegas for a job interview. Having recently graduated from college with a diploma in Retail and Leisure Management, she arrived at her destination, only to be told that the vacancy had been already filled, and that the date on her letter must be a simple typo, as the interviews had been held on the 11th of the month and not the 17th. She'd tried to argue about the injustice of the situation, but to no avail. Down on the cost of travel and out of patience, Marianna finally accepted defeat – bitterly – realising that the journey had been a complete waste of time. After her disastrous day she'd found a cheap motel, as far away from the bright lights and noise as she could, and checked in for the night.

Just two doors down, Joseph was already enduring his second night there. *Enduring*, because the motel wasn't exactly one that could be found in the Zagat Guide. With only paper-thin walls to separate them, he'd already spent two days playing third-party to a young, recently married couple, who were hourly in danger of thrusting themselves headfirst into his room during the ongoing consummation of their new marriage.

Sometime late into the night, Joseph was awakened by something other than cries of passion. Jumping out of his bed, clad only in his underwear, he threw open the door to his motel room and found a semi-naked Marianna clutching a pillow against her bare breast.

"Inside," she stuttered, her free hand aimed towards the darkness of her room.

"What is it?" Joseph asked, wide-awake and alert to trouble.

Marianna just stared back, terrified.

Joseph quickly returned to his room and reappeared armed with a scuffed boot. He inched over to her, keeping his eyes fixed on the wedge of darkness that filled her open doorway.

"What is it?" he whispered, joining her.

"On the bed," was all Marianna could say.

Joseph turned to find her face full of blind terror. What lay inside to have spooked her so? He contemplated returning to his room and dialling 911, but then a rush of bravado hit him, and he decided that he'd investigate things himself, in the hope that he wouldn't look either cowardly or heartless. He took a breath, whispered, "Wait here," and then stepped across the dark threshold.

Marianna waited outside, her teeth chattering, even though the night verged on being uncomfortably warm. A few seconds later, Joseph returned, stepping out of the room backwards, the boot slipping from limp fingers. He doubled over, hands clasped to his thighs, mouth wide-open as if he was about to retch. Yet, rather than emptying his stomach, he instead threw his head back and roared with laughter.

Marianna stood motionless for a second before tugging at the hem of his shorts. Joseph turned to her, his eyes full of tears and laughter.

"What the hell's so funny?" she demanded.

"On… the… bed…" Joseph managed to say, between howls of amusement.

"And?" she asked, colour turning her face an angry shade of red.

"On the bed," Joseph repeated, now finally getting control of himself.

"Well?"

"I thought I'd find a body or something worse."

"And?"

"And, all I found was… a mouse. A tiny little mouse!"

"Tiny? Little? Are you serious?" Marianna asked. "The thing's as big as a cat!"

Finally, Joseph gathered his senses. "I'm sorry," he apologised. "It just took me by surprise, that's all."

Marianna stood gaping, but then their bizarre situation became apparent: she, almost naked, fearful of a creature a fiftieth of her size; and he, there to rescue her, armed with only an old boot for protection, wearing little more than she was. Her apprehension wavered, and she began to laugh at herself. This set Joseph off again, unable to control the tears that slipped down his cheeks. Eventually their laughter died, which left them both suddenly conscious of their exposed state.

With his attention focused now on her, Joseph felt an unexpected swell within his groin. Her legs were long, dark and sleek, giving way to rounded hips and, although she held the pillow tight, he still got a hint of the fullness of her breasts. Having to forcibly peel his eyes away from her body, it was her face that eventually stole his breath. Beautiful without doubt, but naturally so. Not a hint of makeup or lipstick marked her face, her skin was brushed by the exotic colours of nature. Her eyes sparkled in the moonlight and, as she smiled openly at him, her face became angelic, framed by a mane of jet-black hair.

Before she noticed his arousal, Joseph returned quickly to his motel room. He reappeared a moment later dressed in loose jeans and carrying a flannel shirt in his hand.

"Here," he said, offering her the shirt.

She took it, one hand still clutching at the pillow, and then turned her back on him to slip the shirt over her head.

"What now?" she asked, revolving to face him.

"Uh…" was all Joseph could say, mesmerised by her beauty.

"About the mouse?"

"Oh, yeah."

Joseph stooped, took up the old boot and then disappeared back into darkness. He seemed to be gone forever. Worried now about the welfare of the rodent and the handsome black stranger, Marianna almost called out for him not to hurt it – or himself – before he re-emerged with one hand placed carefully over the boot.

"You caught it?" Marianna asked, impressed by both his skill and compassion.

"No point in killing it," Joseph replied. "Wouldn't make much of a meal. Or a scarf, for that matter."

She grinned back, pleased by his kindness, and yet took a step back as he passed her. "Where are you going to let it go?"

"Out in the bushes," he replied, heading towards the side

of the highway.

"Be careful," she called to him.

He returned a few minutes later with the empty boot strung over his shoulder. The hard contours and muscles of this handsome black man struck Marianna.

"You sure it's all clear?" she asked, her throat dry.

Joseph paused for a moment. "Never can be too sure," he told her.

Marianna fidgeted awkwardly, unable to be quite as direct as she wished.

"Listen," Joseph began, "I've got a couple of cold sodas and some potato chips in my room. I could fetch them and make sure Mickey Mouse isn't entertaining the rest of the Magic Kingdom tonight."

Marianna paused, just long enough so she didn't look too desperate. "Great," she replied, simply.

They spent their first night together camped out at the foot of her bed, eating an improvised picnic, laughing, talking endlessly and, quite simply, falling in love.

Now, as he lay cocooned in this tight drum, Joseph smiled ruefully to himself. Even after fifteen years of being happily married, he'd never told Marianna that the mouse had actually disappeared, nowhere to be found, and he'd only pretended to catch it in the hope that she would be impressed by his valour.

The loud knocking that surrounded Joseph stopped, abruptly, and the table that he was strapped to began to retract from the tubular-shaped chamber. He held his breath, fearful that he'd been changed, both internally and externally, and there would be gasps of horror as he emerged in some hideous altered shape from the machine. Nevertheless, when Marianna and his son appeared before him, their faces showed nothing but relief.

"Hey, handsome," Marianna said. "Back in one piece."

Chapter Thirteen

An intertwined canopy of trees sheltered Presley Perkins from both the elements and prying eyes. Shoulders hunched, he hid in the cover that the trees offered and watched carefully as the few people braving the weather walked past. Most were accompanied by partners, pets, or police officers on patrol. Central Park was beautiful in the daylight, but would become a dangerous landscape after nightfall. The clouds above the city rolled by, fat and lazy and darkly ominous.

The day plodded towards mid-afternoon. The park began to empty, most of its visitors heading back to work or returning indoors to their homes to take shelter from the harsh February cold. A few joggers rolled by to the buzz and crackle of oversized headphones.

Presley stood with his feet stomping up and down, quietly in the thick underbrush, and waited for the safest of opportunities to present itself.

It came, eventually, in the form of a large tuft of candy-floss.

The bright splash of colour, set against the sombreness of the day's grey palette, made Perkins stop his foot stomping and forced his attention onto the approaching pedestrian.

An old woman, hunched over in her heavily insulated fur coat, and wearing gloves thick enough to weather the Antarctic, walked casually towards him with her arm pulled straight by the strain of a dog leash. Although she had covered herself against the weather almost totally, her hair was open to the elements in a bright pink curly perm. Like its owner, the little mutt was wrapped in a thick jacket, leaving its four little legs racing in a blur. The mutt pulled against a long retractable length of cord, forcing the old woman to take a couple of quick steps forward, subsequently jerking her handbag off her shoulder. An expensive looking handbag, Presley noted. This is the one, he thought, stepping out from cover.

The old woman came to a halt, alerted to his presence. "Oh, dear," she gasped.

The little dog barked a yap of caution, too. The mutt turned to him, its face scrunched into a permanent show of disdain, which made it look as if it had just buried its nose in a big pile of dog crap.

"Cute dog," Perkins said, as he made his way over to the woman and her Pekinese.

The mutt tugged against the over-extended leash and pulled itself closer towards this newcomer. As it got to within striking distance of Perkins, the dog bared its teeth.

"Heel, Truffles!" the old woman commanded, activating the leash's mechanism. Squealing, Truffles returned to the woman's feet, where it growled continually.

Perkins gave the woman his best smile. Truffles growled louder.

"Now, now, missy," the woman began, addressing the Pekinese. "We don't behave in such a manner. Not when we have people around."

"Hey, no worries," Perkins said. He slipped his hand into his jacket and wrapped cold fingers around the stock of the Derringer. "Gee, it's one cold day, today," Perkins said, scanning the length of the park. A couple of young teenagers were huddled together on a park bench about a hundred yards away. Other than that, the park was deserted.

The wind changed direction, enough to carry Perkins' stench to the old woman's nostrils. "Oh my," she gasped, her nose obviously used to finer scents. The mutt jumped up onto its hind legs, twisting violently against the short length of cord.

"Thing's a little jumpy," Presley acknowledged, nervously, understanding that the dog could quite easily take a bite out of his leg. And, with no wish for that kind of pain, he took a step back before withdrawing the pistol.

"Gimme your goddamn bag, lady..!"

The dog launched into a frenzy, barking and twisting in circles, while the woman just stared back blankly.

"What?" she asked, her face as serene has the Holy Mother's.

"Your bag. Give me your *bag*."

"Why?"

"Because I have a gun."

"Where?"

"Here," Perkins said, jabbing the small weapon towards her.

The old woman squinted, her eyes forming into tight slits. She strained over the ten yards or so which separated them. "Don't see it."

Incredulously, Perkins took a step closer. "See, look. A gun!" he said, twisting the weapon around in his hand for her to get a more detailed look.

The woman shook her head. "No, still can't see it."

Jesus Fucking Christ! Why the hell had he picked this crazy old blind bitch to rob? He took another step closer, his intention to ram the fucking thing up her nose, but the second his foot left the ground, the small mutt shot forwards.

The old woman released the leash's mechanism, "Go get him!" The nasty little dog darted across open space and snagged the hem of Presley's pants in its teeth. Then, as her would-be attacker was pulled off balance, she snatched a small can of mace from her pocket. Stepping forward, she launched a spray of liquid directly at his face.

Presley screamed as liquid fire consumed his eyes. "No… Ah… It burns…" he shrieked. Instinctively, he pulled the trigger. Two small hollow clicks answered as the hammer fell against empty chambers.

"Why you..!" the woman said, now understanding that the weapon wasn't even loaded. She surged forward and rammed her knee into his groin, sending him to the ground in a twisted heap. Truffles released his cuff for a more satisfying mouthful of flesh.

"Call it off! Call it off!" Presley begged. The sting of pain at his groin paled against the fresh agony of the dog's teeth. Truffles snapped at the tender meat of an exposed calf.

With nothing in the way of mercy in her immediate thoughts, the woman slipped the bag from her shoulder, and then started to whack Presley over the head with it. "Young man," she said, hitting him with a downward swing of her handbag between each word. "I suggest you get yourself a real gun, next time you try to rob someone!"

"Christ, lady, please!"

The storm that was her anger quickly blew itself out. "Release," she said, and Truffles backed away obediently. However, as the dog did, Perkins kicked out instinctively, catching the mutt on the chin. Truffles yelped in pain and surprise, and tore away in the opposite direction, hanging itself and spinning the old woman in a circle. Both handbag and mace clattered to the ground.

With tears streaming down his face, he reached out blindly. Mercifully, his fingers grabbed the small can of repellent first. Unable to make anything out clearly, Presley caught the dark blur of the woman's legs. In a fit of vengeance he pointed the nozzle outwards and sent a jet of pepper-spray in the mutt's general direction.

Pain sent the dog running. It pulled the leash from the woman's hand, and took off across the park. With bag and spray forgotten, the old woman followed, hysterically shouting, "Truffles! Come back here. Come back to Mommy!"

Presley reached out blindly to rake in two handfuls of

snow. He pressed the melting snow into his eyes, and whimpered in agony as he did so. The burning at his eyes was finally quelled. He climbed to his feet. He squinted and found the park had become completely empty. His little act of violence had gone unnoticed.

He bent to retrieve the Derringer and bag. Before the woman had a chance to return with cops in tow, he hurried through the park and exited out onto Broadway. Understanding that he would look suspicious carrying an expensive handbag, he stopped for a moment to gather his wits. The bag would look too obvious stuffed under his thin jacket and, if the cops were to stop him, then he'd be in real deep shit. He'd be arrested and it wouldn't take them long to identify their clumsy mugger as a notorious cop-killer. He thought about emptying the bag and then tossing it into a nearby bush, but the thing looked way too expensive to waste, and would probably score a fair sum of money if pawned at the right shop. Looking inside the bag gave him an idea – the only one available to him at such short notice.

Then, he put as much distance as possible between himself and Central Park, passing many a blank face as he went, only a few curious as to know why a homeless-looking guy would be walking the streets with a red bow in his hair, pink lipstick splashed across his lips, and a stylish handbag hanging from his shoulder.

A couple of horse-mounted cops watched the lipstick-wearing gentleman pass by, both following him until the crowd of people gathered him within its multicultural embrace.

One cop turned towards his partner. "Gee – I've seen it all now."

"Yep," replied the other. "City's definitely gone to the dogs. That's for sure."

Chapter Fourteen

A black and white photograph had imprinted itself on the insides of Joseph's eyelids. The picture, clear and crisp, refused to dispel, no matter how hard he tried to focus his attention elsewhere. Standing with hands clasped together were two young girls, grinning sheepishly. He opened his eyes and stared out towards the window. The small block of daylight that filtered through looked grey and dismal: a monochrome block that held the projected picture of the girls in Joseph's imaginary eye. He huffed and turned towards the opposite side of the room. Nothing there apart from Profit, slumped in a chair at his side and snoring softly.

Joseph huffed again, and then allowed his eyes to close. The girls smiled back at him in a duplicated fashion. Joseph squinted, scrunching his eyelids tighter to get a better look. They were dressed in thick clothing, animal skins cut to fit snugly, and wore identical pairs of fur-lined boots. The boots weren't the only identical things. The girls possessed an uncanny similarity, mirror images of each other, with broad Mongolian features. On closer inspection, Joseph noticed that the sisters, twins no doubt, were not holding hands but joined at the hip – literally. Now, Joseph knew where the image had come from: his memory.

Although he couldn't remember their names or anything of any real importance, he figured that at some point in his life he'd read about the pair; that he'd seen this picture before. The significance of the photo hit him. Joseph opened his eyes and glanced at his left hand. He turned it over so his palm faced him. Then, he formed a tight fist, feeling power within his grasp. In contrast, his right hand was limp and lifeless, resting upwards, fingers partially curled, like an overturned crab. Joseph focused his thoughts and tried to force his fingers to move. They resisted. He huffed a blue streak of expletives under his breath.

This was what the picture signified: himself. Two people trapped within the one body. One was fit and strong, the other weak and infirm. Without warning, Joseph began to panic as the full meaning of the Siamese twins analogy set in. One of the twins had died, unexpectedly, leaving the other to fall fatally ill with blood poisoning. They had shared just a single organ, the liver. Today, a relatively simple procedure would have separated them, but not back then. The remaining twin had died some days later when septicaemia destroyed her organs. Only in death had they been separated, and only then in the interests of science.

The photo in Joseph's mind melted away, leaving behind it a wealth of terrible images. Most, if not all, were formed by Joseph's own dark imagination. He watched in horror as a black decaying disease shifted into the left side of his body. Quickly, this malignant entity destroyed the healthy side, leaving behind a festering carcass.

Joseph shuddered.

Using all of his willpower, he turned his mind away from these worrying thoughts. His eyes came to rest on his old coach's features. Once again, Profit had stayed by his side. They had a bond now; one that Joseph hoped would never be broken, no matter what the future held for them.

By the time he'd made a full recovery from his neck injury years ago, Joseph had not only missed his golden opportunity but had also found himself down by one promoter and manager. Only Profit had remained beside him, as he did so now, and Joseph felt a flood of affection and gratitude towards his aging friend. Not for the first time, Joseph thanked his lucky stars as to how Profit had come into his life.

In the late 1950s – when only one championship belt had existed – Eugene Profit had been a world contender. Number Two in the world rankings no less. Back then, Profit had cut a dashing figure; handsome, with an uncanny similarity to the Hollywood actor, Cary Grant. *Time Magazine* had listed the young fighter as one of America's most prolific sportsmen.

By the time he was just seventeen he'd already turned pro and had quickly risen within the ranks. At twenty-one he boasted a scorecard of twenty-one wins, eighteen by knockout, and zero losses. In a sport that had become predominantly dominated by African-Americans, the public and promoters had fallen over themselves to get at this handsome, enigmatic, young white fighter. And by his twenty-third birthday, was working his way to a serious shot at the title.

What followed became the stuff of legend.

Profit, unmarked, touted as being too wet behind the ears by some and well out of his depth, had stepped into the ring that night as a 10-1 underdog. The then current champ had been an ugly, flat-nosed French-Canadian named Maurice 'Mad Dog' Russo. Mad Dog had laid waste to all that had stood before him, having defended his crown no less than eleven times already. A seasoned champ who knew every trick in the book – and then some.

For the first five rounds, Profit was forced to question his current occupational choice many times over. His straight, finally chiselled nose was busted by the end of round two, and a cut that was deep enough to shove dimes into had opened up above his right eye by the beginning of the fourth. Twice his corner men pushed to end the fight. Perhaps the masses had been right, and Profit was not ready for such an undertaking. But something had the young fighter in its grip and was unwilling to let him go. Profit shook off his fears and, with blood dripping from both nostrils and brow, he stepped into the centre of the ring.

Profit got on his toes and worked the ring like a matador. He utilised his strengths: speed and stamina, and concentrated on using his sticking left jab to maximum effect. Every time Mad Dog held them in a clinch, Profit stepped back and countered with simple straight lefts and rights. By the eighth round the fight began to swing towards the newcomer. The ninth saw both opponents floored – Profit by a swinging right hook that he failed to duck, and Mad Dog by a vicious right cross delivered with such speed that even the rolling cameras at ringside were unable to pick up clearly.

Rounds ten, eleven and twelve came and went in a blur of leather, with so many punches landing, the statisticians had difficulty keeping count. The current champ had two factors working against him now: age and tiredness. His guard began to drop and his shots were rapidly losing their power and accuracy. With fire in his belly and lightning in his fists, Profit backed his opponent up against the ropes.

The fifteenth round was Mad Dog's undoing. Knowing now that only a knockout could save his championship, he came storming out of his corner like a man possessed. Within thirty seconds, though, he'd blown himself out, leaving himself wide open to a counterattack. Profit happily obliged. His simple combinations of left and rights eventually reduced Mad Dog to a spent force. And, with only seconds remaining on the clock, he'd landed no fewer than thirty punches that were undefended and unanswered. With no other option, the referee jumped in to end the fight.

The American dream now lay subserviently at Eugene Profit's feet. He took hold with both hands. In less than a year, he had defended his title successfully on three occasions. The film studios of that time were falling over themselves to include him as a bit-part player in countless films. More importantly, he met the love of his life on the parking lot at Paramount Studios.

Elizabeth Montague, a B-movie actress, was herself on the verge of international success. Their first date had been awkward and unnerving, both in awe of the other, desperate not to make fools of themselves, and holding back in an unconscious way as to not suffer too greatly if rejected. However, captivated by this young man's enthusiastic smile, Elizabeth had agreed to see Eugene again, a decision that in some respects would eventually cost her her life.

A string of more successful dates had slowly brought them closer, and in no time at all they had become Hollywood's B-list dream couple. Elizabeth continued to work on gritty, low budget cult features, whilst Eugene made a number of successful defences. Fame and fortune courted them both equally. They married in the late summer of 1959 under a sky bluer than a tropical ocean.

In the 1960s, the film studios started to shift away from the formulaic romantic-dramas/comedies and hired a team of younger, more ambitious directors, eager to take the industry to new heights and along uncharted paths.

Already established as a serious actress, Elizabeth had landed the main role in a gritty movie about a courageous single mother who found love with a black inner-city teacher. The film opened to rave reviews and acclaim, and earned both Elizabeth and her screen partner – a handsome black actor – Oscar nominations.

Awards night should have been an evening of celebration. And had Eugene been there, it probably would have. Yet the promise of even greater successes had lured him away from the ceremony altogether. Instead of arriving at Elizabeth's side, ready to share in her moment of splendour, he'd been almost 3000 miles away, stepping into the ring to the chant of *'Champ! Champ! Champ!'*

Old Mad Dog had returned, unwilling to let either time or defeat get the better of him. A string of recent wins had pushed him back within contention. Eugene had brushed the contest aside at first, with no wish to entertain the aging fighter. A succession of publicised comments, regarding his only career knockdown, and the promise of more lucrative financial endorsements, had worked its way inside his gut. Eventually, pride and desire won out, and Eugene finally agreed to take on the ex-champ again, ready to prove once and for all that he was now the best fighter of his generation. The fight had been a farce. Profit stopped his man within two rounds, before even breaking into a sweat. Only ten minutes after stepping into the ring, he was back in the changing rooms, feverishly searching for a spare dime. By the time he'd been connected to the hotel that was hosting the awards, Elizabeth had left – the ceremony drawing to a close – and had already begun to make her way to the after-party.

She never made it.

Her producer, a ruddy-faced middle-aged gentleman with a passion for film, liquor and fast cars, had escorted her to the after-party. Amazingly, even after downing over a quart of scotch, he almost made it. Yet somewhere high up in the Hollywood Hills, the vehicle had lost control, smashed through the side barrier, before plummeting to ground, killing the producer instantly and critically injuring Elizabeth.

Grief-stricken, Profit rushed back home, catching the first flight available – but arrived too late. His wife, the newly crowned queen of Hollywood, died an hour before he reached her.

Torn apart by both grief and guilt, Profit turned his back on the life he had, blaming himself for Elizabeth's death, and had shunned the world, drawing the curtains of life closed. Until, that is, being discovered by a gangly young black kid named Joseph Ruebins.

Joseph, then just a lanky shadow of what he would become, had found the old fighter in the hope he could convince Profit to return to the world as his coach. It had been a very hard task. At first, the aging ex-pro had flatly refused to answer his door, never mind speak to anyone, particularly this annoying black kid. Still, Joseph had returned first weekly, then daily, before eventually drawing Profit out. They'd simply walked a few blocks at first, giving

Joseph time to explain why he'd chosen the old man as a potential mentor.

That was simple: Joseph's mother had brought the younger, enigmatic and handsome Eugene Profit into Joseph's world through her passion for the old black and whites – particularly the films starring her idol, Sidney Poitier.

Joseph's mother had been giving her son her usual monologue, of how brave the young black actor had been to take on such powerful roles at a time when the industry would ordinarily see Joseph's forefathers as incapable of portraying anything other than bellboys or hoods or servants. Hell, the actor hadn't even had the right to vote by the time he was receiving his nomination for an Oscar. And Joseph's mother truly believed that the actor and those as brave as he had been instrumental in their battle for equal rights.

A casual comment about Poitier's co-star, a beautiful young white girl, had started Joseph on the path to allying himself with the ex-champion of the World.

"Such a sweet looking thing, and such a shame she died so young, leaving her handsome champion all alone…"

This was so different a statement from the one he was used to hearing that a teenage Joseph Ruebins had pressed his mother to tell him all. She had.

And only hours after discovering that an ex-pro, a World Champion no less, could be living practically on his doorstep, Joseph found himself spinning through countless reels of microfiche, late that afternoon, at the local library. Within minutes of reading about the old champ's heroics, Joseph had decided that he wanted this amazing yet tragic boxer to lead him towards a world title fight.

Eventually his determination had won.

Profit started to help Joseph, just a few hours a week to begin with, in the gym, showing him how to throw solid jabs and teaching him the important techniques of defence. By the end of their first year, their fragile partnership had blossomed into Profit working Joseph's corner full time, and the old fighter looking upon Joseph as the son he'd never had.

Now, as Joseph looked upon the sleeping ex-fighter, he understood that Profit had become his guardian angel, there to protect him, and see that success and all its hidden dangers didn't destroy this son of his.

It almost had.

Joseph felt his eyelids grow heavy. He closed them and listened to the rhythmic breathing of the man at his side. Less than a minute passed before Joseph was asleep.

Chapter Fifteen

Detective Thomas Carter flipped his cell phone shut, ending his brief conversation with Captain Mendoza. He returned to Tyler's side, and both stood looking down at Joseph Ruebins' physician.

The desk he sat behind looked way too big for him, took up almost the entire room, and left just enough space for both the detectives to fill the compact office. The desk, though big enough to perform open-heart surgery upon, had very little on display apart from a brass name plaque, which read: *'Doctor Martin Greenwood'*, and a pencil and penholder.

"So, Doctor Greenwood, what can you tell us about Joseph Ruebins' condition?" Carter asked.

Greenwood turned to the window of his office for a moment, the expression on his face sombre. Clearing his throat, he said. "Truthfully, I'm still not sure."

"Meaning?"

"Until all our tests have been completed, I cannot give you – or Ruebins – a satisfactory diagnosis. Or prognosis, for that matter."

Carter leaned over, placing his hands flat against the desk. "Doctor, is it at all possible that Joseph Ruebins is faking this whole episode?"

Greenwood grinned slightly. "Nothing's impossible, Detective. The brain is a very complex organ. Joseph may be suffering from anything as mundane as a mini-stroke, or experiencing a series of schizoid embolisms."

"No, that's not what I mean." Carter said, shaking his

head. "Is it possible he's faking it, knowingly? Consciously?"

The doctor's frown deepened. "Why would he do that?"

Carter shrugged. "Who knows, attention?"

Greenwood shook his head. "In fairness, Detective, I don't think you can get much more attention than becoming Heavyweight Champion of the World."

"Tell that to Charles Manson or William Gacy," Carter countered.

"Is that who you think is laying in that hospital bed, a potential Manson or Gacy?"

"That's what I'm here to find out."

"Okay, Detective, let me tell you this. Joseph Ruebins has most definitely suffered some sort of haemorrhage or stroke, but until the results of his MRI scan return, I just can't be too sure what?"

"So he's definitely not acting?"

"Not even Denzel Washington could force just one side of his face to collapse, not even if there was an Oscar in it for him."

Seemed like a fair point. However, the handprint he'd found left a nagging sensation that Ruebins wasn't telling them everything. "How long before his test results come in," he asked.

"Tomorrow morning."

"Okay, I'll have a guard posted at his door for the night. Until we know what it is we're dealing with."

"I don't like the idea of putting one of my patients under house arrest," Greenwood said.

"No – you're right," Carter agreed. "But if what you've just told me is true, then you are putting a witness into protection."

"What?" Greenwood asked.

"If Joseph Ruebins didn't kill our man, then he's just become our star witness. And one I'd rather keep alive – if that's okay?"

"This is insane. If Jones's killer knows Ruebins is a threat, then why not kill him too? Why leave a witness – any kind of witness – to chance?”

Carter leaned closer to the doctor, their faces only inches apart. “Because, Doctor, he should have died by now, shouldn’t he?”

This obscure question sealed the doctor’s lips closed for a moment or two. “What?” he managed to say, once he’d peeled them open.

“The mix-up,” Carter clarified.

Whatever the doctor planned to say never emerged.

Carter stood back, allowing Detective Tyler to take his place. She smiled warmly, which bled away some of the tension that had been there.

“Doctor,” she started, “my notes show that a Mister Rueben Jackson should have been sharing the same room as our victim. But instead, Mister Ruebins was put there.”

“So?” Greenwood asked, the obvious eluding him for now.

“So, where is Mister Jackson now?” Tyler asked.

“He’s deceased. Passed away some time last night.” He spread out his hands. “Terminal illness, may I add. He’d have died whether or not he spent the night in intensive care, geriatrics, or even in the hands of God himself. Bowel cancer. Secondary tumours had spread to every major organ in his body.”

“Exactly,” Carter agreed, drawing alongside Tyler.

The doctor looked from one face to the next. “And?”

Carter said, “And would a killer have wasted precious time adding another victim to his list, knowing that they weren’t going to see the night through, anyway?”

“But that would mean the killer…” he trailed off, finally understanding the ramifications.

“Precisely our point,” Carter said. “That would mean the killer must have had access to all the patients’ history or medical notes.”

“But…”

“Yeah – but, only the hospital staff have access to them,”

Carter finished.

"My God…" Greenwood breathed.

"So who *does* have access?" Carter asked.

Greenwood pursed his lips. "Almost everyone working on this level – nurses, doctors, even the orderlies."

"I need a list, Doctor. And sooner rather than later."

"Okay," Greenwood acknowledged.

"I also want the names of every visitor that came to see Henry Jones, relatives, friends, colleagues, unknowns."

"I'll contact the nurse who was in charge."

"Good," Carter said.

The doctor flashed him a quick, nervous smile, glad to be of help. Then his face resumed its serious look. "But what about Joseph, how much real danger is he in?"

"One thing's for sure, even if Ruebins didn't get a look at our man, the killer got a hell of a good look at him. I don't want anyone entering his room alone. Not you, not his wife and kid, not even me – not until we've posted a guard outside. Okay?"

"I understand," Greenwood said.

"If our killer *is* part of this hospital, then they're gonna find out about the mix-up soon enough. And once they do, things might just get even uglier for Mister Ruebins."

"Christ," Greenwood cursed.

Carter stepped back away from the desk and folded his arms across his chest. "Now, I need to know who deals with the patients' bodies, once they've passed away."

"The morgue. Why?"

"Because Doc, I want to know where in the hell half my evidence has got to," Carter responded, harshly.

"Like?"

"Like the original bed sheet, for one thing."

Chapter Sixteen

The small hospital bed had become Joseph's entire world. Jake and Marianna sat at the bottom playing a game of cards, while Eugene Profit lay slumped in a chair at his side. His dinner, a plate of cold ham and mashed potatoes, with peas soft as sludge, was mostly untouched on the tray just to his left. The TV in the corner of the room was switched on, but with the sound muted, the flicker of changing pictures went mostly unnoticed.

It had been a few hours since his MRI scan, and now understanding that nothing new would be revealed until tomorrow, they were filling the hours until visiting time was over. Joseph had spent the last few hours fearing another attack was close, but so far, he'd stayed bright and alert and hadn't as yet felt the presence of darkness or dizziness.

Throughout the day his right arm had continued to gain sensation, to the point were Joseph was able to feel the bed sheet underneath his fingers. His face was still a Halloween mask, swollen on one side and a collapsed mess on the other, but his words fell with less confusion tied to them and were clearly heard by those around him.

Joseph looked up and caught Marianna's eyes. They were filled with worry and doubt, and Joseph reached out to pat her free hand. "Everything's fine," he said, hoping to reassure her.

She nodded, the fact that her husband could now speak clearer, proof at the very least that Joseph's condition wasn't deteriorating. Still, the sudden appearance of an armed police guard outside the room was worry enough. Detective Carter had stated that it was for Joseph's protection – possibly thinking that that would soothe Marianna's nerves, now understanding that her husband wasn't in trouble with the authorities – but it had actually magnified her concern with the fear that he was in real danger from someone outside. The detective had said he would return later to offer an update. Marianna checked her watch constantly, waiting for news that the killer had been caught, and all that they needed to worry about now was Joseph's recovery.

Eventually, just as day was giving way to night, the detective entered the room, alone this time. Understanding that all were doing their best to protect Jake, he looked straight at Eugene Profit, nodded slightly, and turned his attention to Joseph and Marianna.

Profit climbed to his feet, making a real show of how hungry he was by rubbing his belly and expressing that he could eat a whole cow if one was available in the cafeteria downstairs.

"You feel like a bowl of cold slop?" Profit asked the boy.

Jake smiled. "Cold slop *and* ice-cream?"

"Yeah, okay." Profit agreed.

Jake jumped off the bed. "Great!"

"Mom, Pop, do you want me to bring something back for you to eat?"

Both shook their heads. "No thanks," they said in unison.

"Okay," Jake said, taking Profit's hand and leading him outside.

Once the door clicked shut, Detective Carter moved over to the bedside. He pulled up a chair, shrugged out of his jacket, and draped it over the back.

"Joseph's doctor says he's making good progress," he said.

"I am," Joseph agreed, directing the detective's attention to him.

"Good," Carter said. "There are still a few unanswered questions I need cleared up."

"Such as?" Joseph asked.

"Mainly, how the handprint got onto the curtain that separated your bed and Henry Jones'?"

"What handprint?"

"Your handprint."

Joseph turned to Marianna, seeking guidance and understanding.

She asked, "What do you mean, Joseph's handprint?"

Carter replied, "The print that somehow found its way onto the partition, a good three feet away from Joseph's bed. A distance that I believe would be impossible for any man to reach, even someone with the reach your husband is capable of."

"So what are you saying?"

"I'm saying, please think hard. Are you one hundred percent sure you didn't get out of bed, even for a moment, and cross the room to the other bed?"

"Why is this so important to you?" Marianna asked.

Carter scratched at the grey stubble on his chin. "Because the sooner I can rule Joseph out of the investigation, the sooner we can focus our attention elsewhere. Meaning, Joseph will remain a lot safer if we're tracking the actual killer."

Joseph held up his hand. "Honey, the detective's only doing his job." Then he tipped his eyes toward Carter. "What can I say that I haven't already? I woke up to find the old guy exposed, so did what I could to get his attention. Unless I blacked out, somehow found my feet, and in a daydream climbed out of bed, then I promise you I just reached out and pulled on the curtain – no big deal."

Carter sat silent for a second, hopeful that Ruebins would add to his explanation, and finally put the issue to rest. But Joseph quieted, too, and looked expectantly towards the detective. A wordless Mexican standoff ensued.

Finally, Carter asked, "Okay, let's move on. When you woke up this morning, what was happening on the other side of the room?”

“What do you mean?” Joseph asked.

“Were any of the orderlies attending to Mister Jones, or were nurses or doctors examining him?”

Joseph shook his head. “I’ve no idea.”

“Why?”

“Because I woke up in here, alone.”

“Great. See no evil, hear no evil, right?” Carter said.

Joseph looked back apologetically. “I wish I had seen something, at least then you’d believe me.”

Marianna spoke up. “Detective, aren’t there security cameras throughout the hospital?”

“Yeah, but only facing entrances and exits, mostly within the main lobby. We’re reviewing them now – but as you can imagine, there’s a hell of a lot of people traipsing in and out all day.”

“What about security? I’ve seen guards in the hospital, a couple of times already,” she added.

“Nothing too heavy,” Carter replied. “There’s a few posted in ER, one or two patrolling the corridors, but this isn’t exactly a high security prison.” Marianna’s gaze turned towards the doorway, the one the armed guard stood behind.

Carter offered a sympathetic nod. “Well – not ordinarily, that is.”

Marianna cut straight to the chase. “How much danger is Joseph in, Detective?”

Carter searched her eyes. They were dark, beautiful, full of fear and, most importantly, desperate for the truth. Carter looked towards Joseph. His eyes were also dark and fearful, but could it be because he was close to being revealed as a cold-blooded killer?

He gave her the most honest answer he could. “I don’t know. I really don’t.” He reached out, taking hold of the lowered safety railing, and then used it to help pull himself up. As he did, his weight forced the bed to move fractionally.

He stopped dead.

"This bed," he began, "is it the same one you slept in last night?"

Joseph frowned. "Yeah, why?"

"Nothing," he answered, but it was obvious this new wrinkle was something.

"What is it?" Marianna asked.

"Wait here," he told Joseph.

Joseph almost laughed. "I ain't going anywhere."

Carter was already halfway out the door.

***

The young police officer turned to face Carter as he appeared. "Sir," he acknowledged, respectfully.

"Don't let anyone inside while I'm gone," Carter instructed.

"Sir?"

"Not even a doctor or nurse – no matter what they say. You understand?"

"Yes, sir."

Carter spun on his heel and headed quickly down the corridor. He took a short ride in an elevator, climbing just the one level, and made his way to the geriatrics ward. Strips of bright-yellow police tape sealed the room he stopped outside. He pulled the tape away, opened the door and stepped inside.

Now that the room had been cleared of its human occupants, it possessed an overpowering antiseptic smell. Carter hit the light switch. The single fluorescent tube flickered to life with a loud electronic buzz and the harshness of the white light jabbed painfully at Carter's eyes for a moment. Two empty beds now occupied the room. Henry Jones, what was left of him, sat chilling in the morgue, awaiting processing and a formal identification.

He crossed the small room and moved directly to the side that Joseph Ruebins had been positioned on. The fluorescent light above cast bright slivers of light across the linoleum floor. He placed his hand on the bare mattress, looked to the floor, and discovered instantly what he'd come to find.

"I'll be damned," he said.

Bending over, he ran his fingertips over the surface of the floor and felt the distinctive groove that had been pushed into the material found there. He stood straight, spotting a second imprint six feet from the first and parallel to the side of the bed. Now using both hands, he pulled the bed towards him, by about eighteen inches, the wheels underneath allowing him to do so with ease, until the rollers fell perfectly into the two small channels.

"Goddamn it," he cursed, chiding himself for being so stupid the first time around.

He jumped onto the bed and laid himself flat, favouring the side closer to the curtain. Reaching out his fingers brushed against the material on the first grab. With just a few more inches, his hand would quite easily be capable of tugging on a handful of curtain. Like Joseph Ruebins had.

"Son-of-a-bitch is telling the truth," he murmured out loud.

Chapter Seventeen

The few colours that had been present in the alleyway earlier leeched away with the arrival of dusk. A thick, impenetrable greyness now filled the alley, as if the dark clouds above had become too heavy to remain aloft, falling suddenly to earth to fill every corner with gloom.

Presley Perkins followed the tight channel of buildings and arrived once again at Moses Prey's hideout. He rapped against the steel door. Like earlier, the small opening slid open and a set of eyes appeared framed by the darkness on the other side.

"I'm here to see Moses again," Perkins said.

The eyes blinked a couple of times, as if their owner was trying to figure out something of a complicated nature. "Wait there."

Presley huffed like a child, reluctant to play the same waiting game twice in one day. The eyes returned almost as quickly as they'd left and the deadbolt from the other side slid open with a muffled squeal.

The door opened to reveal Timothy's bulk. "Moses is busy with another client."

"But I brought more money – look," Presley whined. He dug deep, withdrawing two handfuls of cash.

Earlier, after his escapades in Central Park, Presley had visited a small backstreet pawnbroker. Having already emptied the bag of its contents, including a purse with fifty dollars tucked neatly inside, he presented it to the broker as an unwanted Christmas gift.

The broker's eyebrows had lifted. "You're a bit late for swapping presents."

"I'm a busy man," Perkins had replied.

"Looks like a lady's bag to me?" the broker said.

"Who the hell are you, the fashion police?" Perkins scolded.

The broker had examined the handbag, muttering under his breath as he did so, and had eventually offered thirty bucks for it. Knowing that the bag was worth at least ten times that amount, Perkins had snatched the measly sum out of the thief's hands and stormed out of the store.

Now, Timothy stepped back to allow Presley entrance. "I guess he could fit you in."

"Thanks," Presley said, with mock sincerity.

He made the same trip as he'd done that afternoon, the bleak emptiness of the building even more depressing now that it was illuminated by the unforgiving harshness of fluorescent lights. The discarded balls of crushed foil glittered against the darkness of the floor, radiantly, as if each ball had actually trapped the soul of its user inside.

They climbed the single flight of steps together, and then Timothy led Presley to Moses' room of business. The door was already open, and voices could be heard coming from within: Prey's high-pitched squeal and two others, deep and threatening.

They entered to see Moses Prey handing over a shotgun to a young black thug. Hands that looked as if they could break skulls in two took the weapon gently, like a father holding his newborn child for the first time.

The black kid's companion turned to see both Timothy and Perkins enter. "Hey – who's the white hobo motherfucker?"

The shotgun holder turned also, his face flipping from wonder to worry instantly. "What's this?" he demanded, spinning the weapon in his hands.

"Now gentlemen," Moses said. "This is just another client – like you two, here to invest in his future." He flashed them his most enigmatic smile - a mouthful of rot and decay.

"Fool smells like my ass," the companion said.

The other laughed. "Yeah Bro, you been takin' a bath in horseshit or what?"

The young thugs broke into laughter, revealing gold-capped teeth and silver fillings.

Perkins just stood there, unwilling to engage them, simply eager to pay for his merchandise and then get out.

The shotgun holder misunderstood his silence as fear. "No worry, Bro, we ain't gonna bite, we not too fond of horseshit anyhow."

They cracked up again, Timothy joining in this time. Only Moses stayed quiet, his eyes shifting quickly from one face to the next. With enough weapons to fight World War III laid out before him, he watched nervously, ready to intervene if the situation got out of hand. Then, Moses did something that was completely out of character and without sense. Understanding that events would run smoother if dealing with just the one client, he reached out to grasp the Derringer's two casings, which stood upright on the table.

"Here," he said, tossing them over to Perkins. "You can sort payment out with Timothy."

Presley caught them in his hand. Again, he was surprised by the size of the casings, heavy too.

And this was how Moses had made his mistake: by permitting a client to take hold of the ammunition, whilst in possession of the weapon, allowing both to come together, instead of Timothy handling the rounds until all were safely outside.

"Gentlemen," Moses said, gathering the attention of the gang-members to him. He spread his arms like a preacher ready to deliver his sermon. "Let's get back to business, shall we?" They turned back to Moses, the dishevelled fat guy behind them instantly forgotten. Moses continued to rant, explaining how all good pilgrims should come and visit this Mecca, this Holy Land.

Presley withdrew the Derringer and clicked open the loader. He slipped both rounds inside and then clicked the weapon shut. The brief noise that resulted pulled at the group's attention.

Moses stopped ranting, his oversight now apparent to him. Timothy stared at the small weapon, his similarly small brain unable to register just what amount of damage the weapon could do. And the two black kids burst into rancorous roars of laughter at the pitiful pistol in Presley's oversized hand.

"Dude is packin' real heat there, Bro," one mocked.

The other, who now had a handful of green bills, nodded animatedly. "Hope that's all his fat white ass is packin'."

"Maybe he's over-compensating in size, 'cos his dick's too small," the other retorted.

This set them both off again.

And that was it. Something inside of Presley Perkins snapped. Having once flirted with some of the most powerful figures of the criminal underworld, rubbing shoulders with made men, feared men, real hard men, and sharing in the fear and respect that their actions had instilled into others, Presley just stared back at them, no longer willing to suffer the indignity of their ridicule, and sick now of the cowardly existence he'd been forced to endure.

"Hey, Bro, we just jokin' with ya," one snickered.

"Yeah, we don't mean to pound against your fat white ass," the other said.

They broke into laughter again, fuelling Presley's rage with fire. The words came out of Presley's mouth before his brain had time to catch up. "Why don't you shut your big black lips?" he said, his whole body trembling with rage.

The laughter ceased immediately.

The thugs froze, too shocked to speak at first. In the next second their mouths burst open and a blue streak of expletives poured out. Their insults came so fast and so many that Presley could only catch the occasional single word or short phrase as they beat against his ears.

"Fat ass!"

"Motherfucker!"

"Honky bitch!"

"Hairy Moby Dick look-alike-whore!"

Finally, the young blood with all the cash stepped forward and threw a crumpled bill towards Presley's face. "Go take a bath, bitch," he ordered.

The crushed dollar caught Presley unexpectedly in his right eye. Already sore from the pepper spray, the contact unleashed a searing jag of fresh pain. Instinctively, he reached up to rub at the sudden pain found there, using the same hand that held the pistol.

The kid holding the shotgun misunderstood the abrupt raising of the Derringer as a threat. He panicked and brought his own weapon up, aiming it directly at Presley's midriff.

Moses Prey had just enough time to cry, "Wait!" before the room turned instantly sour with a mixture of gun-smoke and guts.

The kid with the shotgun pulled his weapon tight. His face flipped between rage, fear, and then back to rage again as he pulled the trigger. A hollow *clank* followed as the trigger fell against an empty chamber.

Too late.

Presley caught the act of aggression through tear-filled eyes. He jabbed his arm out, levelling the Derringer straight, and fired. In such a small space the noise sounded like the burst of thunder. The .357 calibre bullet caught the kid across the forehead, tearing flesh and bone as it went. Scraping across the hard surface of the youth's skull, the bullet changed direction, ever so slightly, and hit Moses Prey flush in the face. The dealer's face imploded, folding inwards instantly, before reforming into a macabre portrait of bright reds and brain matter, as it spattered against the wall behind.

The black kid went down heavily, his skull split into two. His pal bolted towards the door.

Timothy's handgun was already out and, as the kid rushed

by, he shot him at point blank range. Three holes the size of fists burst from the kid's chest. Then, in a heap, the kid skittered across the floor. He finished half-in and half-out of the doorway. A brief shower of green bills fell all about them.

For a second, both Presley and Timothy stared at each other. Presley's gun wavered. Timothy took a quick look towards the body of his boss, and then whined hysterically.

"You fucker! You killed Moses!"

"Wait!" Perkins offered.

"You gonna have to pay for that," Timothy cried.

Presley saw the gun draw towards him. He ducked instinctively and dived for the exit. A chunk of masonry the size of his head exploded above him. In the next instant, he was back in the corridor and running for his life.

He tore through the passageway, expecting a bullet to rip through his back at any moment. He reached the stairs landing before the first shot came. A barrage of bullets peppered the wall to his right. He dropped to all fours and skidded to a halt, as another hail tore the wooden banister at his side into a thousand pieces. Presley chanced a look behind him. Timothy was at the other end of the passageway, coming fast now, having traded his handgun for a fully-automatic assault rifle.

Presley scrambled forward, and then took the stairs on his front, sliding down quickly like a kid would do on his belly. Wooden splinters ripped through his jacket as he careened downwards. He almost lost the Derringer halfway down, as it slipped from his hands, but, having already succumbed to the laws of gravity, it bounced and clattered to the foot of the stairs. Presley snatched it up quickly once he'd arrived there. He jumped to his feet and then took the ground floor passageway at full speed.

With half the distance covered, he heard the *rat-tat-tat* of bullets from behind, and then felt them explode into the floor directly at his heels. Changing direction, he threw himself into one of the empty rooms.

"Where you hiding?" Timothy yelled from the hallway.

Presley heard the boots stop, followed by loud gunfire, somewhere behind him. Frantically, he searched the room he now found himself trapped in. Just a few pieces of rotten furniture filled the room: an old sofa, with its guts hanging out of its underbelly, lay to one side, and a round table with multiple scars scratched into its top was propped along the wall closest to him.

He tried to visualise how far the main door was from his current location. At least ten yards, he realised with sickening certainty. Would he have chance to distract his hunter and then make a break for freedom? Not a chance! The heavy-duty bolt that held the door tight would take precious seconds to slide free, giving Timothy all the time he needed.

The words, "You're gonna pay!" echoed around him.

He pushed himself against the wall. The wall, now little more than a barrier of mush, almost gave way under the additional strain of his weight. Holes dotted it at irregular intervals like ulcerous sores, black and raw, and the plaster around them was flaking away like sheets of dead skin. He glanced back at the table and sofa, and then towards the wall again.

An idea formed – the only one available to him.

He reached over to grab the table, dragging it over to him. Another clatter of bullets sounded. Now, as the room beyond was torn apart, and, under the cover of fire, Presley hammered furiously against the wall. With little effort he punched through into the next room, ripping open a large tear. Wasting no time at all, he opened out the hole large enough to fit through. Then, pulling the table, he slotted it into the gap. Now, hopefully, his escape route would go unnoticed at a glance. If not? He could kiss his aforementioned fat ass goodbye.

Heavy footsteps thundered towards him. They moved with more caution, now that Timothy sensed he was closer to his prey. Presley laid himself as flat as he could, hugging the floor with his hands over his head. Another hail of bullets cut the room up adjacent to him, some punching holes through the wall at his side in an explosion of wet plaster and wooden splinters. The assault lasted just a few seconds, but the damage was devastating. Half the wall lay in ruins, allowing Presley to see clearly into the next room. Timothy stood there with white plaster dust and grime covering his face, and the assault rifle at his side expelled a weary breath of gun smoke.

For one terrible second, Presley thought their eyes met through the remains of the wall, but, in the next moment, Timothy turned on his heels to re-enter the hallway.

Presley got to his knees, pushing the table out of the way as he did so. He crawled through the hole and then scrambled deeper into the next room. Belying his size, he skipped soundlessly to the doorway and cautiously stuck his head out.

Timothy was at the next opening, the rifle against his shoulder.

Presley held his breath.

Timothy entered.

There was a deafening clatter as bullets ripped their way over every inch of the room. Steeling himself, Presley dashed to the next doorway, the one that Timothy filled, and brought the small Derringer up behind the heavy's ear.

"Move, and I'll blow your goddamn brains out," he warned.

Timothy froze.

"Drop the weapon," Presley ordered.

Timothy remained still for just a second. Then something changed in his stance. He became more rigid. His breathing stopped and, with sickening dread, Presley knew he was about to do no such thing. The muzzle of the assault rifle began to turn in a wide arc. Time seemed to slow, everything happening at only half the speed it should. The weapon continued to come, and at the same time, Timothy started to spin away from the Derringer.

Presley heard his own warped voice cry, "No!" an instant before all hell broke loose.

The rifle started to tear the wall up at Presley's side, huge chunks of plaster and wood and masonry filling the air with a thick, clogging cloud. Timothy's lips parted and a fearless roar escaped from deep within his throat.

In a blind panic, Presley squeezed off a shot, his last, and then rushed towards the sealed doorway. He almost lost his footing, sliding surprisingly too fast as he stepped on an empty glass bottle. Somehow, he kept upright, and in the next second his fingers scratched frantically at the deadbolt. The hairs at the nape of his neck bristled with fear, and his heart threatened to give, but his fingers continued to grapple with the bolt. With a sharp scrape, the bolt eventually gave and, in the next instant, Presley was outside. He fell to his knees, his feet finally tripping over themselves, and he went down hard.

The steel doorway stood ajar – corridor empty.

Timothy hadn't followed, nor fired a single shot towards the exit. Presley remained frozen where he'd fallen, but he felt safer with the main sidewalk only ten yards away from him.

Another quick look towards the corridor confirmed it was empty. Presley climbed to his feet, slowly, the Derringer tight in his hand. Had anyone even heard the shootout over the general noise of the city? There were no tenants, or commercial businesses – Moses' not included – around the immediate vicinity, and the noise of rushing traffic would have drowned out any sounds of gunfire easily. And when you got right down to it, would anyone have cared, anyway?

Presley took a single step back towards the doorway, believing now that somehow Timothy had been stopped in his tracks. His heart still pounded in his chest, but less painfully so, and a cold sweat had broken out long his spine, making his shirt cling to his back. His attention returned to the sidewalk. The clever thing would be to get as far away as he could. Unfortunately, the present situation he found himself in dictated otherwise.

His original plan had been to come here, to buy protection, in the event that he was cornered again. Now, the weapon in his hand was empty, pathetic, and of no real use. The sounds of sirens reached his ears, but they were distant and harmless. No cops were on their way to arrest him, because nobody cared about this part of the neighbourhood.

He stepped back inside the doorway, keeping his eyes peeled to the open room he'd escaped from. Had Timothy simply given up? Presley reached inside to take an empty soda bottle. Simultaneously, he threw it into the corridor and readied himself for flight. The bottle landed with a crunch of broken glass.

Nothing.

Presley took another step inside. He made his way along the corridor, his back pressed against the wall, keeping one eye on the room, the other, on his escape route. The last few yards were the hardest. He imagined gunfire would erupt at any moment.

It didn't.

Taking one final deep breath, Presley stepped into the doorway.

The room was empty.

Timothy was nowhere to be found.

Chapter Eighteen

Detective Tyler stared at her open notebook. A short list of details had been scribbled down in untidy handwriting, some of which had already been struck-out, Joseph Ruebins amongst them.

"So what have we got?" Carter asked.

Both detectives sat at Carter's desk, awaiting the autopsy report on Henry Jones to come through, along with the provisional findings from the Crime Scene Unit.

"We've got surveillance recordings from the hospital – about 36 man-hours worth of CCTV," Tyler began. "We've also got a long list of names of employees taken from St Mary's. And patients – Joseph Ruebins included."

Carter asked, "Who's analysing the surveillance recordings?"

"I've got Audio Visual looking through them. Told them to pay attention to the cameras positioned within the corridors first. Too much traffic around the entrances. It would have been mayhem, what with the R.T.A. and all."

Carter nodded. "We could still be onto something with Ruebins though."

Tyler frowned. "So far, I'd say Ruebins' involvement - or lack of it - is the only sure thing we *do* have."

"Yeah, I agree," Carter said. "But the chance of another patient being capable of the murder is still a discrete possibility."

"You're right," Tyler agreed. "The murder took place out of visiting hours. So that should greatly reduce the chance of a visitor's involvement."

Carter nodded. "What about security personnel?"

"A relatively short list to work through. I'll check it out personally."

"Okay. So for now, our only known witness is Joseph Ruebins. And he's playing see no evil, speak no evil."

"Yeah," Tyler agreed. "Still, he's the one link we have to the actual killer."

"Or killers?"

Tyler frowned. "Killers?"

"We can't rule out that this was done by more than one individual."

"What makes you say that?"

"Seems too convenient that the original bed sheet found its way to laundry so fast, and Jones wasn't found earlier, considering he was wired to a monitor."

Earlier, Carter had finally found the whereabouts of the missing blanket. A young orderly had removed it after finding Henry Jones' body. Deeply inexperienced and thinking that the blood found had been a simple result of him passing away, she had allowed the bed to be changed, not wishing for relatives to arrive to find their loved one in such a way. The soiled sheet had then been washed in the hospital laundry.

"But what about the orderly?" Tyler asked. "She seemed genuinely upset?"

"Yeah, embarrassed even," Carter said. "Doesn't mean she isn't connected somehow."

"So you think the whole hospital is trying to conceal a murder?"

"Not necessarily," Carter replied, with a shake of his head. "Maybe they're more worried about being sued for malpractice. Neither Ruebins nor Jones received adequate care last night, and perhaps the hospital is simply trying to keep the damage to a minimum."

"So what are you getting at?"

"Maybe the orderly was told to remove the sheet, clean up the patient and then make it look as if he'd simply passed away in the night."

"Okay, that makes sense," Tyler agreed.

"And then they find our killer's calling card – and call us, forgetting their little cover-up in the panic."

"Agreed," Tyler said. "Finding such a thing would have thrown anyone."

Carter shuddered slightly at the memory of the patient's tongue. "Got ourselves one sick son-of-a-bitch, that's for sure."

"What do you think? We got a serial killer at work here?"

Carter paused for a second. "In all the time I've worked here, I've only ever known of one genuine serial killer. They're not as common as films or books would make you believe."

"Go on," Tyler pushed.

"Okay, we need to understand what we mean by a serial killer. A person who kills multiple people, or, a person who kills for pleasure – for some sort of sick purposes? A purpose usually only known to them."

"What's the difference?"

"You could pull any gang member out of any prison, or the streets, and chances are they've probably killed more than one person. But that wouldn't make them a serial killer. Wouldn't qualify them as a Ted Bundy. No, nothing unusual in street killings or gang wars or even intentional hits. We're not looking for someone here who kills for profit or power. More like for passion."

"So you think Henry Jones could be the first for our killer? His baptism of blood."

"I'm not sure," Carter responded.

"Then why the dramatics?" she asked. "Why go to all that trouble, if you didn't have something to say. A statement to us?"

Carter drummed his fingertips along the tabletop. His face

flipped between emotions: thoughtful, confusion, and then too understanding.

"I don't think the killer *was* leaving a message for us."

"Then to whom?"

"I don't know," he admitted, his face returning to confusion.

"But the killer must know we're not likely to go to the press with this. Not yet."

"No," he agreed. "But we're not the only people to have seen the work of our killer, are we? At least a half dozen people at the hospital saw what happened to Jones; any one of them could be on the phone right now, negotiating exclusive rights to the story."

"So you think the message could have been left for a relative?" Tyler asked. "Maybe as a warning of things to come."

Carter nodded absentmindedly. "Maybe…" he muttered.

"So let's get digging on Jones, see what comes up," Tyler said.

"Good idea."

"Okay, what else have we got?" she asked.

Carter stopped drumming against the table. "We're waiting for forensics to come back with a list of fingerprints – see if anything stands out. They're also running tests on the morphine drip and pump, to see if there could have been a malfunction, or if they were tampered with. Seems a bit pointless, I know, considering the way the victim was found, but we need to collate as much information as possible."

"Right. I'll start to compile witness reports, see if anything stands out. Late visitors, staff working in the wrong area and such."

"Okay, I'm gonna see what the coroner's come up with. Find out if a special type of instrument was used to cut the tongue. Something that might only be found in a hospital."

They stood, and Tyler flipped her notebook shut. She slipped it inside her jacket. "Meet back here in an hour?" she asked.

Carter took a quick look at his watch. "Make it two."

"Two?"

"Yeah," he said. "I need to look at past cases – both open and closed, see if there's been a similar kind of crime in the city over the last few years."

Tyler looked back at him. "Thought we'd agreed it wasn't a serial killer?"

"We have. Still, records might just throw some light onto this."

"Like what?"

"Like, motive, for one."

Chapter Nineteen

Fear threatened to drag Presley out of the building, self-preservation ordering him to get as far away as possible while he still had the chance. Chance dictated otherwise, because fate had presented him with the opportunity for a serious score. Yet it was desperation that eventually spoke loudest. His original plan to buy a weapon to protect himself from the cops that hunted him by day, and from the Russians who hunted him both day and night, now seemed part of another life.

The debt he owed had made Presley too much of a known commodity, and his creditor wasn't about to let such a large tariff simply walk away. No, there were people on the streets looking for him. The most worrying one of all was Detective Thomas Carter, a man who was going to stop at nothing until he was dead and zipped up cold in a body bag.

Presley couldn't afford to walk away. And the arsenal of weapons and stash of cash upstairs demanded he risk it. That's how he found himself at the foot of the stairs. He looked up, standing on his tiptoes, in an attempt to get a better view of the landing above.

He'd quickly checked the rooms on this level, finding nothing of the heavy or his assault rifle. Perhaps Timothy had returned to the weapons table in haste, ready to reload and continue his pursuit. Still, minutes had gone by now, with no sound or sight of him.

This is lunacy, Perkins thought, as he took the first step upwards. The board under his foot creaked slightly, a sound he hadn't been aware of during his first two trips through the building. Now, though, his senses were at their highest.

He took a breath and started to climb.

What could he do with the money and weapons, even if he took them? The protection a firearm could offer was simple. If backed into a corner, like the night before, he would at least have options. The option to kill? Maybe? Although he didn't consider himself a violent man, Presley knew now, without doubt, that he could never allow himself to go to jail. A life of privilege had taught him that. No, he understood that freedom was his only option. And what lay above could be his ticket towards winning it.

The landing came into view. Chunks of masonry littered the floor all along the passageway. The banister at the top of the stairs had been blasted into a toothpick. As he ascended, Presley looked along his pathway in the hope of spotting blood. Maybe his single shot had somehow caught Timothy, wounding him sufficiently enough to make him retreat? Not a single drop stained the stairs, nor was he able to find any on the ground floor. Timothy may have also reached the same conclusion as had Presley, and was already making his way outside with a bagful of loot. Moses would have been savvy enough to have given himself more than just the one exit to escape from, if the need ever arose. Timothy could be long gone by now, already planning his future and how to invest his newfound wealth.

This worrying thought spurred Presley on.

He reached the top unscathed and then paused for a moment, his beating chest forcing his lungs to work overtime. He waited until he'd caught his breath. Finally, he took a few steps away from the staircase and inched his way towards Moses' room. His footsteps thudded noisily, masonry crunching under the weight of his shoes, and his breath came out in a tight, constricted wheeze. He reached the doorway to find one of the black gang members sprawled across the threshold, blood pooled out around him.

The stench of blood, innards and cordite was almost overpowering. Presley held his breath as he stepped inside. What he found there was the stuff of nightmares.

The second gang member lay where he'd fallen, his skull open to reveal a mess of orange-grey tissue. Pink, watery fluid had leaked out from the wound, staining the floor around him. However, the most terrible thing to hit Presley was the desperate wheeze that emanated from the kid's lips.

He shuddered, understanding that what lay at his feet was his doing. His attention turned to the table. Moses Prey had been thrown back into his chair, and he sat there, faceless, grinning a ghastly smile from what was left of his lower jaw. Only the bottom half of his face remained intact, along with his bald scalp, and just a few hairs framed this ghastly sight with a greasy dark frame.

The cash that one of the kids had held was now scattered across the room, some soaking up puddles of blood, others gathered in small heaps like the winnings of a jackpot. All three victims lay where they'd fallen, the money sat untouched, and the cache of weapons still formed neat rows and columns.

Presley stepped over the wounded victim, careful not to tread in brain matter or blood, aware that any trace of his footprints would implicate him to the horrific events of the evening. He checked behind him, but nothing threatening appeared. Quickly, with his hand drawn into his sleeve, he moved around the table and opened one of the table's drawers. Inside were a dozen or so small boxes, each with a calibre stamped on them.

What had Moses said about the Derringer? Something about it being the smallest Magnum in the world. He forced his brain to remember the recent conversation, but the scene before him pushed any reasoning out of his mind. Instead, he began to open boxes, carefully though, using just the rough tips of his fingernails, in the hope that any prints would go unnoticed. Then, once he'd opened a few, he clicked the

Derringer's loader open, retrieved the two spent casings, and began to withdraw single bullets, before trying them for size. They were all too small. He tilted the Derringer back, catching the incorrect bullets in the palm of his hand, before slipping the casings inside his jacket, leaving no possibility of fingerprints. Eventually he opened a box of .357s. The first round fitted perfectly, so Presley retrieved the entire box and then quickly loaded the second chamber. He clicked the loader shut before pocketing the box of rounds.

Now back in business, he turned his attention to the carpet of green bills scattered around the room. Most were twenty-dollar bills, some ten, and just the occasional five. All were stained by splatters of red. Presley figured that Moses must have a stash of cash readily available to him. He looked away from the scattering of blood money, and focused his attentions to the table before him. There were another three drawers to examine. The first was empty. An arrangement of wicked looking knives filled the second, ranging from small butterfly-knives to foot-long hunting knives. The last drawer presented Presley with what he'd come for: tightly wrapped rolls of green bills – and lots of them.

"Bingo," chimed Presley.

His dirty fingers reached out greedily, snatching up as many bundles as he could. He raised the handful of cash to his nose and then breathed in deeply. A long exhale of pleasure escaped from his lips. One roll looked to be made up of hundred-dollar bills and, by its thickness, Presley guessed it to be worth at least five thousand. Another roll promised at least another few grand. In all, Presley guessed he was richer by somewhere in the twenty-five grand range.

The kid on the floor groaned again.

Presley's arm rose slightly, and the Derringer wavered towards the kid's open skull. A mercy killing, Presley told himself. That's what it would be if he pulled the trigger. The firing mechanism felt in need of a hundred pounds of pressure to work it. The gun began to waver. Perkins took a deep breath and readied himself.

"Okay," he said. "This is for your own good."

His thumb clicked the hammer back to halfway.

The scrape of a boot pulled his attention upwards. In the doorway, blocking the only exit was Timothy. The assault rifle was clasped in his hands, and his eyes looked directly at Presley. Timothy's face looked ghostlike, white and gaunt. His eyes appeared red-rimmed and hollow. Then, with deadly intent, the weapon began to rise. Timothy opened his mouth and a single word came from between grey lips.

"*Moses…*"

Chapter Twenty

With night falling and visiting time almost over, Joseph held onto Marianna's hand with an intensity born of fear. Darkness filled the window completely, and it pushed against the glass with overwhelming conviction. Worried about the safety of his wife and son, Joseph had convinced her to spend the night across town at Eugene Profit's place. She'd agreed without comment, although not overly keen to do so, in an attempt to ease Joseph's anxiety.

"What about you?" Marianna asked now. "Are *you* going to be okay?"

Joseph flashed her a crooked half-smile. "I'll be fine."

Marianna's brow furrowed slightly. "I'm worried, Joseph. What if this killer decides to come back?"

"Then he'll have to get through hospital security and the armed officer outside."

"The kid's barely out of his teens," she responded, referring to the fresh-faced officer guarding his room.

"Honey," Joseph began, "I'll be fine. I'll watch a bit of TV and get some sleep. And before I know it, you'll be back here. Nothing's going to happen, I promise."

"Okay," she sighed.

Already asleep, Jake was curled up on the chair at the side of his father's bed. The old coach had gone to bring his car around to the front of the hospital. Marianna bent to kiss Joseph on his lips and then moved over to Jake.

"Hey sleepyhead, time to go," she said.

Jake murmured something meaningless and opened his

eyes. He lay confused for a moment, his surroundings strange, before remembering where he was.

"What about Pop?" he asked.

"Pop's staying here for another night. To make sure he's all better," she replied.

"Aww. I want to stay, too," Jake moaned.

"Hey," Joseph said. "Do as your mother says."

Reluctantly, Jake climbed off the chair, kissed his father goodnight and took his mother's hand.

"So, we'll see you first thing in the morning," Marianna said.

"I'll be right here," Joseph promised.

Marianna nodded, and then escorted Jake outside.

***

The guard looked up from the magazine at his lap, the one Eugene Profit had given him with Joseph on the cover – and smiled.

"Mrs Ruebins," he said, climbing to his feet. He closed the magazine and placed it carefully – respectfully – on the seat behind him.

Marianna relaxed a little. Profit's use of the old magazine seemed to have worked, and now the guard had a deeper understanding of the man he was here to protect.

"I'll make sure Joseph stays safe and sound," he said with utter conviction.

Marianna gave him a warm smile. She quickly read the officer's nametag. "Thank you, Officer Gore, we appreciate that."

Officer Gore reached up to activate a walkie-talkie at his shoulder. After a short bout of static, he requested for a guard to make his way up to room 2b. He clicked his radio off, ending the brief conversation. "It's probably better we escort you to the lobby, just as a precaution," he said.

Marianna's heartbeat quickened slightly; the officer's

request once again proving that their world had become terribly dangerous.

After only a minute or so the elevator opened and a guard appeared before them. He walked over casually, and then with careless ease, ruffled Jake's hair. "You up for a ride in the elevator, kiddo?" he asked, flashing a smile made from finely chiselled white teeth.

"Yeah," Jake said.

"Okay, let's go," the guard said, leading the way.

Marianna took Jake's hand and then followed close behind. The elevator doors trundled open. All three stepped in together. Jake stood facing the mirrored wall, pulling a series of funny faces.

"All aboard," said the guard like the captain of a ship. His index finger pointed out towards the bank of buttons. Like an elevator itself, his finger went from the lowest button, marked 'B', to the highest which was numbered '8'. He seemed confused for a second, as if unsure which level to press. His finger hovered at the '8' button for a noticeably long time. Then, as it appeared he was about to hit the highest button, a flash of starched material hurried through the doorway.

"Wait for me," called the young doctor. He squeezed through the elevator doors just as they were about to close. He looked from one face to the next then turned his attention to the row of buttons. Seeing that none had been illuminated, he asked, "We going down?"

"Yeah," Marianna replied, stepping forwards to hit the ground floor button.

Something above their heads whined quietly for a second and then the elevator began to descend. The journey was brief; the elevator slid to a stop and the doors opened with a metallic *ping*.

Marianna grabbed Jake's arm and pulled him quickly out of the booth. The guard hesitated for a moment and then followed them as they made their way towards the main lobby. At this time of night, the main entrance bustled with droves of leaving visitors, and the nightshift workers were arriving in groups of two or three, some tired looking, even though their twelve-hour shift hadn't yet started.

Marianna and Jake stepped out into a chilly February evening. The honk of a car horn drew their attention across to the fire lane.

"Over there," Marianna said, pointing towards Eugene's battered Chevy. She turned to find the guard looming behind them. He appeared to be looking over at the Chevy with interest.

"That your ride?" he asked.

"Yeah," Marianna answered.

"Okay, guess you guys can take it from here," he said, eyes focused on the Chevy.

"Thanks," Marianna said, before leading Jake to the car. They crossed the short distance together and climbed inside the old vehicle. Marianna leaned into the backseat to make sure Jake was secure. As she did, she caught sight of the guard standing just inside the main foyer. And even though at least twenty yards of darkness separated them, she could have sworn she could still make out the flash of a smile filled with white teeth.

Then, in the next instant, the car pulled away and the hospital front became just a blur, dark and distant, but one that was etched deeply into Marianna's mind.

Chapter Twenty-One

Presley froze. The angry look on Timothy's face intensified. His weapon continued to climb, and all Presley could do was watch in horror. The weapon levelled out and then came to rest, aimed at his midriff.

"Hey, boss – we got us a real mess here," Timothy said, his head lowering to the floor, jerkily, like an automaton's.

Presley was rooted to the floor. What the fuck was happening?

Timothy's head came back up to eye level, but it took what seemed like a great amount of will to do so. "Yeah, a real mess." The heavy took a step through the doorwell, barely able to pick his feet up high enough to step over the dead kid, who lay halfway inside. He entered the room rigidly, both arms fixed tightly around the assault rifle. His legs looked incapable of bending at the knees correctly. He stopped in the centre of the bloodbath, covered in a layer of powdered chalk and plaster and looking like a Stormtrooper from one of the *Star Wars* movies.

Presley just stared back, unable to understand what was going on. Then, as Timothy turned to take a look at the body behind him, he caught a glimpse of an open wound at the side of the other man's head. A neat hole, just above the temple, appeared. Blood was already crusting around its edges. Presley stared open-mouthed at the ghastly wound.

Unbelievably, the last bullet fired from the Derringer had found its mark. It took only a moment for Presley to understand that the bullet had lobotomised Timothy. A wave of nausea crashed over him. At every turn he seemed to face death and destruction.

"*Mosssesss…*"

Perkins stepped to his right, Timothy's looming presence stood, oblivious. Another few steps brought Presley back into the hallway. He paused for just a second, to make sure that Timothy wasn't following, then turned his back and quickly made his way towards the ground floor.

Taking the stairs two at a time, he got out of there as fast as he could.

Chapter Twenty-Two

Carter rubbed his tired eyes. The room went out of focus. He squinted heavily a couple of times and when the world again stabilised, he turned his attention back to the computer screen. He'd been trawling the VICAP database for an hour now, in the hope of finding something that would aid in his investigation, but so far nothing. No similar killings and nothing on this side of the coast or out West. Nor had he been able to find anything that vaguely resembled this recent grisly killing.

His trip to the city morgue had proved just as fruitless. The instrument that had been used to sever Henry Jones' tongue could have been done by anything from a sharpened knife to a razor-sharp scalpel. No trace had been found within the wound either. No oils, no fibres, no chemicals, nothing. As for the tongue itself, that, too was still a mystery. Understanding that some killers liked to take trophies, Carter hadn't been surprised to find the lump of flesh in question missing. The pathologist had even checked the guy's stomach and anus for it.

Blood samples were now being processed by toxicology, and the rest of Jones' autopsy would be completed later that evening. With clear signs of haemorrhaging to the eyes and specific bruising around the jaw area, the pathologist had stated quite confidently that the old man had likely been suffocated. He'd also concluded that the severing of the victim's tongue had happened posthumously; based upon the sheer lack of blood that had leaked from the wound site.

Carter looked down at the pad before him. The top line had the old man's name written on it, underlined three times with a large question mark after it. So far, nothing about the old man's past had jumped out and screamed for attention. No immediate relatives had visited him in hospital. Therefore, as of yet, nothing other than the basics had been added to Carter's short list. He had the old man's social security number, taken from hospital records, but nothing amazing or enlightening had come up yet.

Henry Jones had been born June 17th 1920, putting him at eighty-six years at the time of death. He'd never been in trouble with the law, had made his tax payments on time, served his country briefly at the end of the Second World War, as a logistics officer, never seeing any real combat, and had married almost as soon as he returned home from overseas. His wife, Margaret, had died eight years ago. They'd registered two sons at City Hall, Jonathon and Edward, both of whom were also deceased: Jonathon died an infant due to meningitis, and Edward, more recently, in a car accident; perhaps explaining why no relatives had visited the old man during his time in hospital.

Henry Jones' health insurance had covered his treatment at St Mary's; therefore, no other third party could be found at this moment in time. Carter had already submitted paperwork to the courts to subpoena Jones' life insurance policies. Only then would they know who was likely to benefit financially by the old man's passing.

Worry gnawed at the pit of Carter's stomach. Maybe they *were* looking at the beginnings of a serial killer? There didn't appear to be any motive for Jones' murder, nothing obvious anyway. And the taking of the tongue was a clear indication of the workings of a sick individual. It wouldn't be the first time in history that a killer had trawled the bleached corridors of a medical institute in search of prey.

Carter checked the time. The small clock in the bottom right-hand corner of the monitor screen showed 7:33 p.m.

Tyler should be heading back anytime now.

As if the young detective had sprung from his very thoughts, Tyler appeared on the other side of the department. She crossed the office, occasionally drawing attention from some of her male counterparts, before seating herself at Carter's side. She dropped a thin folder onto his desk.

"Anything?" she asked, looking at the list of information scrolled across the screen.

"Nothing interesting. You?"

She huffed a sigh, giving Carter his answer.

Carter nodded absentmindedly. "Yeah – got ourselves a real mystery here."

Tyler pulled her notebook from her breast pocket. She flipped it open. "Lots of names, hospital staff, coming and going, some agency staff – which I'm having checked out as we speak, but nothing that stands out as untrustworthy."

"Nobody acting suspiciously?" he asked.

"Too early to say. Place was under loads of stress, what with the R.T.A. Greenwood referred to, lots of unfamiliar faces in unfamiliar places."

"Ideal situation for a killer to slip in unnoticed and do his ghastly deed."

"His?"

"Sorry," Carter said. "To do his or *her* ghastly deed."

Tyler smiled, but the gesture lacked humour. "That's okay. I know we're most likely dealing with a male unknown subject."

Carter nodded; history dictated that most serial killers were of male gender, and only occasionally did the female sex act out such heinous crimes.

"Okay what about Audio Visual, they come up with anything?" Carter asked.

Tyler reached out to open the folder out on his desk. "Got some stills to start with. They ain't great, but it's the best they could do at short notice." She spread seven grainy black and whites out across the table.

"What are we looking for?" Carter asked.

"These are the security personnel."

Carter took the first photo, raised it to eyelevel, held it there momentarily, and then placed it back with the rest. "Okay what am I looking at?"

All the photographs held a single figure in each, captured in a downward angle, and of sufficient distance for the subjects' faces to remain mostly unclear and almost unidentifiable. The one thing apparent, though, was the fact that all seven wore a distinctive dark blue uniform. NYPD. New York's finest.

"Okay," Tyler started, "it's a simple case of elimination."

Carter stood back, arms folded across his chest and watched as the younger detective took lead.

"First photo," she said, placing her finger against the still to the left. "Guy looks to be about 200 pounds, slightly taller than average. Maybe six-three. White."

Carter tilted his head to get a better view. "Agreed," he stated.

Tyler flipped over the photo to reveal a hand-scrawled list of details. "Lieutenant Greg Grillo."

"Go on," Carter prompted.

She began to read each item off. "Greg Grillo, twenty-eight, approx 200 pounds, Caucasian. Studied at NY City Academy. Works the night tour, and has done since his induction two years ago."

Reaching out, Carter re-took the photo. He studied the picture for a long moment. "Okay, assuming I don't know Officer Grillo, how can I be sure this is actually the guy?"

"Had his Chief study these photos long and hard, until he'd made a confident ID on them all. All six of his night officers. Took him awhile, but you'd be surprised how much information can be gleamed by size, posture and stance alone."

Carter nodded a slight concurrence. He'd had a few cases broke by a witness's ability to identify a suspect with little more that a blurred image to work with. Although the photo would rarely hold up in court, it was sometimes the one thing that would blow open a case, leading them to the perpetrator and a whole catalogue of admissible evidence.

He offered the photo back to Tyler. Then counted the photos on the desk. Six remained.

"You said 'all six of his officers'?" he questioned. "There are seven in total."

Tyler placed the image at the end of the spread of photos. She reached over and took the one at the opposite end of the row. "This guy doesn't seem to fit any of the Chief's officers." She turned the photo around to give Carter a look. There wasn't much on offer. The guy's cap was pulled down tight. Shadows filled in where the cap finished. The face was unidentifiable. Still, the uniform was relatively clear in comparison.

Nothing unusual sprang out at Carter.

"Could have been a municipal cop, off the streets, maybe having arrived in attendance to the R.T.A." he said.

Tyler shook her head. "Don't think so."

"Why?"

"Look at his hip."

"What?"

"His hip," Tyler pressed.

Carter took the photo. He brought it up close and squinted. Something about the weapon's shape got the detective's interest.

"What model is hospital security issued with?" he asked.

"Glock 17 or Glock 19," Tyler responded. Her hand moved to her side. She undid the clip to her holster and slid out her service revolver. A Glock 19. She placed it on the table.

Carter looked harder at the photo. The weapon against the guy's hip was no Glock. The clip looked too long – possibly long enough to hold 20 rounds, 8 more than a Glock – and the muzzle pushed out beyond its holster by at least an inch.

Tyler watched as Carter's face took on understanding. She retook her weapon and slid it back into her holster. Clipping it shut, she turned for her partner to inspect. The Glock was a secure fit. Just a hint of its grip was visible. The muzzle concealed within its holster.

Carter's attention returned to the photo. This weapon had either been modified or was some sort of foreign make that neither of them recognised. The one thing that was clear was that no New York City cop would be walking around with an illegal firearm strapped to his hip.

"We need to find this guy," Carter said. "And real quick."

"I've got the Audio Visual Unit working on it now. They should be able to pull some details off the photo in a few hours."

"How long exactly?" Carter asked, eager to find out who this individual was.

"I'll chase it up," Tyler responded.

The older detective reached out to open a drawer. He snatched up his car keys, deciding that he had time to pay St Mary's another visit. Knowing that time alone in his apartment would tick by with agonising slowness. Understanding that time was the one thing he had a plentiful amount left to suffer, he hoped that his time as a grieving parent would mercifully come to an end – and soon. No matter how brutal that ending may be.

Time.

A luxury for some.

A death sentence for others.

Chapter Twenty-Three

An unnerving silence filled the hospital corridors. Now that visiting hours were over and the usual daytime chaos had drawn to an end, the white passageways fell bleak and sombre. Only the occasional nurse or doctor walked the corridors, alone, their rubber-soled shoes squeaking as they passed.

Officer Gore stretched in his seat, positioned outside the door to Joseph Ruebins' room. Only Doctor Greenwood and the nurse were allowed to enter. The nurse had administered a shot of medicine – a cup of dark blue liquid – that Gore had prayed wasn't hiding some sort of poison. Now that Gore appreciated whom he was protecting, he felt concerned about Ruebins' well-being and was committed to overseeing the ex-champ's protection. The blue liquid turned out to be nothing more menacing that a simple anti-inflammatory, to help with his facial swelling.

Doctor Greenwood had arrived shortly afterwards. Sitting beside Joseph, he delivered a long monologue. Gore had caught little of the conversation and even less of its understanding. Something about a transient ischaemic attack – or mini-stroke, as the doctor had kept referring to it. Still, the Doctor's tone had sounded somewhat optimistic and once he'd left, Ruebins appeared a lot brighter.

Gore checked his watch. At eight o'clock another uniformed officer would take over for the night shift. Only fifteen minutes remained.

The elevator arrived on their floor and the doors opened

with the sharp-sounding *ping*. Gore instinctively turned towards the noise. The doors clacked open, but the elevator was empty. Nobody exited, no one entered, and in time, the doors slid shut and the elevator resumed its journey to a different floor. Gore turned his attention back to the old magazine and began to read an article about a young white middleweight sensation, now retired for over half a decade.

***

Inside the hospital room, Joseph fidgeted. His worries had now been countered with some degree of hope. Doctor Greenwood had stated that the first set of tests had returned with good news: Joseph was not suffering from any sort of heart disease, albeit he did have a somewhat high cholesterol count, nor was he a victim of diabetes. So far, apart from the slight worry of his cholesterol level, Greenwood could only speculate on what had caused the blackouts. He was still optimistic that the MRI scan would show any abnormalities, even of the slightest kind, which would then give them a much clearer picture of Joseph's condition. Perhaps, Doctor Greenwood had suggested, Joseph's illness had been a result of a couple of tiny clots, which had now been dealt with by the combination of antiplatelet and anticoagulant drugs. If the results came back positive, Greenwood had told Joseph that he would consider discharging him as early as next week, providing he continued to make steady progress.

Now, all Joseph could think about was going home. Although he didn't think Marianna and Jake were in any real danger, he still wanted to be with them, sure in the knowledge that no harm could come to them if he was there.

The TV in the corner of the room flickered silently. Joseph reached over to the nightstand and picked up the remote. He turned the sound higher and then flipped between channels until he found something interesting enough to distract him from his thoughts. HBO was showing a documentary about the talented yet hot-headed football star, Michael Tucker. Joseph turned the volume higher. Tucker was acting out his signature move on the screen. With both fists tight and thumbs pointed upward, Tucker chanted, "Show Time!" The mantra was normally a precursor to Tucker dishing out his own favourite brand of pleasure: Pain.

***

Officer Gore heard the sound of voices coming from Joseph's room. He jumped to his feet, the magazine falling to the floor in a flutter of pages. Gore stepped over it and rapped gently against the door. Without waiting for a reply, he pushed open the door and stuck his head in.

"You okay?" he asked.

Joseph looked towards his unexpected guest. "Yeah, why?"

"What you watching?" Gore enquired.

"Something about football and Michael Tucker."

Gore grinned knowingly. "Show Time!" he said. "Guy's got a temper on him – that's for sure."

"Yeah," Joseph said. "Real glad he doesn't box."

"I heard that."

"You want to watch the rest?" Joseph asked.

Gore looked at his watch again. "Sorry buddy, replacement's coming in ten minutes."

"You have a good night."

"You too. I'll be back first thing in the morning."

Joseph nodded. "Going home to a wife and kids?"

"Nah… I like peace and quiet, got me a nice pack of Bud and a New York Rangers game."

"Sounds good."

"Okay, you get some rest."

"Will do," Joseph replied.

The policeman disappeared as abruptly as he'd arrived, leaving Joseph to enjoy the show.

133

Gore scooped up the magazine and placed it face down on the seat. He paced around for a few minutes, stretching cramped muscles. He checked his watch again. It was almost eight o'clock. Where the hell was his replacement? Then he heard the elevator doors roll open again. Like the last time, the carriage was empty. Was the damn thing malfunctioning in some way? He took a few steps closer, catching a small reflection of himself in one of its mirrored walls. Understanding his duties, he halted, about-turned, and then returned to the chair. The elevator's doors rolled shut. A faint whine of machinery sounded as it continued on its way.

Irritated, Gore grumbled and swore beneath his breath. He checked the time again. 8:05 p.m. He reached up to activate his two-way radio. Static ripped through the air with a jarring metallic screech. The officer winced at the grating noise. He twisted the volume to its lowest and then tried again. And again, he was rewarded with a jumble of crossed airwaves. Gore began to pace impatiently. The return of the elevator stopped him in his tracks. Surely this must be his replacement? The doors opened; the wall of mirrors inside the elevator again reflected the corridor at him.

"What the hell?"

He stepped closer. As the officer drew nearer, he became abruptly and inexplicably fearful. There was something decidedly wrong with the continued malfunction of the elevator. Why did it keep returning to the second floor empty? Something scratched at the back of his mind, desperately trying to claw its way to the front. The answer was there, plain to see, just waiting to be discovered.

"Hello?" he hissed, unwilling to shout and disturb any sleeping patients.

No reply came.

The carriage was now just a few feet away from him. Two adjoining corridors broke away from his present position, stretching away in a gleam of white walls and polished floors. Both were empty. Gore stopped for a moment, trying to visualise what lay behind him.

He'd been on his butt for most of the day, leaving his post twice to take a bathroom break. Both times, he'd called for security to come and replace him before heading for the washrooms. The first time, while Detective Carter and Tyler were present, a single guard had arrived ready to take over. The second time, just after visiting hours ended, Gore had excused himself, and then quickly tended to his needs. On the opposite side of the corridor were two alcoves. One led to a washroom; the other to a utility room with a supply cart. Only a couple of orderlies had entered on that side of Joseph Ruebins' room. There was a single fire exit at the end of one short passageway, but it had a breakable catch, which would then activate an alarm system throughout the hospital.

Confident that the rear offered no real threat to Ruebins, Gore stepped into the elevator. His attention turned to the bank of buttons. None were illuminated. Frowning, he tried his radio again, but received nothing on the airwaves, now confined and insulated within the elevator shaft. He stepped outside, and it was then he noticed the outside call button. A tiny sliver of plastic had been jammed between the button and its housing, holding the button in a permanent CALL position. Gore reached around the doorway and fumbled until his finger hit one of the inside buttons. He stood back and waited.

The doors closed a few seconds later with a chime, and then the whir of machinery took the elevator to the selected level. Gore waited and watched as the level indicator situated above the doors changed from '2' to '6'. A few moments passed and then the call button before him illuminated automatically, as if just pressed, and then the indicator dropped back to this level. Another short chime sounded and the carriage reappeared empty.

"What the fuck?" Gore muttered.

The light around the call button died, and the doors started to close again. However, as they did another doorway opened, immediately behind and to the left of the young officer. The elevator's ring hid the slight noise of cracking hinges. Then, as the whir of moving parts filtered through to Gore, he missed the soft patter of shoes coming from behind.

Gore's head exploded with an unholy pain. His entire body jolted in uncontrollable agony. His lips peeled back in a hideous grimace and every muscle contracted as 10,000 Volts racked his body. He heard the crackle of electricity and smelled a tinge of burning ozone. The scream that threatened to form never left his lips, as the pain proved too great to tolerate, and instead, he collapsed to his knees, before tipping forwards onto his front. As the Tazergun pumped high voltage into Gore's flesh, he twitched and thrashed involuntarily, unable to fight against this agony, before he slipped mercifully into unconsciousness. And, as he did, bright lights flared before his eyelids. It was then, with his last thought, when Gore came to understand what had otherwise eluded him. All evening the elevator had been returning to this level, preceded by the illuminated call button. A button that he had been aware of, constantly ringed by light, as if pressed down permanently.

Powerful arms scooped Gore's limp form up and carried him into the nearest empty room. Darkness filled every corner of the room. Just a slight labouring of breath could be heard. Not from overexertion, either, but from excitement.

Gore's attacker waited for his eyes to adjust to the darkness, then he moved towards the empty bed in the centre of the room. The sheet had been pulled back already, and Gore fell limply onto the bare mattress.

Thick fingers clad in latex yanked out the prongs that had embedded themselves into the officer's flesh. He wrapped the leads running from the Tazergun around the main body, and tucked it safely away. The meagre light cast a pale sliver against the polished surface of stainless steel.

With the precision of a surgeon, the razor-sharp blade was drawn along the sleeping officer's throat. Blood burst outwards in a dark bubbling froth. Gore's severed windpipe gurgled in a ghastly inhalation of breath, and then his lungs filled quickly with his own blood. Within seconds, his chest shuddered one final time and the young officer lay still.

The blade dropped away from Gore's ravaged throat, disappearing from sight, and the figure took a step back. The killer stood poised for a second before drawing the sheet up over the corpse's chin. The white hem turned quickly to red.

If someone had walked in at that moment, at first glance, they would have thought that one of the City's finest was here to pay tribute to a fallen comrade. The figure was dressed in a spotless dark blue uniform, buttoned smartly up to the chin. Pants that were pressed to military precision ran in parallel creases to shoes that gleamed with polish, even now, in this near-darkness.

The killer reached up to straighten his cap. Eyes that were cold and merciless peered out from beneath the peak. He spun on his heels and crossed over to the doorway. He paused only slightly, his eyes turning to another body, this one crouched into an awkward sitting position inside an empty shower stall. Gore's replacement. Then, without pause, the killer opened the door, stepped outside, confidently, before striding purposefully towards room 2b. He reached the single chair just outside of Joseph's room, and his thigh caught the corner of the magazine that lay there. With a flutter of heavy wings, the magazine fell to the floor. In the silence of the early night, the sound echoed like a clap of thunder. The killer paused.

But all was as it should be.

He stood outside the doorway and listened for any sign of movement. Only silence reached his ears. A smile broke across his face, an uncommon expression for him.

He reached out, spreading his fingers like a hideous oversized spider, and pushed against the thin barrier. The door opened without a sound. He took one last look behind him before stepping into the hospital room. His trailing hand gripped the scalpel, which reflected like a spark of lightning.

Chapter Twenty-Four

The TV documentary that Joseph watched barely managed to hold his attention. His thoughts – worrying thoughts – simply refused to go away, hovering closely over Joseph's mind, circling around his consciousness like a wake of hungry buzzards. He turned the sound down to its lowest. Then he let his mind wander, shifting his attention away from the colourful screen and its animated people, who spoke to him now in silent tongues.

He placed the remote at his side. The small digital clock built into the TV's plastic housing flashed 08:14 p.m. Joseph sighed. What had happened to his otherwise simple life? He should have been at home now, financially secure and ready to dedicate the rest of his life to his family. Instead, here he lay, limp and useless, no good to either his wife or his son. Now, he would have to remain in this hospital, reliant on others, while Marianna and Jake were left to fend for themselves.

Joseph's hand clenched itself into a tight fist. In a fit of rage, he brought it down hard, pounding against the mattress. His fist rose for a second time, ready to deliver another blow. It stayed motionless for a long moment. Joseph looked upon it. He opened his fist and then spread his fingers wide. They opened out, stiffly, before closing again to form a tight fist.

Joseph gaped openly at this unexpected control of his right hand. Only now did he realise that he'd actually been using the same hand to operate the remote control.

"I'll be damned," he said.

His heart pounded quicker. The painful tingling sensation

from earlier was still present, but less so now. He reached up to prod at the right side of his face. It still felt numb, like he was jabbing his fingers into a lump of clay. The smallest twinge of pain flared across his cheek. Yes, now that he thought about it, the right side of his face was starting to ache. He smiled, pleased with this unexpected development.

He pushed back the bed cover until the blanket had gathered to just below the knees. The white of his boxer shorts stood out in stark contrast to the dark ebony of his skin. Now confident with the control of his right arm, he prodded at the large lump of muscle of his thigh. It was still numb, barely registering the presence of curious fingertips, but there was the slightest acknowledgment of feeling. Sitting up straighter, he ran his fingers along the length of his leg, finishing at his ankle. He pulled the blanket to one side, exposing both his feet.

The toes on his left foot wiggled with ease. His attention turned to his right. They were less responsive, remaining rigid, which put the picture of a cadaver's foot into mind, now requiring just the addition of a toe-tag. Joseph shuddered slightly. He focused all of his attention onto his foot. He imagined his foot had become a hand, and what he needed to do was form a fist out of his toes.

Nothing happened.

He huffed with frustration.

Lying back against the pillow, he remained quiet for a moment, beaten.

The crackle of a radio came from outside his doorway. Joseph turned towards the noise. He heard a mumble of words, Gore's voice, and assumed the officer's replacement had arrived and was now being given instructions.

Not wanting to be found half-naked, Joseph bent forward to draw the sheet over his chest. As he did so, his right leg slipped from the edge of the bed and fell towards the floor. A burst of pain ripped along the length of his leg, starting from his thigh to the very tips of his toes. He winced in agony, bolting upright, half-sitting on the edge of the bed, and began to rub vigorously at the limb.

Cramp, Joseph realised, as he continued to massage his thigh. He could feel that the muscles underneath his fingers had contracted into short lengths of steel. He continued to rub at them until he felt the pain subside and the muscles relax again.

He sat on the edge of the bed, with his back to the door. His feet dangled just a few inches off the floor. He slid forward until the tips of his toes connected with the cold surface. He continued to move forwards, placing both feet flat on the floor. Coldness gnawed at his left foot. His right felt mostly impervious to the chilly surface. Still, finding himself in an upright position, Joseph decided he'd try to stand.

Using the bed for assistance, he climbed unsteadily to his feet. His left leg took most of his weight, and he tottered for a moment until he managed to balance himself straight. The right leg was unwilling to assist, just a straight length of flesh, which gave no real control over his movement. Nevertheless, Joseph grinned stupidly at this small triumph of standing unassisted. He turned to the doorway, wanting to call Gore in, ready to show someone – anyone – this unexpected achievement. But he heard the distant chime of a bell and understood instantly that it was the arrival of the elevator, here to take Gore on the first part of his journey home. He thought about calling to the officer's replacement, but the gesture would probably go unappreciated.

Using the bed to remain upright, he manoeuvred slowly around to the other side, so that he was now only a few feet away from the doorway. It stood tantalisingly close. Just four or five steps separated Joseph and freedom.

Could he make it outside and find a nursing-station, or even better, a payphone? There, he could reverse charges and surprise Marianna with a call. However, he remembered the possibility of the danger he was in, and paused for a second, understanding that the correct thing to do was stay within his room and keep safe.

What the hell, he thought. If the guard didn't like it, he could follow close behind with his weapon drawn. Nothing was going to stop Joseph from sharing this news.

Now with a greater resolve, Joseph focused all of his attention onto the door. He took his first step, unsteadily, and was forced to throw his arms out in an attempt to maintain his balance. He wavered for a second, placing most of his weight onto his left leg. With arms still spread wide, he took his next step, using his hip to throw the limp right leg forwards by a few feet. Then, quickly, he hopped forwards and thrust his left leg in front of the other. To his surprise, he didn't crash to the floor in a heap. He grinned again, pleased with his ability so far.

It took a few uncertain steps for Joseph to reach the closed doorway. Now – the hard part. He reached out to take the handle. He pulled the handle towards him and the bright corridor outside filled the gap with a flood of white light. Joseph squinted against the glare. He pulled open the door, using it to keep his balance, and then slid along the doorframe until he had successfully vacated his room.

He found the passageway empty. The chair was empty, too, and the magazine that Eugene had left had been placed face-down against the seat. Gore was nowhere to be seen. Nor his replacement for that matter. Joseph cursed under his breath. A fine amount of protection they were offering. Still, at least there'd be no awkward or embarrassing scenes, or arguments about Joseph's stupidity.

The elevator at the end of the corridor was open.

With his back against the wall, Joseph scanned both left and right. The corridor to his left was short and branched off in a T. What secrets were hidden on that side? He'd already endured a couple of trips via the elevator and knew the other side to be populated with staff and amenities.

Would the other passageway offer the same?

Maybe?

"Okay, right it is then," Joseph said, deciding that the elevator was just too far for him to handle. He half slid and half walked along the wall, using his right shoulder and left leg to keep him upright. Eventually, just before his strength abandoned him, he reached the end of the main corridor. Two short passageways revealed themselves.

One led straight to a fire door, which Joseph thought would then lead onto an emergency stairwell. A couple of shut doors could be seen on that side, but as they bore no numbers, Joseph guessed they were possibly used for storage or something similar.

His attention turned to the other passageway. More doors, and only one with a number or sign stencilled across its surface. From his position, though, he was unable to read it clearly. He looked back the way he'd come, debating if he should go back. Curiosity finally won. What the hell, if he fell on his ass, then at least they'd have less distance to carry him back to his room. Whoever *they* turned out to be. The elevator had stayed open, and as yet, neither Gore nor his replacement had shown themselves.

Joseph reached out with both arms, giving himself a Frankenstein-like stance then lurched over to the opposite wall. He rolled onto his back and then scooted around the corner and into the adjoining passageway. Now tiring considerably, he took a while to get close enough to read the sign on the door.

The sign read: *Visitors' Washroom*

Joseph laughed out loud.

It would be highly unlikely for him to find any help in there. He huffed with both tiredness and disappointment, and then began to make his way back towards the main corridor. As he did so the slight tinge of ozone brushed past his nose.

Joseph summoned as much strength as he could, breathing heavily from the continued exertion, and pushed himself along the main wall. The smell of ozone got stronger. He reached the doorway opposite his, 4b, and stopped for a moment to take a breath. The chair was still empty, but the magazine had now fallen to the floor.

At last, Joseph thought, Gore's replacement had arrived. Maybe there was still a chance of calling his wife, especially if the replacement officer was willing to help? Excitement got the better of him. He pushed away from the wall without first finding his balance, and managed just the one step before his right leg failed him. Throwing his arms out, he tried to redistribute his weight onto his left side, but the effort was too late. Joseph hopped foolishly on one leg for a moment before falling backwards, against the doorway to 4b.

The door gave way under Joseph's weight, and he toppled backwards and into darkness.

Chapter Twenty-Five

Thomas Carter was seated in his car. About two inches of the driver's window had been cranked open, and a steady stream of smoke billowed out in a grey cloud. Carter closed his eyes, allowing his thoughts to drift away, as if they themselves were caught on the mist of cigarette smoke, to be taken away up into the heavens, where perhaps the person of Carter's interest would be able to read them. His son.

Both Carter and Tyler had called it a night an hour earlier, and the young detective had taken her leave almost instantly, eager to get home and spend time with her family. She'd paused for just a second, to ask if Carter would like to join her for a late supper, but when he declined, she had quickly headed out of the Department.

Carter had lingered at his desk with little or no reason to leave. Where would he go tonight anyway? He'd promised Captain Mendoza that he'd stay out of trouble for the next 48 hours. That left all tonight and tomorrow night to fill. And tonight, he just couldn't bear the thought of spending the dark hours alone in his empty apartment. He'd waited long enough for the Audio Visual Unit to generate the photo and then made his way to the hospital.

The detective opened his eyes and then shook his head in an attempt to clear away the feeling of guilt. Since being handed the case this morning, Carter had had little time to focus on his grief. For most of the day his thoughts and attention had stayed on the present, not on the past. He'd had little time to stop and ponder Billy's death and, now, sitting silently alone in his car, he felt an overwhelming rush of betrayal for not having done so.

Only three months had gone by since he'd been forced to walk along the bleak corridors of the city's morgue, assisted by Captain Mendoza, as he headed towards the pathologist's lab on trembling legs. That was the place where they'd taken Billy, and the last time Carter had seen his only son.

His son's face formed within his mind. It wasn't a picture full of pain or brutality, either, just a desperately sad one. Billy had been prepared in one of the adjoining rooms, away from the main examination area. Laid out on a bed, he'd appeared to be merely asleep, ready to be woken and join the living at any moment. Pale, yes, but not overly so. Only a few hours had passed since the fatal shooting, and Billy had not had sufficient time to take on any real characteristics of a cadaver. His face didn't look sallow, or wax-like, the need for an undertaker's hand not yet apparent. Instead, his face had been recently scrubbed, the pathologist's attempt to save Carter the pain of seeing his son covered in blood. He'd done a good job, too. A single crust of dried blood in Billy's ear was the only slight indication of injury. Even the gunshot wound looked nothing too severe – little more than a dark red scab.

Now, he found himself parked in this near-empty lot, with his thoughts turning almost as dark as the night sky. He patted at the holster that lay just under his right armpit. His usual Smith and Wesson snub-nose had now been replaced by Presley Perkins' discarded weapon. A weapon that had been taken from the collection of evidence. Taken without anyone ever knowing about it.

Detective Thomas Carter had replaced the original small revolver with one almost identical to it. It had been a hard task considering the importance of the weapon. Both that and the pile of excrement found near the crime scene were what had led the investigation team straight to Perkins. A simple DNA test and fingerprints had conclusively put Perkins near the scene, followed by ballistics on the bullet that had killed Officer William Carter, and that was all the authorities needed to secure a conviction.

Considering his background, Perkins had only once brushed against the law. As a young teenager, he'd been arrested for taking his father's Caddy, unbeknown to old Dolly himself, and had subsequently been arrested for grand theft auto. The arresting cops had taken prints and a DNA sample and put these on record. Dolly had then sworn he'd simply suffered a severe but short bout of amnesia, explaining that he'd knowingly allowed his son to take the car. Unsurprisingly, all charges had been dropped. Still, Presley's identity was stored for all eternity in the police database.

Having all they needed, the detectives running William Carter's case just had to bring in their number one suspect.

Only Perkins wasn't willing to play ball.

And now, Thomas Carter had taken charge as lead detective – unofficially, of course. It had taken a great amount of cunning and resolve to get his hands on the weapon used to kill his son, replacing it with one that looked identical. A task that he would have to do in reverse, replacing the original gun, once he'd carried out his plan. Not a plan as such, but a punishment.

Carter checked his watch. 8:20 p.m. He pulled on the cigarette one last time before stubbing it out in a half-full ashtray. Then, after winding the window back up, he popped open the door and stepped out into the night. The cold wind battered him for a moment, grabbing his coattails and whipping them about his thighs. He tucked his head down and headed for cover.

A set of automatic doors opened for him. He stepped out of the dark, windy night and into the glare of overhead strip lights. The hospital lobby was relatively quiet; just a few staff filled the entrance, either taking a cigarette break or milling around the coffee machine. For a second, Carter just stood there, not really sure why he'd chosen to come here. He unbuttoned his coat, shrugged it off his shoulders and draped it over his arm. A few hospital staff had gathered around the elevator, waiting for it to arrive.

Carter stepped over to join them. He looked up and watched as the indicator dropped from the eighth floor to the second. The light held at Level 2 for what seemed like a long time, before it fell to Level 1 and then finally to ground level. The doors opened with a metallic ping.

Carter climbed in with the rest of the passengers.

Chapter Twenty-Six

The floor underneath Joseph drew heat from his body like an elemental magnet. He pushed himself into a sitting position and then scanned around. The room was almost a mirror image of his. Same size, same layout, albeit everything opposite to his, and the window in this room had the added effect of snow blowing against it.

The bed behind him was empty. Not even sheets could be found. A bare mattress lay flat on bedsprings, and a couple of coverless pillows had been piled at the foot of the bed.

Joseph shivered. The temperature in this room was almost as bleak as the room itself. Barren, soulless, empty, were words that formed in his mind. The room was clean, too clean, as if it hadn't been graced by a human soul for quite some time. He shuffled over to the bed, sliding on his butt until his back pressed against the cot.

Favouring his left side, he drew himself onto the bare mattress. The bedsprings beneath him sung a short, high-pitched tune, as they contracted under his weight.

What now?

Should he wait here for a while and gather his strength? And, in doing so, alarm his present guardian. Surely by now Gore's replacement would have arrived – to find Joseph missing. No, Joseph realised, the right thing to do was to return to his room and rest. He wiped the sweat off his brow. As his hand dropped away, he spotted a mop propped up in the corner of the room. Just to the side of the mop lay a rusty old bucket. Joseph nodded in understanding. The room had recently been cleaned, and that's where the overpowering smell of chemicals had come from.

An idea sprang to mind. Once again, he climbed onto unsteady feet. He shuffled over to the corner of the room and took the mop. Then, spinning it around, he fixed the mop head underneath his right armpit. Perfect. The wooden handle reached to the floor, allowing Joseph to use it as a makeshift crutch.

He laughed slightly, pleased with his ingenuity.

Maybe there'd still be time to call Marianna after all?

Finding movement easier now, Joseph hobbled to the door and pushed it open. The glare of the lights outside stabbed painfully at his eyes, forcing him to blink a couple of times. He stepped out into the bright passageway, and as he did so the door to his room opened. The unexpected arrival of another person caught him by surprise.

"You," the guard said, raising something metallic for Joseph to see.

The guard jabbed the sharp blade out to show his intentions. Joseph reacted by taking an awkward step back. Matching him, the guard stepped forwards, keeping the distance between them equal. Joseph raised the mop handle off the floor, and then levelled it out in front of him in an attempt to hold the guy back.

The guard laughed maliciously. "That all you got?"

"What do you want?" Joseph asked foolishly.

No explanation came. Instead, the sharp weapon was jabbed aggressively in Joseph's direction. And although the motion was only meant to intimidate, merely an exaggerated gesture with no real threat, Joseph still jolted back instinctively.

The cackle of cold-blooded amusement came again. "Not such the tough guy after all." The words were broken and clumsy and full of mispronunciation.

Joseph's mind flipped into overdrive, his heart pounding quickly in his chest. It was obvious to him who this guy was. His intuition washed away the guard's façade immediately.

The uniform looked all wrong: too neatly pressed, too new, and worst of all, a perfect fit. Gore's had been tight around the midriff and washed to a lighter blue. This guy looked too seasoned to be a rookie, his face was deeply lined and greying hair, cropped closely to his scalp, bristled at the sides of his cap. His shoes reflected bright white slivers of light off their polished tips, and the peak of his cap looked like glazed ebony. This guy had never seen the streets, let alone served and protected them. In all, he looked like he'd just stepped out of a TV cop show.

"Tough guy," he said again. His words were unclear, like a drunkard's, and laced with Slavic undertones.

"The guard'll be back any minute," Joseph said.

The guy just shook his head with a resolute no. "He's got a sore throat. Not be back tonight, or any other night." He drew the blade across his throat to show Joseph what he meant.

"His replacement's on his way now."

The guy's eyes crinkled at the corners. "He busy too. He got himself a splitting headache." Two fingers and a thumb formed themselves into the shape of a gun. He placed his fingers to his temple and then dropped his thumb. "Kaboom..!"

Joseph looked at the guy's belt. A dark leather holster held a firearm tightly against his hip. His heart skipped a beat, and the corridor tipped forwards slightly as fear threatened to force him into the killer's embrace.

The attacker recognised Joseph's terror. He reached down with his free hand and patted at the weapon. "No worries. I like to get up close and personal."

The blade waved backwards and forwards a few feet from Joseph's face.

"I wrestle with big bear – like back home. You big brown bear," he said, flipping the blade over in his hand. Now, the blade pointed to the floor, and the guy had the option to either hit out with his fist or strike down with the knife.

He made the wrong choice. He threw a punch towards

Joseph's head. Standing square-on, Joseph managed to block the punch by catching it with the inside of his left wrist, then immediately launched his own counterattack. His left hand skipped over the failed assault and landed squarely against the guy's jaw. The counter-punch carried speed but little power. Still, the man staggered back, caught off guard.

Wasting no time, Joseph swung the wooded handle towards his assailant's head. Again, his attack carried little power. His right side was still weak, and the handle bounced uselessly off the guy's shoulder.

The guard grabbed at the handle. He caught it under his arm, trapping it in a tight embrace. Then, pulling it towards himself, he tried to rip it out of Joseph's grasp.

Joseph used the momentum to his advantage. Instead of trying to resist, he pushed the mop forwards and forced the attacker against the closed door of his room. It opened with a hollow boom, and the guy fell backwards, losing his grip. He back-pedalled, lost his footing and then landed heavily in the centre of the floor.

Joseph stepped forward to grab the door handle as it swung back. He pulled it tight and then fed the wooden stick through the handle, turning it into a makeshift deadbolt.

Now, in the centre of the corridor, Joseph scanned quickly right and left. The elevator lay to his right, both doors closed now, and out of reach. The left side offered either the washroom or the fire escape. Joseph took a few steps to the left, hobbling dangerously, before stopping.

Behind him, the elevator arrived. He spun around to see Detective Carter stepping into the passageway. Joseph changed direction, and then staggered awkwardly towards the detective. He passed his room and heard the muffled sound of gunfire come from within. Chunks of wood exploded outwards in a hail of splinters, and the mop handle snapped down the centre, breaking into two. In the next second the door flew open and the guard stepped out into the passageway.

Moving with too much momentum, Joseph tipped forwards and went down hard. It saved his life. A bullet zipped over his head before punching a hole into one of the elevator doors. Another bullet whizzed by, this one going in the opposite direction. Joseph heard a cry of pain. He chanced a look behind him and saw his attacker stagger against the wall.

In the next instant, Carter was at Joseph's side. He aimed and fired again, but the guard was already rounding the corner. A second later the corridor was filled with the deafening wail of a fire alarm.

Carter yelled over the noise. "You okay?"

Joseph nodded. "Am now."

"You hurt?"

"No."

Carter remained poised, clearly unsure if he should remain here to assist or give chase.

"Go," Joseph said, understanding the detective's dilemma. "I'm okay. He was alone."

"Okay," Carter said. "Help will be on its way." Almost as quickly as he'd arrived, the detective disappeared from view.

Chapter Twenty-Seven

Carter took the stairs with reckless disregard. He'd already left Level 1 behind him and was now a single flight of stairs away from the ground floor. All around him came the insistent ringing of fire-bells, piercing to hear, which threw his senses off somewhat.

He slowed now, understanding that the shooter could have vacated the stairwell in favour of the many corridors the hospital had to offer. No trace of blood could be found on the stairs or walls. Body-armour, Carter thought, understanding that the killer must be wearing a bullet-proof vest. How else could he have taken a direct hit and still be standing? Stepping away from the handrail, he pushed his back against the wall and trained his weapon towards the access doorway. It was closed tight – just like on Level 1. They were thick, insulated fire doors.

Carter brought himself up against the doorway. A small reinforced window revealed an empty corridor beyond. He moved away, taking the first steps towards the basement.

The standard fluorescent lights were replaced by smaller bulkhead fittings, which made Carter feel as if he was heading deeper into an underground labyrinth. Also, the whitewashed walls faded into a dismal grey, as if light from above was not a requirement here, in the deeper bowels of the building. Carter didn't like it one bit. He felt as if he was leaving the safety of civilisation somewhere above him. Then, mercifully, the ringing bells stopped. His ears filled instantly with the sound of silence.

The slam of a door stopped him short. The detective waited for a second to see if any other sounds came from below. Maybe the perpetrator had intentionally allowed the door to slam shut, only to tiptoe to a lower level, taking that door silently instead?

The stairwell was dead quiet.

No, his quarry had taken the first route available to him. Carter bounded down the stairs and reached the basement doorway in four or five long strides.

Unlike the two previous doors, this one was operated by a simple push-bar. Carter dropped the bar and opened the door by an inch or two. Darkness prevailed on the other side. Had the suspect hit the switch on his way, now waiting in darkness, ready to shoot anything that came through?

Maybe?

Carter scanned behind him. A fire extinguisher hung just off the floor from a heavy-duty hook. He took it, momentarily tucking his weapon into his holster. Returning to the door, he cracked it open slightly. No shots rang out. He undid his tie, quickly loosening the knot, and then slipped it over his head. Dropping to one knee, he wrapped the length of material round the operating handle. The short nozzle fixed itself to the body of the canister. He pulled it clear before withdrawing his weapon.

Ready for action, he stood, pushed open the door, yanked the safety pin away from the handle and then launched the extinguisher into the room. Thick, white powder exploded from the nozzle, instantly filling the room with a choking, dry mist. He waited for just a few seconds before reaching inside, now under cover. His fingers found the light switch just inside the doorway. He pressed it and then quickly retracted his arm.

The room beyond became a flare of bright lights. A shot rang out, barely distinguishable over the high-powered jet of powder, and a chunk of wood splintered just as Carter's hand was clear. He kicked the door open, spinning away from the opening, to take cover behind the wall opposite. Another shot sounded and a bullet thudded loudly as it buried itself in a chunk of masonry.

Carter dropped back to one knee. He leaned quickly away from his place of safety and fired a single shot at the extinguisher. The expected explosion didn't happen. No ball of fire to engulf the perpetrator or flying red-hot shrapnel to rip skin from bone. Instead, Carter heard the canister crack open and the powder filled the stairwell in a billowing white cloud. Silence followed.

The calm was finally broken by the sound of running feet. In the next instant, Carter was up and giving chase. He barged into the room, falling to one side, dropping low with his arms out straight in a shooter's stance. The powder had already started to fall, its density too great for it to remain aloft for any real length of time. Just a light mist lingered, most having covered the floor and contents with a thick white blanket.

Carter found himself in a laundry room. A fleet of carts took up one side of the room almost entirely, soiled sheets, pillowcases and hospital gowns filled most to overflowing, and large, industrial-looking washing machines were crammed closely together on the opposite side. They stood idle, large circular doors open to reveal deep drums.

The room funnelled into a tight passageway on the opposite side, and Carter spied another door swing shut. He climbed to his feet and continued his pursuit.

He arrived at the doorway, his intuition knowing almost certainly what would lie beyond. He could smell it from this side already. A pungent reek of dampness filled his nostrils. Again, he paused on this side, uncertain whether the shooter was waiting on the other side. With no other option this time and little cover available to him, he simply kicked open the door and barged through. With the agility of a gymnast, he dropped to one knee before rolling sideways, away from the open doorway.

No sudden flashes of gunfire erupted; no heads popped up from behind the available cover.

The room was humid, warm. In some corners dark patches of mould could be seen, too rampant to be hidden by a mere additional coating of paint. Large pressing machines stood with their lids poised, ready to iron out any creases within the linen sheets. Like the adjoining room, no workers could be found here.

Carter stepped into the centre of the room. Now, he had a choice of two doorways. One shut tight by his side, the other slightly ajar. He checked the one to his side but found it locked. A heavy-duty mortise lock barred entry. It would be unlikely the suspect just happened to have the right key, even if it was an inside job. Intuition steered him towards the open doorway. As he drew near, a slight draught brushed against his face. It carried with it the faint odour of gasoline and burnt oil.

Expecting to discover a boiler room or some other type of utility service, he was surprised to find himself once again at the top of a flight of steps. The stench of motor-oil became stronger. He took the steps carefully, fully alert to danger, and eventually they gave way to a simple opening. A large yellow stencilled sign read: Parking Level 1.

Instantly, Carter understood the origin of the smell: cars. He poked his head around the throughway just for a second, before pulling back. Still, he had enough time to register a dozen or so lines of parked vehicles. This, it seemed, was the hospital staff's car parking area. Carter guessed the primary access to the parking bay must be located elsewhere, possibly by both the elevator and stairs. Meaning, the shooter could now be doubling back towards Room 2b. Would he be bold enough to do such a thing?

Most likely, considering the state of panic the hospital had been thrown into. He took one step into the parking bay, in the hope of seeing a retreating car, or fleeing fugitive, but the area was silent.

Quickly, he re-entered the stairwell and began a hasty ascent back the way he had come.

Chapter Twenty-Eight

Neon signs scratched bright effects into the canvas of the night. The swirls and loops of luminous reds, blues, pinks and greens offered a dazzling array of colour, which belied the dark festering reality that could be found here. Young girls some barely out of their teens, stood with midriffs exposed and legs clad in dark stockings. Lipstick almost as bright as the neon signs could be found smeared across their cracked lips, while eyes that were the windows to troubled or lost souls looked out upon the night with bleak despair.

In this part of the city, immorality ruled absolute. Strip joints and peepshows could be found in every other doorway, separated by shops that advertised adult merchandise, or shuttered doorways, which were makeshift beds for the night's unwanted and forgotten homeless.

How strange then that Presley Perkins felt so comfortable as he trawled along these illicit storefronts. The night was busy, drawing together a mixture of young and old, some to sample the tempting things that were on offer, others brought by mere curiosity – and the rest, like Presley, had come here with only business in mind.

While Presley made his way along the sidewalk, he was stopped countless times by many a face: black, white, oriental, youthful and aged, haggard or fresh-faced, but all presenting him with the same service – sex. Presley kindly rejected all their offers, smiling and bowing submissively in apology, then continued on his way. Maybe there would be time for such pleasures later. But for now, he stayed focused on the task at hand.

Finally, just before the bright strip gave way to a main avenue, Presley arrived at a closed doorway. The solid-looking door reminded him of Moses Prey's place. He shuddered at the thought of the carnage he had left there. Then, raising his fist, he hammered noisily against it.

A familiar scene played out before him. A peephole slid open to reveal a pair of eyes, full of cold contempt.

"What you want?" the muffled voice asked from beyond the door.

Presley took a step closer. "I wanna speak to the Boss." The light from the sidewalk cast half of Presley's face in shadow.

"And who might you be?" asked the voice, which had a distinctive Slavic tone.

"It's me – Presley."

The eyes widened, contempt replaced instantly by confusion. "Presley?"

"Yeah."

"Is that really you?"

"It's me," Presley replied.

The voice on the other side became a guarded whisper. "You shouldn't be showing your face around here. The Boss is really pissed with you."

"I know, but I need his help."

"Help?"

"Yeah. I need to disappear."

The eyes turned to astonished amusement. "Viktor would happily do that for you, free of charge..!"

"I know he would. But he may be willing to help if he gets his money back."

"Money?"

"Yeah, from what I borrowed."

"Presley, I'm not sure you're aware of this fact. But Viktor has people looking for you. You know – not with good intentions, either."

"I know. That's why I'm here – to have him call off the dogs," Presley explained.

The speaker's eyebrows rose slightly at Presley's audacity. "You sure of this? We could keep this to ourselves."

"Look – Nikolay, I'm in a real jam and need the Boss's help. You gonna open up or what?"

Presley heard Nikolay's lips purse on the other side of the doorway. "Okay, Presley, but don't say I didn't warn you. The Boss is in a foul mood tonight."

"I'll take my chances."

Nikolay shook his head, as if silently reproaching a foolish child. The loud noise of a heavy-duty bolt sliding back sounded from the other side. Next, the door swung open to allow Presley's entrance. Nikolay, a slim, old man, stepped to one side, giving Presley room enough to move deeper inside. The door swung shut and the bolt returned to its housing.

"You'd better follow me," Nikolay ordered, taking the lead. Shades of Moses' place could be found here, as if all lawbreaking 'entrepreneurs' hired from the same interior designers. The corridor was long and dark, but carpeted, and the rooms that led off the main passageway were closed tight. With names like Crystal, Suzy Star, Mercedes and Candy stencilled on their doors, it was obvious to Presley what type of transaction went on inside. Indeed, as he traversed this corridor, the muffled sounds of pain and pleasure could be heard.

Nikolay took Presley the full length of the passageway. At the end, Nikolay turned and asked, "You carrying?"

Presley pulled his jacket to one side. "Just this," he replied, showing him the small handgrip of the Derringer.

"Hard times, indeed," Nikolay said. "You wait here, while I see if the Boss will see you."

Presley nodded, confident that Viktor would make time to see him – no matter how busy he might be. He stood alone for a few minutes, enduring the grunts and moans that came from closed doors. Seemed like Viktor's business was thriving as ever.

Nikolay returned shortly and simply gestured for Presley to follow. He was led into another short passageway and then directed to the single doorway at the end.

"You not coming?" Presley asked.

Nikolay shook his head apologetically. "No."

"What about this?" Presley asked, pointing towards the Derringer.

"What about it? That ain't gonna be of no concern to the Boss." The old guy turned on his heels and simply disappeared back around the corridor and out of view.

Presley took a deep breath – perhaps his last – and then stepped inside. The room he entered was familiar to him. Plush furniture filled most of the space available. Elongated sofas, long enough to seat whole football teams – or so it seemed – were laid out at irregular positions. Each had an expensive table or stand at either end, and along one entire wall TV screens flashed with bits of imagery, forming a large, single picture. The New York Rangers were filling up most of the screens with their red, white and blue uniforms.

Five people sat watching the game, the central figure almost as broad as the two who sat on his right. Another two were leaning forward on the opposite side, engrossed in the early match statistics. A sixth person, a thickset Georgian named Pyotr Krylov, stood just in the open doorway, his attention focused directly on Presley. For someone with such a muscular figure, Pyotr's face looked skinny and long in comparison. Pyotr smiled slyly, as if he was already privy to Presley's fate.

The guy sitting in the middle of the sofa cursed loudly at the screen in a language that was mostly unfamiliar to Presley. He knew it to be Russian, but had little understanding of what had actually just been said. Another hail of abuse – its tone unmistakable – fell from the man's lips, and his round face turned slightly red under the verbal assault.

Yeah, Presley thought, the Boss is in a real foul mood tonight.

Not good.

Not good at all.

Chapter Twenty-Nine

Although Joseph did not consider himself overly politically motivated, his recent predicament presented him with a small measure of sympathy towards the nation's leader. Five armed police officers accompanied him, each with his weapon drawn and eyes alert to trouble. Detective Carter led the way, a two-way radio pressed tightly against his ear, as he barked out instructions to waiting officers. Joseph found it difficult to draw breath. The tension was unbearable. Sitting in a wheelchair, pushed by a sixth officer, he felt totally exposed. His escort did little to make him feel safe. This, Joseph thought, is how the President of the United States must feel on a daily basis, under the constant threat of harm.

Immediately after Carter had taken off in pursuit of the killer, Joseph had been swamped by a group of overeager staff, all offering help and assistance, quickly getting him back into bed. It was the last place he'd wanted to be: flat on his back, surrounded by strangers, any of whom could be plotting to kill him. Thankfully, not long after he'd disappeared, Detective Carter had returned, red-faced and out of breath. He'd ordered all but one of the hospital staff out of the room, and had then called for back-up. Within the space of five minutes a team of armed police officers had arrived.

The bodies of Officer Gore and his missing replacement had been found, prompting Carter to shut down the hospital instantly. It was highly unlikely the killer would still be in the building, but the detective wasn't taking any chances. Half of Carter's department were either here already or on their way.

Detective Tyler was making her way across town to pick up Marianna.

With the elevator out of bounds, now cordoned off awaiting the forensics team, Joseph had had to endure an agonising trip down the stairs. He'd been forced to suffer the indignity of being carried by two burly officers, each taking him by one arm and a leg. Wanting to tackle the steps alone, Joseph had been silenced by Carter, stating that they didn't have time for such a thing and to shut up and allow himself to be carried. The detective had also flatly refused to allow them the use of an alternate elevator, unwilling to have them caught in an enclosed box, and unable to see what lay ahead. At least Joseph had been able to find time to dress. He'd slipped into a clean set of clothes that Marianna had brought him the day before. This small measure of mercy had saved Joseph the embarrassment of being manhandled, and, having his ass on show for the whole world to see.

Now, Joseph was back in a wheelchair and heading for the lobby. A scattering of staff looked on, surprised to see one of their patients being wheeled out, flanked by an armed escort. The hospital's security manned the exit and, as Joseph's party arrived, they stepped aside.

"You got this place shut tight?" Carter asked one of the guards.

The guy looked worried and out of his depth. This wasn't your average security job. He shrugged his shoulders. "Place is a big institute. Would be impossible to do such a thing with so few men."

"Great…" Carter grumbled. "What about missing vehicles or hospital staff?"

"Nothing so far."

Carter shifted his attention to Joseph. "We're getting out of here. This guy could be anywhere – just waiting for another chance."

"Where?" Joseph asked.

"I'll take you to the precinct. We'll figure something out

from there," Carter explained.

"What about Marianna and my son?"

"Detective Tyler will bring them. Don't worry, Joseph, we'll get you all safe."

Joseph nodded, reluctantly, feeling inadequate and angry that he couldn't protect his own family.

Carter read his distress. "They're in good hands. Now, we need to get out of here."

The detective turned towards the outside lobby, ready to call for a car to take them to safety. As if conjured from his very thoughts, a black-and-white patrol car pulled up outside the lobby entrance. The passenger side opened and the bulky figure of Captain Mendoza climbed out. He made the short trip to the entrance.

"Captain," Carter acknowledged.

The captain wore his badge on the outside of his shirt pocket, and his sidearm was strapped at his hip. He looked phased but still in control. Losing two officers in one night had shaken him to his foundations.

"What we got here, Detective?" he asked.

"Never seen anything like it," Carter replied. "Place is a bloodbath."

"What about the two officers?" Mendoza asked, hopeful that his initial information had been wrong – somehow misunderstood – and the two young rookies would be found here safe and sound. Carter's frank reply quashed any hope of that.

"Dead," he responded. The word seemed strange to Carter, not real, and didn't seem to convey what he'd witnessed up on corridor 2 – not nearly enough.

"Who the hell did this?" Mendoza demanded.

"God only knows," Carter said. "Didn't get a look at the killer. I've no idea who we're looking for or what the hell his motives are."

Joseph spoke up. "He was Russian – I think."

Both Carter and Mendoza turned to him.

"What?" they said in unison.

"That's how the guy sounded – Russian."

"You sure?" Carter asked.

Joseph nodded. "Yeah – positive."

Carter turned back to Mendoza. "What do you think?"

"Could mean anything, but you need to get out of here – right now. Take Ruebins back to the precinct and start digging straight away. Get as much help has you can. Call everyone in if you have too, I don't care."

"What about my family?" Joseph asked. "They can't stay there."

"You want them safe?" Mendoza asked.

Anger crept into Joseph's reply. "Of course I do."

"Then follow Detective Carter and do as he says." Mendoza turned his attention away from Joseph, his thoughts on more urgent matters. He nodded to Carter, signalling for him to continue with the task at hand, and then strode purposefully into the maelstrom that was waiting for him, ready to take charge.

Carter gave the signal for the armed guards to carry on. Just before they did, Doctor Greenwood came rushing over, his face ghost-white and wide-eyed.

"Detective – wait," he called. Greenwood now looked more dishevelled than ever. He had dark sweat rings underneath both arms, and his tie had been removed, the top two buttons of his shirt undone. What had started as a bad morning had now descended into the realms of a nightmare.

"Detective, where on earth are you taking my patient?" he demanded. "You can't simply take my patient out of here without medical assistance."

"What the hell are you talking about?" Carter responded, angrily, now eager to put this place behind him.

"Joseph may still suffer a relapse. I just cannot allow it," Greenwood stated.

"It's not your call, Doc. If we don't move him, you may not have a patient for much longer."

This uncompromising statement sent fear running down Joseph's spine. Carter patted Joseph on the shoulder, as if to dispel this most disturbing predicament.

"Look – Doc," Carter began. "Something's going on here that none of us can understand. Or predict. Whatever happened last night in Joseph's room goes beyond comprehension. But I do know that if he was to stay here, then he'd be in serious danger."

"But what about his treatment?"

"Like what?"

"He needs antiplatelet and anticoagulant drugs every few hours, plus what if the MRI results show something tomorrow? We still do not know what caused the initial transient ischaemic attack."

Carter looked back blankly.

"What caused the mini-stroke," Greenwood explained.

"Then call us when you do know," Carter replied abruptly. "Get me his medication and a nurse, and hurry. We ain't got all day."

Greenwood stood for a moment, not used to being given instructions so forcefully. Then his professional instincts took over, and he quickly headed off in search of a nurse and Joseph's medication.

"Hurry, Doc," Carter called after him.

They held position in the lobby for a few agonising minutes, watching carefully as different teams of law enforcers arrived in their droves. Crime Scene Units appeared, some already suited in protective jump-suits, and more patrol officers filtered through to take up positions throughout the hospital.

Eventually, just before Carter's nerves gave out, Doctor Greenwood returned with an attractive nurse in tow. The nurse had a pack in her arms, and was struggling to keep up with the consultant.

"Okay," Greenwood said. "Nurse Walton will go with you. She's one of our most trusted staff. She can report to me directly if anything happens to Joseph."

Carter acknowledged the nurse with a simple, courteous nod. "Right, let's go." He spoke into his radio, ordering a patrol car to move around to the front, and then turned to lead the way.

"Just one more thing," Greenwood called.

"What?" Carter asked, already halfway outside.

"If Mister Ruebins suffers another attack, or worse… Then *you'll* be responsible."

Joseph and Carter looked at each other.

Carter grinned apprehensively.

And Joseph shuddered with dread.

Chapter Thirty

Viktor Mikhel looked away from the TV screens and at Presley standing by the open doorway. His face remained impassive for a second. Then, as if addressing a welcome friend, he jumped to his feet and strode towards Presley with open arms. The Boss was an imposing figure. Short yes, but thickset with a bull neck and broad shoulders. His eyes were two slashes of Mongolian heritage, cut on either side of a flat face.

"Comrade Perkins, you have returned to us unharmed," he said, his words thick with Slavic tones.

Presley twitched nervously.

Viktor put his arms around him in a crushing embrace. "You fell out with old Viktor? You seemed quick to forget who your friends are."

Presley truly believed Viktor was no such thing. A friend to him extended to no more than an obedient dog. Still, Presley grinned back and said, "I had business to attend to."

"Business?" Viktor quizzed.

"Yeah."

"You know old Viktor, he respects people who appreciate good business." Viktor stepped back to look over Presley's face. "You lost weight since I last saw you."

"Had a lot on – you know, this n' that."

"This n' that..." Viktor echoed. His Mongolian eyes narrowed slightly with amusement. "This n' that," he said again, finding something funny with the simple saying. He turned to the four heavies on the sofa and laughed: "This n' that!"

They broke into an uncomfortable bout of laughter; clearly knowing that it was expected, but not sure why.

Viktor turned back to Presley. "Come – sit," he said, with a gesture towards the sofa.

Presley moved over to the sofa, having to forcefully drag his feet just the few yards to get there. Now, in the presence of the Russian crime boss, his idea of atonement seemed foolhardy, desperate, *suicidal.*

The four heavies shuffled over in anticipation of his arrival. He wavered for a moment, knowing all too well what kind of mind games Viktor was capable of, before sitting unwillingly between them.

Viktor clapped his hands like an excited child. "Good – good." He stood looking down at Presley for a moment before bringing one finger in front of his face. "Tut, tut – Presley been a bad boy," he said, waving the finger from side to side.

Presley gulped.

"You take old Viktor's money and then disappear without letting me know where," he reprimanded.

Presley's hands rose in submission. "I got your money, Boss. All of it."

Viktor's hands rested against his hips. This was an unexpected development. "You got Viktor's money?"

"Yeah."

"Where?"

"Safe."

"Where, Presley?"

"Here," Presley said, digging in his pocket. He presented Viktor with a thick roll of green bills.

Viktor just laughed coldly. "What is that?"

Presley misunderstood Viktor's apparent confusion. "It's money. What I owe you."

Viktor snatched the roll of bills out of his hand. He rolled the rubber band off and then began to count the amount.

"Comrade Perkins, there is only five thousand here?"

"I've got the rest."

"Then let me have it."

"I don't have it on me, but it's somewhere safe."

Viktor shook his head. "What is this? What are you trying to do?"

Presley shuffled awkwardly on the sofa. "Viktor, I need your help."

The Russian's face almost collapsed with shock. "What?"

Presley shifted to the edge of his seat, leaning forward now, ready to make his play. "I need you to set me up – in Mexico."

Viktor looked shell-shocked. He turned to look at each of his men, individually, to make sure that what he'd just heard was indeed correct. All stared back at him equally amazed.

"Mexico?" Viktor echoed.

"Yeah," Presley replied.

Viktor's face started to lift. He went from complete confusion to total amusement in a matter of seconds. "Presley, you had me going then. What is this, a trick?" He spun around to face the bank of TV screens. "Am I on camera? Candid Camera?" He started to look towards the corners of the room, in an exaggerated pantomime show of surprise and delight, looking for the hidden lens of a camera.

Presley twitched nervously. "I'm serious."

Viktor stopped his performance instantly. "What – with this?" he said, waving the handful of bills in Presley's face.

"Like I said – I got the rest."

Viktor stood back.

For the first time since Presley's arrival, Pyotr Krylov stepped away from the entrance and moved towards Viktor. Bending into his boss's ear, he spoke in hushed tones. Viktor nodded as they spoke. Pyotr took the handful of cash and then disappeared towards the rear of the room.

"Mexico?" Viktor asked, now turning his attention back to his surprise guest.

"Yeah," Presley croaked.

"They have lots of girls," he said, winking to Perkins and to the men flanking him.

Presley endured a short bout of laughter from the heavies. "So you can help?" he asked, after it had died down.

Viktor paced up and down before him. "I am not an unreasonable man. You get me the rest, come back and we'll talk."

Presley relaxed a little, understanding that he wasn't about to be harmed. Yet, he also knew that it would be foolish to just return with his pockets bulging, leaving him little or no leverage.

"How long will it take to get me tickets, and somewhere to stay – once I'm in Mexico?"

Viktor's brow creased as he worked it out. "Not long, comrade Presley. I have friends in many places. I can get you tickets, papers, and an address for a safe-house for as early as tomorrow."

"Tomorrow?" Presley repeated.

Viktor's head flicked from side to side. "Mmm – yes, this I can do."

"And we'll be okay?" Presley asked. "No hard feelings. You get your money and I get a simple bus ride out of here?"

"Simple." Viktor said, his face forming into a smile – eyes tight unreadable slits.

"Okay," Presley said. "Where do you want to meet?"

"When?"

"Tomorrow, for the money and tickets," Presley prompted.

"Oh – yes, we should meet somewhere beneficial to us both – yes?"

"Yes," Presley agreed. He had no wish to return here with the rest of the money, only to have a bullet waiting for him, ready to send him on his way.

Viktor stood thoughtful for a moment. Then, after nodding to himself, said, "Union Station?"

It took a few seconds for Presley's mind to calculate the

potential of Viktor's suggestion. "Union Station?" he echoed.

The Russian's face became impassive.

"Okay – sounds good to me," Presley conceded.

Viktor beamed now. "Let us toast tomorrow." He moved away from the sofa and crossed to the opposite side of the room. There, he busied himself with the task of pouring out two drinks. With a glass in each hand, he returned to offer Presley one. Viktor raised his glass high, said "Salut!" and then downed the shot of Vodka in one.

Presley tipped his glass back and drank. And as the fiery liquid burnt his throat, he sat there, praying that this wasn't the start of his descent into the flaming bowels of hell.

Chapter Thirty-One

Considering the kind of events that had happened at the hospital, the homicide department was almost empty. Chairs were left scattered, some with forgotten jackets resting over them, and desktops had been left cluttered. The room looked as if it had been vacated – en masse – in a hurry. No doubt it had, once the call had come in from St Mary's.

Joseph shuddered. The night seemed to have worked itself inside the building, searching out warm bodies to drain heat from living tissue. Joseph sat at Carter's desk, alone, watching, waiting for the arrival of his wife and son. He turned towards the department's clock. Only three minutes had ticked by since he'd last looked. It felt like three hours.

The nurse who had accompanied them was now dozing in Captain Mendoza's office, stretched out in the captain's chair. Earlier, once they'd arrived, she'd administered Joseph his medicine and then carried out a series of simple motor-functional and neurological tests. Joseph had been forced to act out different positions with both arms and legs, recite a short passage that was printed on a card – the body of text printed in tiny letters – and finally, identify certain objects throughout the room, to prove he wasn't suffering any form of dysphasia. His brain worked fine - apparently. Although he could not be considered as being in 'good health', he was at least not slipping any further towards sickness.

Joseph checked the time again. Two more minutes had ticked by slowly. He turned his attention to the object before him. Folded up and propped up against the desk was the wheelchair he'd arrived in. Joseph grunted slightly with disdain. Doctor Greenwood wasn't taking any chances of legal action, should Joseph receive injury whilst still in the hospital's care. Once they'd entered the department, Joseph had swapped chair with wheels for one with legs, not wishing for Marianna or Jake to find him in such a state.

Detective Carter appeared on the other side of the Department, carrying two cups of coffee. He reached his desk to place both down, before absentmindedly licking at his fingers in an attempt to clean away a trickle of the dark liquid.

"Hope you like it black," Carter said. "'Cos that's all we've got."

"Black's fine – as my mum used to say," Joseph responded. "*She* wasn't a big fan of cream. Said her hips liked it though – liked it a lot."

Carter laughed slightly. "Yeah, I like cream too. The machine out in corridor must love it also, as there never seems to be any left."

Joseph reached out to take the hot brew. He took a sip, swallowing a mouthful of muddy liquid. The stuff had more bite than a rattlesnake – and he imagined this is what was used when long hours into the night were required. Like tonight.

"Any news on my family?" he asked.

"Hey – sorry, should have said, Tyler just rang to say they're gonna be here shortly. Got caught up in traffic. Rangers game just finished."

"Oh."

A few moments of silence stretched out before them, both lost in their own thoughts, thoughts that were dark, worrying and full of dangers.

Finally, Carter said, "You've had an eventful couple of nights, to say the least."

Joseph nodded. Felt like an eternity had gone by since he'd been slugging it out with the Warrior from Queens. He sighed, understanding for the first time that that had been the end of his career – carried out on a stretcher, unconscious for the entire world to see. A harsh laugh escaped him.

"What?" Carter asked.

Joseph shrugged the act of bitter amusement away. "Nothing – just thinking, that's all."

"Right," Carter said, absentmindedly.

"It usually this quiet?" Joseph asked, scanning around the room.

Carter looked around too, as if he'd not had the time to register something as mundane as whether or not people were at their desks.

"Nah… Usually five or six work the nightshift, ghosts who like the darkness almost as much as night itself."

"They busy tonight?" Joseph asked, foolishly, forgetting that the two bodies left by the killer were work enough for a hundred cops.

"You could say that," Carter responded. His face softened slightly and he said, "It's better that they're not here. Some of them are a bit pissed with you."

"Me?" Joseph asked, a stab of fear twisting in his gut. What had he done wrong?

"They lost money."

"Money?"

"Yeah – from the fight."

"Oh – right, sorry." He paused. "For the misunderstanding. Not the fight."

The corner of Carter's eyes creased slightly. "No worries. Everyone gets tagged sooner or later."

Joseph opened his mouth, ready to defend himself, eager to explain that the fight had been stopped because of the mini-stroke and not by the hands of the 'Warrior'. His lips came together. Not a single word left them. What would he say? Did it matter? If he started now, justifying his defeat to the ignorant, uninformed masses, then he'd never stop. Because individuals out there, he realised, thrived on other people's misfortune.

"Tell them they can take it out of my ribs," Joseph responded. "Once I'm better."

The faintest suggestion of humour flickered across the detective's eyes. "Don't worry, they will. Me too, I lost fifty bucks on you."

Joseph just grinned back, then gave the detective a shrug of his shoulders.

They fell silent again, each focusing on their steaming cups. Finally, Joseph was unable to contain the worrying sense of responsibility.

"Did those two cops die because of me, Detective?" he asked.

Very carefully, Carter placed his cup on the desk. He looked at Joseph straight and held his gaze for a long moment.

"Did you get out of bed and kill them both with your bare hands?"

Joseph sat back in his chair, the question almost too obscene to answer.

"What?" he managed to say.

"Did you kill them with your bare hands?"

"Hell no."

"Then don't ever ask yourself that again," Carter said, understanding that Joseph hadn't been looking for just an answer, but more an atonement, a purging of his soul – the very same thing that Carter had asked and sought many times during these last three months. Was he responsible for William's death? Had he in some way been partially responsible for the shooting of his son? He'd come to understand after many nights agonising, that he wasn't.

"Look," Carter began, "whatever's happening has nothing to do with you. Not directly anyway. The old man's fate had been sealed well before you arrived, and I guess the killer returned tonight to make sure he finished what he'd started."

"Which is what?" Joseph asked.

"His cover-up."

"What?"

"Our killer revealed something tonight by his actions. He came to the hospital to cover up a mistake. And went to great lengths to do so. Goes against every profile we've got with regard to serial killers."

"I don't understand."

"Okay. Serial killers are very meticulous about choosing their prey. They go to great lengths to select the right candidate: right age, hair colour, shape, eyes, and then plan down to the minute detail how they're going to torture, rape, brutalise their victim. But, surprisingly, they use very crude techniques to capture the victim."

"Such as?"

"Pretending they need help, a flat tyre, unable to carry groceries to their car, wrapping an arm in bandages to fake injury, or just tailing the victim until an opportune moment arrives."

"And then what?" Joseph asked.

"And then they usually knock them out cold or use a sleeping agent like chloroform. It's when they arrive at the killer's house that all the preparation starts to take place."

"Okay, so what did *our* killer reveal tonight?"

"That he was desperate enough to return to the hospital, two nights running, risking detection, to carry out what should have been finished the night before."

"What, to kill me?" Joseph asked, fear tightening around his chest.

Carter shook his head. "No, you were just an oversight. Wrong place, wrong time. The killer was there to slay Henry Jones, or more correctly, get the attention of someone close to the old man."

"Like who?"

"In truth, Joseph, I don't know – yet."

"But why come back for me, if his message had been sent?" Joseph asked.

"Because this guy's a pro – a real talent – and doesn't like the thought of leaving potential witnesses behind."

"But I didn't see anything, remember?"

"Yeah – I do. But how certain was he? Considering you were meant to be someone else, waiting to die that very night."

"So I'm just a loose end – nothing more?"

"It's a shitty world we live in," Carter said. "Conversely, Joseph, you may have just become the pivotal point in this investigation."

"Why?"

"Because now you *have* seen the killer, and he isn't gonna like that – not one bit."

"Christ…" Joseph cursed. "Who the hell is this guy?"

Carter scratched at his chin for a moment. "Wait here," he said finally. He stood and worked his way over to Detective Tyler's desk. He rummaged around for a second, clearly looking for something in particular. Then, putting a thin folder under his arm, he returned to Joseph.

"Thought you might want to take a look at this guy," Carter said, slipping out a black and white photograph.

Joseph took it. Turned it to the light to get a good look. The picture was mostly filled by shadow – of deepest inky black – and the rest a mass of grey shapes. This was hardly an award-winning portrait, something with artistic flare, or something to be found on the cover of a magazine. The face – if that's what it truly was – was barely distinguishable.

"Is this a joke?" Joseph asked. "This could be anyone. Or any*thing*."

Carter grumbled, "Agreed. The Lab's still working on it. It takes the digital recognition software an age to process the light and shadows available, and then turn it into something more accurate."

"Tell them to keep trying," Joseph advised, before handing the photo back.

Carter slipped it inside the folder. "Maybe we'll have

something better to work with later – once the techs have done their thing."

"So, who is this guy?" Joseph asked.

Carter raised the folder off the desk slightly. "What – the guy in the photo?"

"No," Joseph replied. "Who the hell is – *was* – Henry Jones?"

Carter looked deeply into Joseph's eyes. "I don't think Henry Jones is anybody. Just your average law-abiding citizen. What we need to find out is who the hell is connected to him, and connected in a big way?"

"So what have we – sorry, *you* – got so far?"

"Well, we now have a nationality. Russian, right?"

"I guess," Joseph agreed.

"So let's start digging – see what we can uncover."

"You think this guy is trying to get someone's attention?"

"No," Carter replied. "I think he's just the hand to the body that is trying to get the attention. And a very large body at that."

"Like who?"

"Not sure, but I'd be guessing the Russian Mafia or some other Eastern European crime syndicate."

"Good God," Joseph moaned, sick by the prospect of unwittingly becoming the target of such ruthless a group. "So who have I got after me? Some sort of hitman?"

"There are a lot of highly skilled, cold-blooded professionals out there. Ex-KGB, Cold War spies, Russian army, criminal underworld, all just looking to get a piece of the action." Carter got up and moved towards another desk. He pulled the chair back, ready to seat himself before a computer system.

"What you doing?" asked Joseph.

"See if I can find anything on recent disputes involving Russian gangs."

"Such as?"

"Similar grisly killings."

"Jeez..."

Joseph ran a hand over his face, as if that simple gesture would be capable of wiping away the vision before him, returning him to the world he'd once known and leave behind this insane alternate reality. He looked beyond the empty desks and a face caught his eye: dark-skinned, elegant, yet tired-looking, but full of strength and determination.

Marianna entered the Department, closely followed by Detective Tyler.

Joseph straightened in his chair, wanting to look strong and in control for his wife and son. He smiled at Marianna and then looked beyond her in anticipation of Jake.

He didn't appear.

"Where's Jake?" he asked.

Marianna stopped at the desk. She switched her gaze from Joseph's face to Carter's, finding concern on both. "What's the matter?" she asked.

"Jake. Where is he?" Joseph repeated.

"He's with Eugene, asleep. I didn't want to wake him. Why?"

Joseph looked back, uncertainty striking him dumb. What were these worrying thoughts and feelings that had him gripped now? Did he really want his son here, when dangerous times were ahead? He turned to Carter to find his own fears mirrored on the detective's features.

"What is it?" Joseph asked, looking for understanding.

"Not sure. Doesn't feel right."

"What doesn't feel right?" Marianna demanded.

"You think they could move that fast?" Joseph asked.

"Who move that fast?" Marianna questioned.

Carter climbed to his feet, his chair scraping noisily along the hard floor.

Joseph reached forward to use the table. He stood on unsteady legs.

"Where are you going?" Carter asked him.

"I'm coming with you."

Marianna grabbed Joseph's arm. "Going where?"
"To get Jake."
"Why?"
"Because we're in trouble, real trouble," Joseph said.
"From what?" she asked.
Carter turned to her and said, "God only knows."

Chapter Thirty-Two

Viktor Mikhel sat alone now. His previous audience had vacated the room, leaving the crime boss alone with his trusted right-hand man, Pyotr Krylov. The Georgian was standing by the main door, sentinel-like, as if trouble could present itself at any moment.

Viktor stared with bleary eyes at the half-filled glass. The clear liquid in it had already done a good job at numbing his senses and had, for the time being, vanquished the demons that scratched at his brain. Hard times were afoot. Things were changing rapidly. And some of these changes were slipping through his fingers like running water.

The Russian crime boss looked around the room, suspicion and tiredness turning his eyes into tight slits. His earlier rant about hidden cameras had not been unreasonable, considering the level of trouble he was in. Both the FBI and Viktor's own boss, Sergei Mikhailov – the head of the Solntsevskaya Mafia based back home in Moscow, were putting the squeeze on old Viktor.

The FBI had him under surveillance 24/7, his phone lines were probably tapped, bank accounts being monitored, and any number of his civil liberties were being breached. Viktor had come to the US expecting free will and democracy: an open market for him to excel in. Instead, here he sat, a prisoner in his own home.

Home?

Yes, Viktor thought dismally, this vile place had become his home.

The Big Apple!

What a joke.

Sergei Mikhailov had sent him here in the early 90s, and Viktor had come without hesitation. Eager to make a name for himself, he'd arrived with enthusiasm and ambition - his two closest comrades - ready to plunder this new Promised Land. Sergei had set him up with both business and manpower, and Viktor had first begun operating in the Russian émigré communities in New York's Brighton Beach district.

Extortion had been his business plan. He'd used the muscle Sergei had obtained for him, a group of hardened Ex-KGB and Afghan war veterans, who had years of experience behind them, and all looking for work and wealth now that the old communist regime had fallen.

Viktor started to demand protection money from local businesses to begin with. A couple of hundred bucks here and there, before extending into illegal gambling dens, some of which were frequented by public figures, their palms already greased by Sergei Mikhailov. Next, a steady flow of sex-workers arrived, some under the promise of stardom, others simply desperate to get away from the economic collapse of a once great nation. All were forced to work off their debt, willingly or not.

Before long, Viktor was amassing a serious amount of annual turnover. The vast majority was returned to his homeland, were the money was quickly laundered. Sergei was a master at turning dirty money into clean untraceable riches. He had inside men, accountants on his payroll, who were adept at filtering these funds without detection. The Afghan War Veterans' Association was one such institution that had been added to the list of business fronts.

Then, in the late 90s, Viktor had struck gold.

Back home, Sergei had laid his hands on a Soviet-era submarine, an old Scorpion b-427. The vessel was earmarked for decommissioning, but the Muscovite crime boss had managed to gain ownership of it. Viktor had returned home briefly, before leading a contingent of ex-navy and army to South America. Their new-found Colombian friends had taken a deal, whereby Viktor supplied them with a small crew and navigational charts, allowing the submarine to enter American waters undetected. Unwilling to sell the vessel directly, Viktor had negotiated 10% profits on all shipments brought into the eastern states.

However, the new millennium had brought many new hazards with it. The newly formed successor of the KGB, the FSB, had started to take back some control. And the police's elite Berkut – or Eagle – force was conducting high-profile commando-style raids. Inevitably, many people were cutting deals to save their own necks, giving valuable information to the authorities, who were more interested in catching the bigger fish. These days, it seemed, nearly every organisation had a mole or rat, making it almost impossible to do business.

Viktor tipped the remainder of his glass back. The fiery Vodka scorched his throat. He placed the empty glass back down and rubbed at his tired eyes. His little empire was now under threat. Someone who once served this enterprise had ratted him out.

The FBI had seized an employee of his – on New Year's Eve of all days – an accountant, who had struck a deal with the District Attorney. This accountant had been working with Viktor for years, laundering money over here by using national and international charities and business start-ups, fronts no less, and maintaining the books for Sergei's pleasure. The Rat, Viktor's way of identifying him, had taken a job in one of their 'charitable trusts', looking to make his mark. The guy had the Midas touch. He'd shown – taught – Viktor's guys how to make vast sums of money by setting up hedge funds, macro hedge funds, no less. The simple premise had been for Viktor and Sergei to target a specific sector – manufacturing, for example – and then they would put the squeeze on the organisations and businesses that operated in such sectors. They'd simply make life hell for that particular division, forcing equity and shares to plummet. The accountant and his team would then invest heavily, buying large amounts of shares at rock-bottom prices. Finally, Sergei would call off the dogs completely, focusing on other areas; and before long, the industrial sector would quickly stabilise, allowing the accountant to cash in on sky-high share prices. It was a simple case of manipulating the local economy – and it was easy.

It hadn't taken long for Viktor to take the accountant under his wing. Then the real fun had started. Viktor had increased his percentage with the Colombians, explaining that the Scorpion submarine required more maintenance and personnel to run efficiently. It had been a small percentage increase, just 0.5%, not enough to draw too much attention back home from Sergei, but enough to keep both Viktor and the accountant happy. In just two years, they'd amassed a small fortune, all at Sergei's expense.

But then things had started to change. Viktor's hold on the organisation was becoming tenuous at best. Some of his men had started to drift away, returning to the homeland, where they were needed to help run Sergei's outfit, now that he was battling against the revived Russian government and the constant threat from rival gangs. The Chechen gang, Obshina, had already started to monopolise the firearms market within East European countries.

Viktor knew without doubt that the FBI were looking to nail both him and Sergei, working in conjunction with the FSB, and were now busying themselves with collating as much evidence as they could. Why else had they not yet come knocking on his door? The accountant must have squealed like a pig, giving them much to think about.

The Rat had just disappeared one day, simply not returning to his place of work after taking his lunch break. At first, his manager had failed to report this fact to Viktor, something that would not happen again, now that he was buried somewhere in the East District of Jersey. Viktor had immediately sent his men looking for the accountant. Then, two days later, an article had been printed in the *Times*, stating that a man had been found dead, burned beyond recognition. The car, though, was clearly identified as the accountant's. Later that week a second article was run, now confirming that the body had been Viktor's man.

Viktor thought otherwise.

Nothing rang true. Everything seemed too convenient. The car wreck had been found twenty yards down an embankment, somewhere just off the I97 turnpike. The news article stated that it was believed the driver had lost control and had gone over the embankment and crashed into a line of trees at the bottom of the hill. Okay, that was more than feasible. But cars just didn't simply explode on impact, nor had there been any reason for the accountant to be so far out of town, at a remote place like Liberty State Park, during his short lunch break.

Viktor had started to dig deeper.

How and why had he travelled from the Brighton Beach area – where he worked – all the way over to Jersey City, with just an hour to spare? No, Viktor thought, the accountant hadn't planned on making the return trip. Something or someone had been waiting for him, over in Liberty State Park. Further investigation revealed that no official funeral had been held for the accountant, just a short memorial at the hospital chapel where his body had been taken. Only his aging father had attended, and then the trail had simply disappeared.

It had taken many calls and heated discussions with many of Viktor's associates for him to discover that the accountant was actually alive and well – now under the supervision of the Witness Protection Program. The accountant and his cohorts were now preparing to tear Viktor's empire down in one fell swoop.

Still, Viktor wasn't going to simply lie down and let that happen. He'd put his own plans into action. Unable to get directly to the accountant, he'd formulated a plan to draw the supergrass out of his vile lair.

Tomorrow would bring its own problems, namely, Presley Perkins. Don 'Dolly' Perkins' son was turning out to be a real pain in the ass – that was for sure. Whatever his criminal involvement, Viktor was in no rush to harbour a known cop-killer. That just brought too much potential exposure, even for him. He should have put a bullet between the guy's eyes the moment he'd arrived here. Yet the promise of returned profit had halted that decision. Presley would indeed get his ticket out of here – that was for sure.

Viktor had a plan for Presley too.

He had plans for everything.

Plans that would involve the slaughter of innocent and guilty alike.

Chapter Thirty-Three

As if time had somehow been unable to find its way inside, kept out by sentiment alone, the room in which Eugene Profit sat in was devoid of anything modern or new. The chair he rested in looked like an antique, thick leather armrests with studded ends, and a back wide enough to seat a colossus. A TV stood silently in one corner, a simple wooden box that showcased dust instead of motion pictures. Black and white photographs on the mantel above the fire showed pictures of a younger Eugene and his wife, Elizabeth.

Although it was still early evening – the hands of a grandfather clock ticking slowly towards nine o'clock – Eugene Profit lay dozing. A man of ritual and rhythm, he was a firm believer in 'early to bed, early to rise'. The old ex-champ's eyes rolled beneath their lids as he dreamt about days gone by. Most nights he was visited by an angel, her face eternally young and always smiling, eager to share these lonely hours with him, unwilling to be forgotten.

Profit muttered something softly. "Elizabeth..." Then a contented laugh slipped quietly from curled lips. Sometimes these dreams turned to despair, as the old pro witnessed his beloved wife slip from his life, taken into the night without chance or forgiveness.

A bullwhip crack sounded, which jolted him awake. His eyes opened wide, first turning to the picture of his wife, before quickly scanning around the room. Darkness pushed against the window. Occasionally the wind scraped snow against it.

Eugene strained to catch the sound again.

Silence filled in the gap as he waited. Briefly, for a second time, the slight sound of a crack reached him. He climbed to his feet. The apartment he lived in was small and intimate, and had no hidden secrets left to reveal. A pipe underneath the kitchen sink gurgled late at night, a symptom of high pressure, brought on by the woman upstairs using her toilet. And Profit knew every loose floorboard so well that he could play out a melody by standing on them in sequence.

Yet this noise was unfamiliar to him.

For a second, he thought it sounded like the branch of a tree tapping against one of the windows. But here on the fourth floor no willow or honeysuckle would be capable of such heights.

He stopped in the centre of the room, waiting. The noise refused to reveal itself. Nothing obvious sprung to mind and he almost shrugged it off – but then it came again, clear and sure. The sound came from the hallway. Profit walked around an old sofa and poked his head inside the next room. The boy he'd come to see as his grandson slept soundly in his bed, oblivious to the dangers that lurked in the darkness.

Profit closed the door gently behind him and then entered the short hallway. A door to the right led towards his kitchen and another opposite offered access to a small closet. Most of the ex-champion's boxing mementos were stored there: memories of another life that the old man had let go a long time ago, too painful to bear witness to, their triumphant meaning now hollow and pointless since the death of his wife. Just one small trophy remained in view, between two photos on the mantel, one which had been awarded to Joseph for representing his country as a young boy.

Profit shuffled along the short passageway, passing the open door to his kitchen and the closed one to the closet. He stopped at the front door. A spy hole had been cut out at head height. He peered through. The magnifying glass revealed an empty landing on the other side in a fishbowl effect. Nobody stood on the opposite side baring elongated features. The landing appeared empty. Perhaps he'd been wrong and the sound had come from elsewhere? Turning his back, he traced his steps back the way he had come.

He re-entered the living room. The snow battered against the window in another noisy torrent. Over at the window, he looked out into the darkness and saw trees bent over with the burden of ice and wind, stooped low, like old men in a Lowry painting.

Eugene was just about to return to the comfy chair when the room turned surprisingly cold. He shivered, the night finding its way inside. The atmosphere changed too: an inexplicable shift in the air. He spun around. He took a short step towards the hallway, silently, instinct warning him to be cautious.

As he entered the hallway, the pages of a calendar, which was pinned to the wall opposite, fluttered slightly. Eugene frowned. Like the fingers of an apparition, a draught scraped cold nails across his cheek, forcing him to look the other way. The door to his apartment was ajar.

Quickly, he backed out of the hallway and into the lounge. His arm reached towards the mantel and gnarled fingers wrapped themselves tight around the boxing trophy. Consisting of a brass statuette on a solid marble base, the trophy weighed heavily in the old pro's hand. He returned to the hall with his weapon ready.

The door was barely open. A narrow strip of darkness ran down one side. Profit stepped closer. The draught howled through the gap like a pack of distant wolves. The trophy rose above his head. Belying his age, he took a couple of quick steps forward and pulled the door open.

The dark landing beyond jumped out at him. Nothing remotely menacing lay in wait. No blood-red eyes of hungry beasts or looming spectres – just the winter's chill snapped at his bare ankles. The weight in his hand dropped to his side.

He felt foolish now, understanding that he must not have secured the lock properly on his entrance. He chided himself for being a stupid old fool. Turning around, he stepped back inside. And as he did so, a dark figure rose from the shadows of the open door opposite, glided effortlessly and silently up behind the old man, then reached out with one gloved hand.

Chapter Thirty-Four

Carter hit the brakes, swerved around the oncoming traffic and then pushed the gas all the way to the floor. The Sedan tore past other vehicles, leaving them behind in a blur. The blue and red beacon flashed in a wide arc and the siren screamed out its warning. This was no covert operation. Carter wanted everyone to hear him coming.

"Almost there," he said, speaking to Joseph.

"Hurry," Joseph replied, from the passenger side.

The heavy evening traffic began to filter away as they entered a more secluded part of the neighbourhood. The squat buildings of commerce gave way to tall apartment buildings.

"Which one is it?" Carter asked, understanding that the old pro lived in one of the high-rises.

"That one, over there," Joseph directed, pointing to the furthest tower. Unlike the rest, this one seemed to stand in total darkness – even the lights from the stairwell appeared to be doused. Joseph's imagination ran wild. "They've cut the power," he said, picturing a gloved hand with wire cutters.

"Calm down, Joseph," Carter urged.

Joseph took a deep breath, pushing his fear all the way down to the pit of his stomach. There, it thrashed about like a fiery serpent.

"You sure you don't have a number to call?" Carter asked.

"No phone," Joseph replied. "Not even a landline."

"How the hell does this guy live?"

"Quietly."

"I hope you're right, Joseph. I hope you're right."

The detective threw the vehicle in a large arc. Twin headlights cast long shadows and the flashing lights granted them macabre faces. The siren gave them voices, screaming voices, which called out an impending doom.

Carter brought the vehicle to a halt. Tyres screeched noisily and the Sedan slid across the wet blacktop, coming to rest at an awkward angle. The detective was out in an instant. Joseph climbed out unsteadily, relying heavily on the door for assistance.

"You okay?" Carter asked, stepping around the vehicle, ready to help him.

"Fine. Go. I'm right behind you."

The detective turned and headed towards the base of the apartment building. He arrived to find a steel doorway at the bottom. A glass window had been cut into the thick metalwork, reinforced by wire mesh. Access would be granted by one of two ways. First, the simple use of a key; secondly, by activating one of the telecom buttons, which were mounted on the wall opposite.

Carter reached out. His finger stopped a few inches short. "Which number?" he called to Joseph.

"Four-D!" Joseph yelled back.

Carter pushed hard against the button.

Nothing.

No indication of operation: no buzz, beep, bell, nothing.

Carter waited impatiently. He allowed a few seconds to pass before jabbing at the button again. Now worried for the safety of the old man and the boy, he began pressing buttons at random.

The speaker before him crackled to life.

"Yeah?" asked a voice full of annoyance.

"Police. Open up. This is an emergency."

"Really?" the voice questioned, the single word laced with suspicion.

"Hurry!" Carter ordered.

"Listen – asshole, you think that one hasn't been tried before?"

"This is Detective Thomas Carter from the Fourteenth Precinct. Now open up."

"Yeah – well. This is Jack Johnson, recently removed unnecessarily from the crapper! Now go away!"

The speaker fell silent.

Joseph reached the doorway, panting slightly, but eager to get inside.

"No answer?" he asked, fearfully.

"Nothing."

"What now? We need to get inside."

"I know," Carter acknowledged. He took another look at the small window, and then turned to Joseph. "You keep trying Four-D, and as many others as you can." He took a step away.

"Where're you going?" Joseph asked.

"Trust me."

The detective quickly headed back the way he'd come. He was gone for just a minute, no longer, but it seemed like an eternity to Joseph.

"No luck?" he asked, finding the doorway still tight.

"No."

"Stand back," Carter ordered. His arm rose from the darkness, and the limb appeared to be two sizes too long.

"Wait," Joseph said, seeing the riot shotgun. "What if we're wrong? Over-reacting and they're merely asleep."

"Then I guess they're in for a rude awakening."

Joseph reached out to press Profit's number again. "One last time," he explained.

The weapon stayed poised.

Finally, unexpectedly, the speaker crackled and the old pro's voice came to them, metallic and distant sounding, over-masked by the hiss of interference, but Profit's nonetheless.

A smile started to form on Joseph's face.

The single word that followed dropped the smile like a dead weight.

"Help..!"

Carter dragged Joseph out of the way. He pushed his face against the glass window, making sure no one was standing behind or nearby. The window was pitch-black, with not a glimmer of light insight. He took a step back, brought the weapon up, pressing the muzzle against the window. He paused for just a second, now understanding that discharging a weapon within city limits would lead to a mountain of paperwork. Yet the urgency of the situation outweighed any promise of a late evening filling in forms.

He pulled the trigger.

The window imploded, glass and wire disappearing instantly. The hallway beyond it lit up spectacularly for just an instant before the gunfire extinguished itself.

Now, a crude hole had been blown into the glass. Taking a short step back, Carter fired again, widening the opening. He jabbed his hand through and hastily felt around for the inside latch.

"Got it," he cried, pushing open the door.

He fell through in his haste to get inside. Joseph found him on one knee, crouched in darkness.

"Hang on," Joseph said. He ran his hand along the surface of the wall, finding a light switch. The corridor came to life in a blaze of harsh white lights. No doors were situated on this level, just a tight hallway with stairs leading into darkness, and an old elevator with a crisscross safety door pulled tight.

Carter climbed to his feet. "Stay here," he said, taking the first of the steps.

"Like hell," Joseph replied.

"There's no time," Carter explained. He paused, reached under his jacket and produced his handgun. "Here," he said, tossing the weapon towards Joseph, who caught it with unsteady hands.

"You know how to use that?" Carter asked.

"Yeah," Joseph lied.

Carter turned his back and started to take the stairs three at a time. The steps gave way to a short landing with four different doorways. Despite the amount of noise his entrance had made, not a single glimmer of curiosity had presented itself. All four doors were locked tight. Sensible living, Carter thought, as he tackled the next flight of steps. Levels 2 and 3 were the same: four closed doorways, offering no hint of life. Was the whole block vacant, or the occupants inside hard of hearing?

Level 4 was entirely different.

Two doors stood ajar, both interiors illuminated slightly by the stairwell lights. Carter reached the first. No number on the doorway. He took a long stride to the next. Again, only frayed screw holes could be found. Wasting no more time, he entered the nearest door.

A dark hallway stretched out before him. He yelled, "Police!" and then, with the shotgun levelled out in front of him, quickly walked the short distance to the first doorway. The interior opened out to a small, compact kitchen. Nothing there. Move on.

The door on his right opened out to a living room. An empty sofa, chair and everything seemingly intact gave no indication of a struggle. The next room was filled with the stench of blood. A figure outlined by bright lights lay on the bed, beneath thick, blood-soaked sheets. Twin reading lamps illuminated the ghastly sight. A shock of white hair played starkly against the deep running red that had begun to pool around the victim's severed neck. In seconds, Carter's analytical mind played out what had happened. The killer had sneaked in undetected and slit the old man's throat whilst he lay sleeping. Then, the switch had been thrown, to reveal the killer had made a mistake.

This wasn't Eugene Profit.

Carter tore back the way he'd come, passing quickly

through the second doorway. Here, he could see the telltale signs of a struggle. A calendar had fallen to the floor, its pages spread wide like the wings of a downed bird. A boxing trophy lay against the wall, the statuette's leading left hand holding it upright.

However, the most obvious thing was the handset to the intercom. It dangled uselessly on its coiled wire, swinging gently, dark liquid glistening off the plastic surface.

Blood.

Carter bellowed, "POLICE!" He repeated the process he'd followed in the first apartment. First checking the kitchen. Then the living room. Both were empty. Next came the bedroom. He held his breath, prayed silently that what lay beyond wouldn't shock him to his core, and then stepped inside.

The bed in the centre of the room was unoccupied. The sheet lay crumpled in a heap at the foot. Similarly, Eugene Profit lay slumped on the furthest side of the bed. Carter pulled open a closet door – nothing there. He ignored the old man for now, concentrating on the last remaining room. The doorway to a washroom offered the last chance of concealment. The detective pushed open the door and dropped to one knee, brought the shotgun up to head height. A showerhead dripped heavy drops of water into the empty white tub.

"Jake?" he called.

The boy didn't respond.

Carter slipped back outside, first checking that neither of the other two doors had opened. They hadn't. He rushed back to the landing. It was then that he heard the whir and whine of old machinery. He pressed his face against the dirty window, cut into the elevator door. The drop of cables before him twitched as the booth continued its descent. He tried to prise open the door, but the mechanical safety held it firm.

Carter returned to the stairwell. He filled his lungs to capacity and then bellowed, "JOSEPH. HE'S HEADED

***

Joseph stood back from the booth, the whine of machinery announcing its imminent arrival. He heard Carter cry out to him and his hand tightened around the gun. The weapon felt surprisingly heavy and the grip had turned slick with his sweat. He braced himself, ready for confrontation. The bottom of the car appeared, and Joseph gritted his teeth.

This was it.

He panicked then, realising that this was beyond anything he'd ever experienced. What the hell, he'd never even held a gun before – let alone fired one! He checked the weapon, now aware that it must have a safety. True, a small notch was fixed to the side of the weapon. Joseph flicked it with his thumb. Damp with sweat, his thumb brushed uselessly over the switch. He tried again, and this time it clicked over.

The elevator arrived.

Through the dirty window, Joseph watched as a gloved hand pulled open the crisscross metal barrier. It slid open with a squeal of dry hinges. Next, the main door opened and the attacker from the hospital appeared.

Clamped roughly under one arm, limp and lifeless, was Jake.

The guy looked up, surprised to see Joseph there with a gun pointed in his face. Cowardly, he pulled Jake up in front of him, using the unconscious boy as a human shield.

"Let my boy go!" Joseph demanded.

The face behind Jake's grinned with unholy glee.

"Let him go!"

The guy changed his grip on Jake, using just one arm, tightly across his midriff, to hold him in place.

"Shoot and boy will die," the killer said.

The slightest glimmer of hope, relief, offered itself to Joseph. Jake must still be alive, or the killer's threat would be meaningless.

"Just let him go," Joseph pleaded. He could not – *would not* – shoot. Not this close to Jake. "Please…" he pleaded.

The killer smiled to reveal his film star's perfect white teeth.

"What do you want?" Joseph asked, trying to buy time, desperate to find an opening, anything to pull his boy to safety.

The killer's smile widened. "I want you."

"For what?"

"This." The killer's other hand appeared holding a handgun. And, even with Joseph's limited knowledge of firearms, he still recognised the silencer that had been attached to the barrel.

"What is this?" Joseph asked, this insane predicament beyond his understanding.

The guy just shrugged apologetically. "Simple case of wrong place, wrong time. Nothing personal."

"My boy?" Joseph asked, fear for himself the furthest thing from his mind.

"Don't worry," the killer began, "he didn't see my face. I'm not a monster."

"Then hand him over."

"Sorry, Joseph. This is where it ends for you."

"Why? What have I done?"

The killer smiled his bright-white smile again. "You have seen Yurius's face. Not good."

This acknowledgement of a name – Yurius – sent a shiver down Joseph's spine. Until now, the killer had been an enigma. Something to be feared, yes. But a figure that could be vanquished, like a fictional creature, nonetheless. Now, though, this inclusion of a name added another dimension to the killer – substance and authenticity – that made him far more menacing and real.

"But I hadn't seen you," Joseph said, referring to the previous night.

"Couldn't take chance. Too dangerous."

"What?" Joseph asked, needing to know answers.

"Too dangerous," the killer said again. His gleaming teeth disappeared, replaced now by the macabre slash of his mouth. The silenced weapon rose high, towards Joseph's face.

Joseph just stood there powerless.

"FREEZE!" Carter yelled.

The killer tensed noticeably. His weapon wavered fractionally, his attention now split between the two of them.

"Drop the weapon," Carter ordered. He pumped a round into the shotgun. "Do it now and nobody gets hurt."

The Russian's eyes stayed focused on Joseph, but his arm whipped around towards Carter. The muzzle coughed gently, two, three times. The attack caught both Joseph and Carter off guard. Carter ducked low as the bullets tore into the wall above him. Each was wide of its mark yet sufficiently close enough to knock Carter out of his rhythm.

The killer's weapon spun back towards Joseph's head. Joseph had little time to think. Reacting instinctively, in the only way he knew how to, he threw a short jab towards the guy's face. It was fast, desperation and fear giving it more speed and power than expected. At the same time, he slipped to his left and delivered a right hook. In contrast to the lightning fast left jab, this punch was weak and slow. Still, the small revolver that was clutched in his right hand gave it added weight.

Yurius's head rocked back and his gun went off, his finger jerking spasmodically around the trigger.

Mercifully, the bullet tore harmlessly over Joseph's shoulder. Instinctively, he shut his eyes, the bright fire blinding him momentarily. The Russian barrelled past him, shouldering him out of the way with ease, which spun Joseph around before sending him crashing to the floor. When Joseph opened his eyes, the lobby was empty.

Neither his son nor the killer, were anywhere to be seen.

Chapter Thirty-Five

The old Ford bucked and swayed like a crazed mustang. Yurius gripped the steering wheel with both hands in an attempt to keep this wild beast under his control. The road was little more than a series of potholes and cracked asphalt. Up ahead he could see only the occasional light, which streaked across the windscreen, warped and elongated by the greasy glass surface.

The air inside the Ford was a mixture of stale sweat and lemon-scented freshness. An air freshener in the shape of an American football helmet swung eagerly from the rear-view mirror. Yurius turned his attention away from the dark, desolate streets, the swinging helmet acting like a hypnotist's charm.

The dark road slipped away before him, replaced now by the dilapidated husks from Yurius's homeland. This American industrial sector became the Russian's playground from memories past: the rundown shanty areas on the outskirts of Moscow, the very place where Yurius and his half-brother had once played. His mother, a burnt-out addict, who was a slave to morphine and poverty-stricken, had given birth to Yurius in a near-empty high-rise, which had discarded its people like a fish sheds its scales. War, economic collapse and crime had reduced those who remained, into the vague shadows of a once proud people.

Both Yurius and his brother had worked tirelessly to escape from their desperate beginnings. While Yurius had channelled his athletic capability towards success, his older brother had found release through the acts of violence and criminal activity.

Yurius had come to America in his early twenties: an athlete who excelled at everything he did. He was a tall, well-built individual, and as bright as a burning star. Or had been. He'd arrived here as a representative of the old USSR, the lead flag-bearer, who proudly led his team into the Atlanta Arena on the first day of the Olympics.

At that time he had been the European champion at 200 metres sprint. He was unbeaten in over thirty competitions, having gained many victories over the American world champion, Tyrone Lewis. It had been the most anticipated event in the track and field programme, and the final didn't disappoint. Both made through the qualifiers with considerable ease, and the stewards had lined them up side-by-side for the final.

Yurius had won by a full two metres.

Suddenly, this young man from the mean streets of Moscow had become hot property. Showing an aptitude for anything physical, Yurius had stayed in Atlanta, having had successful tryouts for the Atlanta Falcons football team.

He'd completed his first season with them, finishing in the top half of the national league. Then, that summer, he had been involved in a training accident. He'd collided head-on with a 250-pound linebacker and, even though he'd been wearing his helmet, he'd suffered a fractured skull.

Worse had followed. An undetected bleed had subsequently damaged the frontal lobe of his brain, nothing too dramatic or even noticeable at first. Nevertheless, Yurius's personality had started to change. He lost interest in football, his attention turning now to the demons of drink and drugs. This had fuelled his change rapidly. And, before long, he lost his contract with the Atlanta Falcons and turned to other forms of contracts to survive.

Contract killings.

Something dark had awakened on the day of the training accident. Something that had slowly taken him over – a dark malignant cancer that had fixed itself to his soul, favouring the eternal spirit rather than mortal flesh.

Yurius had once again been reunited with his older half-brother. Together they had formed a secretive partnership, where Yurius added muscle to an organisation that required a necessity to work outside the law. Living under his mother's maiden name, the younger brother had operated as a ghost, working throughout New York state. Untraceable, he was known by only a few as a dark presence that added substance to an ever-expanding empire.

Now, Yurius pulled the Ford to a halt. He popped the door open, pulled the keys from the ignition and climbed out. Only a few buildings surrounded him. Most were crumbling shadows. One or two lights burnt their way through the darkness, but Yurius was confident that he was sufficiently alone.

Alone?

No, Yurius thought, not alone.

He moved around to the rear of the Ford. With one final check to make sure the coast was clear, he activated a button on the key-ring. The Ford's hazard lighting flashed twice with an audible *bleep, bleep.*

The trunk popped open.

Yurius pulled something from his jacket. Its cylindrical shape caught what light there was available. He cranked open the trunk to reveal Jake's motionless body. The young boy was curled up in a tight ball. He didn't raise his head, move, flinch in terror, or show any indication of life.

Yurius reached out to take Jake's limp wrist. He felt for a pulse. Then, as the hypodermic needle punctured young flesh, Yurius grinned to reveal his shark-white teeth.

"Not monster," he said, with cold, soulless detachment.

Chapter Thirty-Six

Joseph's legs threatened to give. He reached out with a trembling hand in an attempt to remain upright. He felt weak and uncoordinated, as if he'd just suffered another sudden attack or bout of dizziness. He filled his lungs and then nodded towards Detective Carter.

"You sure you're ready for this?" Carter asked.

They were stood outside the hospital morgue. Only a set of double-doors separated them from what lay beyond.

"I'm ready," Joseph responded. He sucked in another breath through gritted teeth. Then he nodded once to Carter before pushing himself away from the wall.

The detective opened the door nearest and allowed Joseph to slip through.

The morgue appeared almost totally barren. There was nothing of an excessive nature on display. White walls magnified the strip-lights above, which filled the area in a cold glare. A reception desk occupied one side of the room. And, the window that opened out to greet visitors or hospital staff was made up of frosted glass, which added to the bitter harshness of the place.

Joseph shuddered, although the room itself was deceptively warm.

"You don't have to do this now," Carter said, drawing Joseph to a halt.

Their eyes met.

Joseph's eyes held a combination of agony and anger. He already knew what lay ahead, and in different circumstances, less desperate times, he may have simply been saddened and angered by this. However, it was the uncertainty of his son's safety that fuelled Joseph's emotions. His jaw had started to ache. The hatred towards the man who had taken Jake was quickly in danger of consuming him.

Carter understood this clearly. He needed Joseph Ruebins to stay focused and, more importantly, in control.

"We'll get him back, Joseph," Carter began. "But we need to stay calm and try to figure out what it is this guy wants us to do next."

Joseph shook his head. He reached up and rubbed his thumb and index finger over his closed eyes. When he opened them, Carter saw that the anger had been put into check.

"Let's get this over with," Joseph said, turning back towards the reception desk.

Carter took the lead. He approached the half-opened window to find a middle-aged woman sat behind. She looked away from the computer screen that occupied her attention.

"Can I help?" she inquired.

The detective flashed his identification. "Detective Thomas Carter. This is Joseph Ruebins." He flicked his head backward slightly in Joseph's direction.

The woman had to push herself out of her chair slightly to get a look beyond Carter. "Saw you on TV," she said, speaking directly towards him.

Joseph just stood there silent, mute, *numb*.

"We're here to identify Eugene Profit," Carter said. He turned towards Joseph and offered him a considerate nod, hopeful that his directness had not pained the man stood behind. Joseph simply offered the detective a slight wave of his hand. Carter turned back to the woman.

"Is he ready to be viewed?"

The receptionist shifted back into her seat. She tapped out a few commands into her keyboard.

"Yes," she replied simply. "Room 2."

Carter stepped back from the desk and turned his attention towards the adjoining passageways. He stood in indecision for a few seconds, unsure of which way to go.

"That way," the receptionist directed, her head poking out through the gap between windows.

"Appreciate it," Carter said, heading towards the correct passageway.

Joseph followed dutifully, trying to put the picture from the old coach's apartment out of his mind.

Profit had taken a horrendous beating. Most of his facial bones had been shattered, so that both Joseph and Carter were barely able to recognise him, and his body had been stomped on until almost every rib had cracked. The paramedics had arrived on the scene within minutes of Carter calling it in, but by then the old man had been taken from them. Joseph had held the ex-pro in his arms as they waited for the paramedics to arrive, feeling the weak beat of his heart grow ever slower and less rhythmic. Just before he'd slipped away, Joseph had witnessed Eugene's eyes flutter open, briefly, and his battered and misshapen mouth form into a weak smile. He'd whispered something, something so faint that Joseph hadn't been able to understand it at first. Then, as Eugene lay still, the single word had become apparent.

"Elizabeth," he'd said with his dying breath.

Now, Joseph stood over his friend's body, his heart aching from the loss, his fists clenched tightly, and his soul swearing solemnly that this atrocity would not go unpunished.

* * *

Marianna was inconsolable. Detective Tyler sat next to her, one arm draped over her shoulders and the other clasped tightly in the distraught woman's hand. The department was bustling with activity. Almost all the available detectives were here, handsets clamped tightly between shoulder and jaw, their hands a blur as they jotted down information.

Captain Mendoza was back in his office, Carter with him, and they were talking animatedly and with conviction. Soon the FBI would arrive, ready to take over the case of Jake's abduction, this being their jurisdiction, then both Mendoza and Carter would be forced into taking a back seat.

This worried Joseph to the core.

He sat at Carter's desk, Marianna and Tyler on the opposite side, the sound of his wife's agony slicing through him like a razor-sharp knife. His heart hadn't stopped pounding since identifying Eugene's body, and a cold sweat had sodden his clothes.

Tears slipped down Joseph's cheeks. Underneath the table his fists were clenched, anger and hatred giving him a strength he thought lost. He chanced a look towards Mendoza's office to see Carter throwing his hands up in exasperation. The detective turned his back on Mendoza and then exited his office with a look of murder on his face.

"What now?" Joseph asked.

Carter looked down at him, and the anger vanished from his features. "We have a name – a start."

"Yurius," Joseph said.

"Yes," Carter agreed.

"So let's find the bastard and get my boy back!"

"FBI are on their way," Carter said. "This is their case now. To negotiate the release of your son."

Joseph looked deeply into the detective's eyes. "We both know there won't be any negotiation. The killer wants me – and me alone."

"We don't know that for sure," Carter said.

Joseph shook his head. "Yes we do." He took a deep breath to help gather his thoughts. "What about Amber Alert? Should we notify the media now, and see if that helps get Jake back?"

It was an idea that the detective had been considering. Would notifying all media channels help them, or send the killer into a panic? For although Jake's kidnapper had thus far proven himself to be adequately capable, would he want to risk detection by holding onto the boy, if Jake's face and description was to flood the TV channels and airwaves? Carter's intuition told him not. The killer may simply despatch Jake and take his chances with Joseph at a more opportune time.

Carter turned back to Mendoza's office. His professionalism held him firm. He was not willing to mess up any chances of getting Jake back safe by overstepping his role as detective. The FBI would be better equipped at handling such a thing: a detail that Captain Mendoza had just made quite clear. Yet, the parent, father, *man* in him demanded that he take action, and take action now.

"I'm not sure that would be wise, just now," Carter conceded.

"I got the Devil on my back – ain't I?" Joseph said.

Marianna's tear-stricken face rose. "Shouldn't we be getting home – in case the kidnapper phones?"

Carter shook his head. "We've already got the lines running directly to here. Any contact and we're right onto it." He pointed to a technician, who was staring ardently at a telephone set. A recording device and tracking system sat next to the phone, and a set of oversized earphones lay next to that.

Marianna shook her head. They needed to be acting now – not waiting for a phone call. "Find this… *Yurius*, whoever he is."

Tyler took Marianna's arm. "We're looking." Half of the department had already spent the last hour trawling the police database in search of a Russian named Yurius. So far – nothing.

"How long has it been?" Joseph asked.

Carter glanced at his watch. "Still less than two hours. It's very early days yet."

Carter and Joseph eyed each other. Both had witnessed the

killer's intentions firsthand. Jake's taking had been a direct attempt to get at Joseph. It was only coincidence that they'd arrived during the act.

"This waiting is unbearable," Joseph announced.

Silence worked its way between them, both men turning towards their own thoughts. The quiet was shattered when the phone near the recording device burst alive with a shrill of noise. A collective gasp followed.

"Here we go…" Carter breathed.

It took all of Joseph's will to stop himself from throwing up, terror boiling away in the pit of his stomach.

The technician reached out to activate the recording device. He slipped the earphones on and then sat waiting.

Pick it up! Joseph screamed silently. As if he'd heard, the young detective looked directly at him.

"Hurry," the technician ordered.

It was then that Joseph realised the call had been rerouted from his home, so the caller would expect either him or Marianna to pick up. He jumped to unsteady feet, and then quickly made his way over to the desk.

"You ready?" Carter asked.

"Yeah," Joseph replied.

"Keep him talking for as long as you can," the technician instructed.

The phone continued to demand attention, ringing with grim determination.

Joseph reached out to take the handset. "Yes?"

There was a pause on the other end. Just the slight hiss of static played into Joseph's ear. Marianna, who was up and out of her chair, stood desperately close to her husband, her ear close to his.

"Hello?" he asked.

"You big bear?"

Joseph almost hung up.

This was no time for crank calls. The handset moved away from his ear by an inch, ready to be slammed back into its cradle.

"You big bear?" the voice asked again. The question had been laced with thick Slavic tones.

"Yeah," Joseph said, understanding the voice belonged to the killer.

"Little bear is safe."

"Where is he?"

"Safe."

"Why are you doing this?"

"It's just business. Nothing personal."

"Give me back my son!" Joseph demanded.

"Little bear will be returned tomorrow, when big bear comes to meet me."

"What the hell do you want, Yurius?"

The phone line fell silent, but still connected.

"Yurius?"

Click – the connection broke.

"Hello?"

Marianna snatched the phone out of his hands. "Let me hear him," she pleaded.

Joseph took back the handset and then wrapped his hands around her, gaining strength from the woman he loved. "He said Jake's alive. I'll get him back – I promise."

Carter turned to the technician. "You get anything?"

The tech shook his head. "Didn't stay connected long enough."

Carter moved away from the recording and tracking equipment. He headed for Tyler's desk and her computer. "We should be looking beyond known felons. Maybe the Internet can help us. This guy may have just arrived from the old Eastern Bloc – here to graze pastures new. Maybe Russian news archives or clips can help us."

Joseph felt unbearably weak. He ambled over to Carter's desk and sat heavily. Marianna remained over by the phone, as if her presence there would somehow force the kidnapper to call back – this time making a fatal mistake, thus revealing

Jake's immediate whereabouts. Joseph ran his hand over his eyes in an attempt to clear his head. Opening them, his eyes came to rest on the thin folder which sat on Carter's desk. This was the same folder the detective had taken the unrecognisable snapshot from earlier. Joseph opened the folder. The same blurred image of a face lay inside. Instinctively, he reached out to take it. Nothing revealed itself to Joseph, and the image stayed a mystery. With a heavy sigh, he tossed the photo back. The air underneath caught the photo in flight for a second, and it glided over the folder to land almost at the edge of the desk. Gingerly, Joseph reached over to retake it. And, as he did so, another picture caught his gaze.

"What's this?" he murmured to himself.

He took the snapshot and brought it up to eyelevel. Understanding came to him immediately. This picture was a clear image of the one he'd just tossed away. And this one now held a recognisable profile within. The dark shadows of the previous photo had been removed and the image brought into focus. The picture had lost some definition – now looking more like a picture that had been photocopied many times over. However, the contrast, brightness and gamma had been manipulated to reveal – and quite clearly – the face hidden within the shadows.

The tech guys had done one hell of a job.

His son's kidnapper, Eugene Profit's killer stared back at Joseph with cold detachment.

Yurius.

This fact, Joseph was certain of. His heart began to race. The photo in his hands began to shake. Memories flooded together inside his head: pictures and video and sounds, all merging together like a multidimensional jigsaw puzzle.

A fist landed squarely against Joseph's forehead. Pain flared across his skull, and for one terrible second he thought he was about to lose all consciousness – downed by another attack. Instead he stayed upright, rocking back in his seat. He was now gripped by the photograph's clarity and meaning.

"Don't bother with the Internet," Joseph advised the detective. His eyes were clear now, and a bitter smile, laced with hatred, had split his face in two.

"What?"

"I already know who Yurius is."

Carter looked puzzled. "You okay, Joseph?"

Joseph formed a tight fist, but left his thumb pointed out. *"Show Time..."* he said, giving the detective the thumbs up gesture.

Chapter Thirty-Seven

The Rat continued to gnaw away at Viktor's thoughts. In the late hours of the night, Viktor often suffered at the hands of his dark imagination and paranoia. Was it because he spent these hours alone, with no one to share the nights with that he toiled with his own tortured thoughts? Most of Viktor's men had returned home, another day of work done, having helped Sergei Mikhailov's empire to grow that little bit bigger.

The bottle of Vodka next to him was now almost empty, the glass that siphoned it empty, too. The aroma of spent sex hung heavily in the air. Earlier, Crystal, one of Viktor's working girls, had put in a bit of extra time tonight. They'd fucked; Viktor thrusting into her aggressively, trying to vanquish these demons through the act of sex, while Crystal had lain there silent and immobile.

Now, alone again, he was stretched out on the bed, the sheets gathered in a crumpled mess at its foot.

He'd paid a high price for his leadership – a position that demanded an impassiveness bordering on cold-blooded detachment. Only once or twice had he allowed himself to get close to some of his employees – his men – but on each occasion he'd been forced to discipline them, when a mistake had been made. And Viktor's discipline came with a heavy hand. It was all about maintaining face – keeping respect and fear as your two closest allies.

And this was the only real reason why Viktor had entertained the fool Presley Perkins. To allow someone to get away with $25,000 would make him look weak, and this was a weakness that Viktor could not afford to have.

Viktor would be sending his top man, Pyotr Krylov, to do business with Presley. The Georgian had requested that he do so. Viktor didn't think Perkins would like what Krylov had to offer, but the thought bent the Russian's lips into a ghastly leer. Krylov had made many 'problems' go away over the last few years, and the Russian boss felt glad to have him here to help when times were hard. No one – not even Dolly's son – could be allowed to make a mockery out of old Viktor.

There was a gentle tap at the door.

The Russian boss reached down to grab his undershorts. The tap came again, louder this time, but still masked with caution.

"What is it?" Viktor inquired, drawing his shorts up to his waist.

"Boss – you have a guest," a voice informed him.

Viktor open the door to find the doorman, Nikolay, standing before him.

"Guest?" he asked.

Nikolay nodded.

"Who?"

The old Russian shuffled nervously from one foot to the other. "A familiar face," he replied worriedly.

Viktor stepped back in the room to gather up the rest of his clothes. "Where is this 'guest' now?" he asked, slipping his shirt on.

"In the TV room."

"What? You let him in?"

Nikolay shrugged. "Said he needed to speak to you – so I let him in."

"At this time?" Viktor said.

"Said you'd want to speak to him. Something about a rat?"

Now, Viktor looked both interested and unnerved. "He's here?"

"Who?" Nikolay asked, the conversation taking a bizarre reversal of direction.

"Never mind," Viktor said, dismissively, with a wave of his hand. "I'll see him."

"You need me to arrange for assistance?" Nikolay asked, meaning protection.

Hell no, thought Viktor, wanting no one but himself to speak to the unexpected visitor. He shook his head. "No, Nikolay, I can handle this quickly by myself."

Nikolay nodded again, and then simply disappeared from view. Viktor dressed quickly before heading towards the TV room. He stopped halfway there, wondering if it would be more prudent to go armed. Yet, after chiding himself, he stepped inside.

Viktor's heart skipped a beat.

A uniformed policeman stood in the centre of the room. His cap was tucked under his arm, casually, like he was making a routine house visit. Then the visitor turned away from the bank of TV screen to look upon the Russian boss.

In a hiss, Viktor asked, "What are you doing here?"

The guy before him grinned back. "Come —Viktor, you're not pleased to see your own brother?"

Chapter Thirty-Eight

The old TV set hissed and a blanket of white fuzz filled the screen. A small group of people sat huddled around it, their faces expectant and eager. The TV had been plonked on Carter's desk and an old VCR lay covered in dust to one side.

Joseph, Carter, Marianna and Tyler were all tipped forward in their seats. The white blizzard that blew across the screen cleared.

"What are we looking for again?" Tyler asked.

Joseph pointed to the screen before them. "Keep watching." He pressed the remote and a picture appeared, warped and broken, and playing at twice the speed. Joseph stopped the tape.

Football sensation Michael Tucker filled the screen, his broad shoulders reaching beyond the shot, clipped off by the edge of the TV set. The tape had lost its quality somewhat, the top part of the screen constantly pulling the picture to the right, a symptom of overuse and an inability to track. The recording had come directly from one of the other detectives, who'd rushed home after Joseph had launched into a frenzy desperately seeking anyone who had been aware of the previous night's documentary.

Carter fidgeted awkwardly. Had Joseph slipped into some kind of dementia? His surprising change in behaviour had unnerved him. All he kept saying was *Show Time* and giving him the thumbs up.

The picture started to fast-forward again. Tiny bodies in

bright uniforms scurried around the football pitch like overexcited ants.

"Here," Joseph said, playing the tape again. Now, Tucker was being interviewed in a locker room, dressed only in a towel, which was wrapped loosely around his waist. By his smug expression it didn't take long to realise that the interviewer was female.

"Turn it up," Carter insisted.

Joseph increased the volume. The football player was halfway through thanking God for bestowing His humble servant with such divine talent. An occasional naked body would appear in shot, black or white butt cheeks, momentarily gracing the camera. Tucker turned to someone out of shot and then launched into a tirade of juvenile banter. The camera panned around to catch a towering white male. The guy was laughing, but his eyes belied a lack of understanding. He was tall and muscular, with a broad face, cut either side by tight Mongolian eyes.

Joseph hit the pause button. "Yurius."

"What?" Carter gasped.

Marianna reached out to take her husband's hand. "Joseph – are you sure of this?"

Joseph nodded, his eyes unwavering, pinned to the TV screen. "That's the bastard who took our son."

Carter examined Joseph's face. He recognised the look – he'd seen it many times over the last three months, in his own bathroom mirror. The hate that radiated from Joseph was tangible.

"Joseph," Carter began, "are you one hundred percent certain of this fact?"

"That's the man who took Jake – yes."

Carter moved to one of the computer monitors.

"What are you doing?" Tyler asked, joining him.

The detective brought up Google. He typed in 'Yurius footballer' and then pressed ENTER. A list of sites appeared instantly. Carter clicked on the first one. The same face that was frozen on the TV appeared on the monitor screen. The caption read: *Olympic Medallist takes America by storm.* Carter started to read deeper.

At that moment, a group of dark-suited individuals entered the Department. There were seven men in all. Six of them carried themselves with an air of self-confidence, self-assuredness, which was borderline obnoxious. The seventh person followed, dressed casually, he moved with slouched shoulders and looked around with nervous eyes. He was short, in his mid-to-late forties, and appeared to be doing his best to stick close to the team of agents.

Like synchronised swimmers, the group split apart, without hesitation or dialogue. Two headed directly for Captain Mendoza's office, one placed a large briefcase next to the detective and his recording equipment, and the remaining three gathered around the edgy civilian as if he was the President himself.

The agent with the briefcase opened it without comment, and then began arranging a second set of recording equipment. These, though, were state-of-the-heart devices: a paper-thin laptop instead of the detective's old analogue recorder, earphones that looked as if they should be worn by some performing pop star, and a small box that, in all honesty could have been anything. Quickly, he arranged a second set-up next to the first.

Whilst Carter's attention was riveted to the confrontation going on in Mendoza's office, Joseph couldn't tear his eyes away from the civilian-looking guy. He looked fearful, sad and annoyed all at the same time. Joseph recognised these emotions as his own. They made eye contact. The guy nodded simply, as if he somehow shared Joseph's internal pain.

The man hesitated for a moment, before stepping towards the occupied table. The three agents shadowed him step for step. Now closer, Joseph found the guy's eyes to be red-rimmed and puffy. He'd been crying, and recently.

The guy opened his mouth as if to speak.

This new inclusion to the group drew Carter's attention away from the verbal exchange that was going on in Mendoza's office.

The guy spoke. "I'm sorry for your loss." He was softly spoken and his words had had genuine sincerity behind them.

Joseph just stared back blankly.

"I've lost someone too," the guy said.

"Who?" Joseph asked, wondering if perhaps he was the brother of one of the slain cops.

"My father…"

"Do I know you?" Joseph asked.

"No. I don't think so," he replied. "But you may have known my father – sort of."

"Sort of?"

"I believe you met my father."

Joseph frowned. "I'm sorry – I don't believe I did."

The guy extended his arm. "I'm Edward Jones. Henry's son."

Carter's mouth dropped open. "Wait a minute – you're supposed to be dead."

Edward Jones turned his attention towards the detective. His hand remained in Joseph's, but his empty, soulless eyes bore into Carter's.

"Dead and gone to hell," he said, in a voice devoid of hope.

Chapter Thirty-Nine

The uniformed officer took a step towards the Russian boss. His face split to reveal bright white teeth. "Come – Viktor, is this any way to greet your brother? Your blood?"

Viktor was half inside the TV room. Subconsciously, his hand patted the side of his hip, where he would ordinarily wear his weapon, on the few occasions when he needed one.

The guy before him laughed openly. "Always the same old Viktor."

Viktor's eyes formed themselves into tight, questioning slits. "What brings you here, Yurius?"

Yurius placed the officer's cap on the back of the large sofa, which overlooked the bank of TV screens. "We have business to attend to, remember?"

"Not here," Viktor hissed. "You shouldn't be seen here."

Yurius's smile widened, reminding Viktor of a Great White shark. "No worry, brother – I came undetected."

Viktor finally entered the room. He moved closer to his brother, but maintained a safe distance.

Yurius said, "I come bearing gifts."

"What?"

"Gifts, for my brother."

"From whom?"

Yurius grinned again. "I bring cub from big bear."

The Russian boss frowned. "What?"

"I bring bear cub, for my brother."

Viktor took another step closer. "You get out now, while I still have my patience."

Yurius just stood there grinning foolishly. Another step took Viktor close enough for him to see his brother's face in detail. He was broad of face, square-chinned, with a thick crop of brown-grey hair. His was cut into a short, tidy style, unlike Viktor's unruly mane. Now, closer, Viktor also saw the thin line of scar tissue that ran from just below Yurius's hairline, down to the top of his left temple. His eyes were deep brown, but the left one ticked constantly, just noticeable if you knew what to look for.

Yurius smiled now with a look of deep affection. "Viktor – you look tired."

Viktor took the remaining few steps before finally embracing his brother. "You shouldn't come here," he said again, but this admonishment had no weight or malice behind it.

Yurius kissed both of Viktor's cheeks. "Come – I show you gift now."

Viktor shook his head. What the hell was his crazy brother talking about? He paused for a moment, looking deeply in his brother's eyes. The burning flame of intelligence that had once been there was now gone.

"What is this gift you speak of?" Viktor asked.

Yurius grinned, his shark-white teeth visible. "I will show you. Come, follow me."

The Russian crime boss followed his brother. He was led to the rear of the TV room, through a storage area, and then along to the bolted back doorway.

Viktor frowned. "How did you get in?"

The white smile cut through the gloom. "Nikolay let me in. Don't worry Viktor, nobody saw me."

Viktor rubbed at his eyes. Tiredness clawed at them with cruel talons. "Hurry, Yurius – it is late."

Yurius reached out to release the bolts. They slid back silently, well greased and maintained: an emergency exit that was kept in good working order. The doorway opened and the alleyway beyond flooded in, dousing them in a pitch-black wash of darkness.

Viktor's heartbeat quickened.

His brother's moods were volatile at best, and Viktor wouldn't have put it past his boss, Sergei, to utilise such a thing, and turn brother against brother. Stepping out into a dark alleyway was not on Viktor's immediate list of things to do. Yurius stepped into the shadows and gestured towards something just out of view.

Viktor poked his head outside, briefly, tensing slightly, half-expecting the quiet cough of a silenced weapon. Instead, he caught a glimpse of a car's rear. The weak lights above, which filtered through from the bright sidewalk, cast slivers of light on the trunk's surface like the multicoloured mix of motor oil and water.

Yurius moved towards the trunk. He activated a button on the key ring that had appeared in his hand. The taillights flashed twice before the trunk lid popped open.

"Look, Viktor – bear cub."

Viktor took a step closer. A slight shape revealed itself to him. Just a small part of the object was visible, but with sickening dread, he knew what lay inside to be human.

"What have you done?" he asked, thinking the unthinkable.

Yurius frowned. "What?"

"Who is this?" Viktor asked, looking down now at the small bundle.

"It is big bear's little cub," Yurius explained.

"What is this big bear you speak of?"

Yurius grinned from ear-to-ear. "It is Joseph Ruebins' son."

"Oh good God…" Viktor cursed. "What have you done?"

Chapter Forty

Edward Jones continued his tale, his small audience enthralled by his unbelievable revelations. He explained his involvement in laundering vast sums of money for the Russian kingpin, Viktor Mikhel; money that had been filtered through various associations, like the Afghan War Veterans' Association. He explained how, after working for just two years with an accountancy firm based in the Brighton Beach District, he'd been given the task of head bookkeeper. He also took a while to explain how he had helped build the Solntsevskaya Empire by manipulating local economies and then investing heavily in macro hedge funds. He then went into great detail about how he and Viktor had made a small fortune, taken from the Colombians, by laundering money through various charitable trusts, without Sergei Mikhailov knowing.

Understanding came to Carter. "So that's why they got to your father, in an attempt to silence you."

Edward nodded. "Yeah. Cowards couldn't get to me – so they went for an ailing old man who couldn't defend himself."

Tyler shook her head. "Everything makes sense now. Why the killer took the tong…" She cut her sentence short, aware of Edward Jones' involvement.

The accountant reached out to pat her shoulder. "It's okay – I've been informed about what happened. Go on."

She didn't need to finish her sentence, as most understood

what she'd been about to say.

Joseph said, "So it was a direct threat to you – a symbol to force your silence?"

"Yes," Edward agreed.

Joseph frowned. "But he said something about his secret – his… insurance?"

"Not his – mine," Edward corrected.

"Explain," Carter said.

Edward Jones pulled a chair towards the desk to seat himself, now including himself into this gathering of desperate people. He gave them a sympathetic look that contained an element of both shame and remorse.

"I've turned a blind eye to things I knew to be wrong. Money is a very powerful motivator. And money's something I'm good with."

"Go on," Carter pushed, eager to understand everything.

"Viktor Mikhel is also very good at what he does – a master. But he has his weakness. Greed. Not for money, but for power, respect, *fear*. Still, money plays a factor in all that. Viktor's ready to start spending his personal fortune – all at the expense of his boss. Word has it Viktor's been planning a return trip home – one way – and is ready to take over as head of the Solntsevskaya Mafia."

"The Solntsevwhat?" Carter asked.

"The Solntsevskaya Mafia – the biggest firm in Moscow."

"Explain everything," Carter urged.

"Okay – Viktor now knows I'm alive, and that both the FBI and FSB are coming after him. I'm just one cog in a whole bigger machine; I didn't think he'd come after me with such ferocity. Not considering what I know about his secret stash. Sergei Mikhailov would have him dead and buried before sunrise if he knew."

Carter said, "So he needs to shut you up – before this goes to trial, and his little secret becomes known. Because if it did, his chances back home would be greatly jeopardised."

"Exactly," Edward agreed. "He'd be dead before stepping

onto the first plane."

Joseph asked, "Can't they just arrest him now? Keep him in prison?"

Edward shook his head. "Things take time. Viktor's connections are too great to let them get away, so they can't risk a botched or unprepared investigation. The authorities won't move on him until they're sure they have Sergei for sure."

Tyler leaned forward, closer to Edward. "I don't understand. Why doesn't Viktor Mikhel just leave the country now, before he's arrested?

"Good point," Edward said. "Thing is, he has unfinished business here to attend to first."

"Such as?" Tyler asked.

"Such as – me. He needs *our* little secret to disappear."

"Hang on a minute," Joseph interjected. "Then why did your father refer to it as *his* secret, *his* insurance?"

The accountant appeared confused for a moment. "We'd spoken, that day, on the phone. Wasn't safe enough for me to visit – so they…" he gestured over his shoulder, "…they set up a line for me to speak to him. A… safe line, untraceable, which was cut the moment the conversation ended."

"Wait a minute," Joseph said. "Now I understand. Your father was repeating what you'd said to him – wasn't he?"

"Must have been," Edward agreed.

"Okay," Carter said. "So why did they kill your father?"

Edward's face collapsed into despair, he answered evasively, "He was dying anyway – I guess I can take some comfort in that."

"Edward, we have to know exactly what's going on here," Carter said, needing the accountant to explain all – and quickly. If he was going to get Jake back, then he must understand precisely what he was up against.

Edward's words had been guarded throughout the encounter, which Carter had thought to be in respect of the present situation. It was only when the accountant lowered his tone to a barely audible whisper that he realised he'd been masking his words from the trio of agents who stood nearby.

"Viktor needs my guaranteed silence," Edward began. "What I know will put him away for a very long time. Or better – permanently."

Joseph still didn't understand. "But surely what he did to your father would strengthen your resolve even more?"

Edward nodded. "Yes – true, but I have my own weaknesses too." He lowered his tone even more. "Do you think I dare mention anything about our scam, to anyone? No, I'd end up as dead as Viktor, and twice as fast. Sergei's reach is infinitely more capable than Viktor's. If he found out I'd been stealing from him, he'd come over here and put a bullet in my head – personally – and laugh while he did so."

"Then why the dramatics?" Carter asked. "Sorry, wrong choice of word. Why kill your father?"

Edward said, "To draw me out. Gain my silence. Kill me."

Carter ran a hand over his face, the long day now washing great waves of tiredness over him. "But haven't you already told the authorities enough to put him away?"

"Yeah," Edward agreed. "But that wouldn't stop him. He's smart, never tarnished his hands with blood, and always had other people to do his dirty work for him. He'd hire a team of the best lawyers money could buy and then flee across the border to Mexico or Canada while out on bail. Or buy the whole prison system if he got that far, and simply disappear."

"But he would require Sergei's help to do all that?" Carter asked.

"Indeed," Edward said.

"Then where does that leave you?" Carter quizzed.

"In a real jam. I've got myself a double-edged sword. If I tell the authorities about our secret funds, then I mark myself for death. Sergei would not allow such a thing to go unpunished. But if I don't say anything, then Viktor will see me dead. He too cannot allow me to continue drawing breath, knowing what we've done."

Carter shook his head. "Dammed if you do, dammed if you don't…"

"True…" Edward said.

Joseph spoke. "What about this Yurius? Who the hell is this guy?"

For the faintest of moments, Edward's face seemed to change. It was so slight, so fleeting, that most didn't have sufficient time to consciously acknowledge the transformation. Only Joseph spotted this shift in facial expressions, and even he wasn't convinced it hadn't been more a trick of the eye then an actual response. In a single heartbeat, Jones's face flipped from humble victim to vicious predator and back again. Then, with a simple shrug of his shoulders, he said, "Sorry – that is a name that I do not know."

Carter seemed to deflate then. He breathed out between puffed cheeks.

"Can you help us in any way to get my boy back?" Joseph asked.

"Not directly, no," Edward replied, his face taking on its usual look of sympathy.

Carter spoke. "Then what are you doing here? Why risk detection by coming?"

"I need to get a message to Viktor. Explain that our secret will remain just that, for as long as I stay alive, and that any direct threat will see Sergei gaining knowledge."

"But how will you do such a thing?" Joseph asked.

Edward reached into his pocket. He withdrew a crumpled envelope.

"What's that?" Joseph asked.

"It's a message – for Viktor." Edward handed it to Joseph, by sliding it flat along the surface of the table.

Joseph took it, and then flipped it over, looking for an address or name. "Why are you giving this to me?"

"Because, Joseph, you'll be seeing Viktor sooner than I will," Edward stated.

"Look," Joseph said, his voice rising in pitch. "I'm sorry about your position, but I need to get my boy back. I cannot get involved with your disputes." He started to slide the letter back.

The agent standing nearest to Jones tensed visibly. The other two quickly took up formation around the grieving accountant. Joseph's little act of aggression towards Jones was met by equal hostility. An agent, square-shouldered, tall and handsome, almost snarled in Joseph's direction when he said, "Keep it."

Joseph's hand stopped half-outstretched. He eyed the agent, noticing a slight scar above his top lip. "Keep it," the agent repeated in a growl. The agent's words were laced with Eastern European undertones.

Joseph's temper started to boil to the surface. "Who the hell are you people? Go and find my son."

"Yeah," Carter agreed. "You know where Viktor is. There's a chance Yurius could have taken Jake there."

"Let's go," Joseph said, climbing to unsteady feet.

Now, all three agents seemed to swell around the small group. And for just a second, Carter thought they were about to reach towards their sidearms.

"No, we stay," Edward Jones said. The short sentence had been full of calm but weighed down by a directness that demanded obedience.

The agents deflated slightly then, realising they'd possibly stepped out of line. The one with the scar gave Joseph a courteous nod before taking a few steps back.

"Sorry, Joseph," Edward began. "This investigation of ours reaches too far – too many organisations involved with much to gain. Both FBI and FSB agents have been working tirelessly to bring this case to a close. I apologise for FSB Agent Vitos' abruptness. But even Jake's taking cannot be allowed to threaten the ultimate goal of taking down Viktor Mikhel and Sergei Mikhailov's empire."

Edward then stood up quickly. Joseph's arm remained

outstretched. "You need to keep that – it will help you to put an end to this nightmare. Trust me." Edward said.

Before Joseph could respond, Edward turned and headed away from them. Like obedient dogs, the three agents followed closely behind him.

"Wait!" Joseph called. "What is this?"

Edward turned back. "Your salvation – and mine," he said, before disappearing out of the Department.

Chapter Forty-One

Four walls, warm sheets and food of choice: three things that Presley Perkins hadn't taken pleasure in for as many months. The bucket of fried chicken stood almost empty, and the corner of the bed sheet had thick smears on one corner; Presley being unable or unwilling to make the short trip to the bathroom to gather a hand-towel to wipe greasy fingers clean.

The TV in the corner of the room flickered with bright faces and beat out an enthusiastic tattoo. *Baywatch* played into the room with its golden beach, blue waters and near-perfect cast. Presley grunted subconsciously as one of the swimsuit-clad girls ran across the expanse of even sand.

He dipped his hand back inside the bucket to retrieve a chicken leg. Half a thigh disappeared in a single bite. His hand returned to the bed sheet as he hastily wiped it clean. What the hell, he thought, dismissing his lack of manners. He wouldn't be here to clean it up tomorrow.

Now, with his newfound wealth, he lay relishing the luxury of a cheap motel room. He'd bought a set of new clothes, simple sweatpants and top, and had invested in a small collection of toiletries. His cheeks tingled, invigorated by the razor and gel that had removed three months of grime.

Presley caught his reflection in the small mirror that faced him. He gave himself a wink, pleased with his current situation.

The credits started to roll on the TV screen. Presley reached over to take the remote. He flicked between channels for a few minutes, staying on each one just long enough for him to decide if the programme warranted his attention or not. Eventually, he chanced upon a spaghetti western. *The Man With No Name* was currently dusting down his poncho.

"Draw!" Presley ordered, firing an imaginary bullet at Clint Eastwood's head. Clint looked back at Presley with unwavering blue eyes, unimpressed.

Presley laughed out loud. "The man with no name," he said, and then glanced over at the mirror for a second time. He tipped his imaginary hat upwards, nodded, and said, "Howdy ladies – you fancy a good time with a cowboy?"

This time tomorrow, he'd be long gone – driven out of town, not by a posse of lawmen, but by the promise of freedom. Mexico and all the Señoritas he could wish for would be waiting for him, ready, willing and able.

He settled back, his belly full and a greasy smile smeared across his lips.

Yes, tomorrow couldn't come fast enough for him – his day of independence.

Then, Presley Perkins would be back on top.

Chapter Forty-Two

The Homicide Department was a hive of activity. A dozen or so detectives were sat with handsets clamped between shoulders and heads, chatting eagerly, scribbling down information onto notepads, blank crime reports, desktops if necessary, anything that they could get their hands on. The first few hours of any investigation, were the most critical. Two of their own had been killed, Gore and his replacement, and their friends in blue were not about to sit idle.

The FBI agents were also running task forces via sleek cell phones, or expensive laptops, or simple good old-fashioned landlines. One blue-suited individual – who busied himself with his open laptop – now occupied the technician's chair. Two agents, FSB Agent Vitos included, were chatting to each other in hushed tones over by one of the office windows.

Marianna and Tyler were talking quietly at the young detective's desk, whilst Joseph and Carter sat facing each other, red-eyed and beaten.

"I'll understand if you want to go home," Joseph said.

Carter yawned, and Joseph thought that was just what the detective had been waiting for – an easy get out.

"Like hell," Carter announced. "I'm seeing this through to the end."

"This isn't your fight – not now. Only I can bring Jake home."

"But at what cost?"

Joseph eyed Marianna. She was busy in conversation with

Tyler. He just shrugged. "This Yurius wants me – dead."

Carter nodded. "I believe he does. But that doesn't mean I'm going to let that happen."

"What can you do?" Joseph asked. "What can *they* do?" he added, indicating the agents.

"They, Joseph, have their own agenda. We'll get Jake back."

Joseph sighed deeply. "How?"

Carter scratched at his chin. "There's a way. There must be a way."

"We both know they're holding Jake to get me. And I don't think they're looking for some sort of reconciliation. Do you?"

"No, Joseph – I don't."

"Then what now?"

"Yurius will call. I guarantee it. He's desperate to silence you, before his identity can be compromised."

"Too late."

"I know. *We* know. But he doesn't. When he calls, don't address him by name again. Act confused, uncertain, and don't for a second let on you know about his connection to Viktor Mikhel."

"And then what?"

"And then do as he says."

"And?"

"I'm working on it," Carter said.

"Detective – this has gone beyond 'serve and protect'. Lives are on the line here. Not just mine and my son's – yours too if you stay involved."

"I am involved. Believe me. I ain't about to let some two-bit punk harm an innocent boy."

Joseph reached out and took the detective's hand. "Thanks."

"I haven't done anything yet."

"No, but most men wouldn't put it all on the line for a stranger – not even a boy."

Carter looked away for a moment. His face flipped between anger and agony.

"What is it?" Joseph asked, seeing something more than just professional conduct was driving the detective.

Carter looked Joseph in the eye. "I have a son – *had* a son."

The pain in Carter's eyes left no question as to what that meant.

Joseph shook his head. "I'm sorry."

"Yeah…" Carter breathed. "William, my boy, was shot and killed in action, recently."

"Dear Lord," Joseph said.

"A hold-up. He wasn't even responding to a call – just happened to chance on it, whilst the robbery was in progress."

"Good God…"

"Billy didn't even get the chance to draw his weapon."

"I'm so sorry," Joseph offered. "I can't imagine how you feel, not even with Jake taken."

The detective wiped at his eyes. "Losing a child is worse than anything imaginable, something that simply does not go away – ever. Even on those rare occasions when something else demands your attention, the pain comes back with a vengeance to remind you of the loss."

Joseph couldn't find his voice. What words could he offer anyway? There wasn't a word in the English language that conveyed enough sympathy or sorrow. However, the agony in his own heart, for Jake's safety, gave him all the understanding he needed.

Carter said, "So now you know why I'll be seeing this through to the end. I'm not about to let anything happen to your son – not while I can do something about it."

"Like what?" Joseph asked, needing some form of reassurance – no matter how desperate.

"I don't know yet, Joseph. But I will, when the time comes."

They made eye contact again, and Joseph felt the detective's determination wash over him. It gave him added strength, and more importantly, made him realise that he wasn't alone in this nightmare.

***

It was almost midnight when the second call came through. Tyler and one of the FBI agents were sleeping fitfully, twisted and bent into uncomfortable positions, dozing in chairs, using hard desks as unlikely pillows. Both jumped awake, their attention snapping back into focus.

Joseph and Carter were already on their feet by the end of the second ring. Marianna joined them, her hand seeking out Joseph's. He took it and then reached for the handset. Already, the agent seated there had activated the recording and tracking devices. The agent's hand gestured in slow circles, silently directing Joseph to keep the caller talking.

"Yeah?" Joseph asked.

"Big bear?"

"Yes."

"You know who I am?"

Carter had already slipped the earphones on and was listening to the exchange. He shook his head vigorously.

"You're the guy who has my son," Joseph replied.

The caller stayed silent for a moment.

"You know who I am?" the caller asked again.

Joseph looked toward Carter for help.

'NO,' he mouthed.

"I know your name is Yurius, and if I don't get my son back... I'll find out who you are, and hunt you down, and kill you. If it takes the rest of my life, I'll find out who – *what* – you are, and not rest until you are dead."

Marianna's mouth opened and her body tensed noticeably. She almost reached up to snatch the handset from Joseph, but Tyler intervened at the last moment, dragging Marianna quickly away from the group.

The line became a hiss of static.

Then the caller's voice returned, more confident now, full of control. "Big words for a big bear."

"Where is my son?" Joseph demanded.

"Safe."

"Then give him back."

"Tomorrow."

"What?"

"Little bear will be returned unharmed."

"When?"

"Will call again tomorrow. Be ready."

Click.

The agent slammed his hand against the desk. "Nothing," he moaned. "This guy knows just how long to maintain a connection before chance of detection."

Joseph handed the handset over.

Marianna broke away from Tyler and stepped forward to deliver a blow to Joseph's face. The slap caught him off guard, and his head rocked back.

"What were you doing?" she demanded.

Joseph was stunned.

Carter intervened. "Marianna, Joseph's quick thinking just saved your son's life."

"What? How?" she asked, tears slipping down her cheeks.

Carter said, "He just confirmed he doesn't know who the killer is."

"I – I don't understand."

"By saying if he didn't get Jake back, he'd find out *who* the killer was. Subterfuge, making the killer believe his identity remains a mystery."

Marianna's hands rose to her face, covering her mouth, her mistake now apparent. She looked to Joseph and her face reddened with shame.

"Oh – Joseph…" she whispered.

Joseph stepped forward to take her in his arms. "Hey – I

love you."

She stayed in his arms, drawing his strength now, tears slipping heavily from her eyes.

"Please bring our boy back," she sobbed.

Joseph's hands tightened into fists behind her back. "I will. Even if the Devil himself stands in my way, I'll bring Jake home," he vowed.

Chapter Forty-Three

Only one person knelt in prayer, head bowed, hands clasped tightly together. The rows of pews stretched out behind him, empty at this late hour. Candles burnt on the Alter in front of him, tiny glittering lights which danced as one synchronised group.

Footsteps echoed hollowly.

Joseph Ruebins looked up from his position. He turned to spot Detective Carter making his way between the rows of empty pews. Carter walked carefully, with measured steps, conscious of these sacred surroundings. What came out of his mouth was in complete contrast. "Joseph, what the *hell* are you doing?"

Joseph turned back, glancing up at the figure of Christ before him. "Hoping God is listening," he replied.

"This is insane," Carter reprimanded.

"You not a religious man?" Joseph asked, his attention pinned to the face of Christ.

"What?"

"Am I mad for being here, looking for guidance?"

"Yes," Carter replied. Then he looked about him, and said, "I mean – no."

Joseph turned back to the detective. "Which is it?"

Carter hovered over Joseph, his feet shuffling slightly, uncomfortable about being here at this hour.

"Joseph, we have a small room for prayer at the precinct. You shouldn't have come here – it's too dangerous. So, yes – I think you're mad for being here. And no, not for looking towards God for direction."

The church, St Andrews, was situated just half a block from the precinct. Joseph had lain awake as Marianna lay next to him, sleeping lightly, whimpering like a terrified child. The noise had sounded too much like the sound of Jake's terror for Joseph to endure. He'd climbed out of the single cot, dressed, then left the open cell and gone to gather his wits. In the cell next to his, Tyler slept, the thick blanket pulled up under her chin, just her shoes visible underneath the bed.

Joseph had stood on the steps leading to the precinct for a while, drawing clean, crisp air into his lungs in an attempt to dispel some of the anxiety that gnawed away at his gut. A slight scattering of snow fell from the dark skies, barely heavy enough to leave its mark on the world below. Just a thin layer of white powder marked the streets and avenues. Tomorrow morning seemed like it would never come, darkness holding on with an impossible grasp. The city had fallen quiet, as if it was now holding its breath in anticipation of Joseph's plight.

The bright steeple of the church had cut through the night like a guiding beacon, and Joseph had followed the light with the same conviction as a lost vessel.

As he made his way towards the church, he encountered only the occasional passer-by, who looked upon him with more concern in their eyes than he had in his. There would be no late-night hits, masked men jumping out of the shadows with silenced weapons. No, the night held no nightmares now – only morning would bring such horrors. It had taken a good few minutes to walk the hundred yards or so, his right side slowing him down considerably.

Inside, Joseph had found the silence that he sought so desperately. He'd seated himself before allowing his thoughts to wander. Jake's face had come to him, happy, bright, loving, and Joseph had wept silently for a while.

Now, he turned his attention back to Carter. "How did you find me?" he asked, wondering why the detective hadn't used such an ability to track down his son.

"You left footprints in the snow," Carter responded.

Joseph sighed heavily. Nothing quite so obvious was going to lead them to his son. "You don't need to be here, no harm will come to me tonight."

Carter nodded. "I guess you're right. Still, the city holds other dangers at these late hours."

Joseph laughed gently. "Not for a six-foot-two black man, there ain't."

Carter smiled despite the tension. "I guess."

"You a religious man, Detective?"

Carter paused for a moment. He didn't want to explain how he cursed God every night for the loss of his son. That would not help Joseph in this, his time of need. "It's Thomas," he replied, simply.

"Sorry?"

"My name – Thomas."

"Oh…"

"And yeah – I believe we're being watched by someone, something."

"You think this 'something' has a kind heart? Or enjoys watching us suffer?"

Carter shrugged. "Both – unfortunately. But even one person's grief can be another's gain."

"At the cost of the innocent, though."

"Perhaps," Carter agreed. "My son, for instance. He died by taking a bullet. A bullet that might have killed the storeowner, had Billy not entered. A storeowner who was due to donate bone marrow to his ailing niece."

"What are you saying? That some must die to protect others?"

"Not exactly. What I'm saying is that there doesn't always appear to be justice or reasoning to God's plans. But everything is connected in one way or another. Something good may come of tomorrow. Something that could not happen if Jake hadn't been taken."

"Like what?"

"I don't know."

Joseph turned back to the figure of Christ. "For everything a reason," he said, praying that the detective was right, that the return of Jake would lead to something both good and decent.

He reached inside his pocket to produce the letter that Edward Jones had given him. "You think there's something good in here?" he asked.

Carter took the creased envelope. "Could be. Maybe." He turned it over, finding both sides blank. "Could be nothing. Or a warning to Viktor? Maybe Edward Jones is trying to make amends?"

"Open it," Joseph said.

Carter looked back with curiosity. "What if we don't like what's inside?"

Joseph simply shrugged. "I don't like anything about any of this. What difference will *that* make?"

The letter was handed back. "It's your call, Joseph. Jones gave it to you."

Joseph held the unopened envelope in his lap. He turned towards the statue of Christ again, hoping for guidance. "What the hell," he said, pushing his thumb underneath one corner of the flap.

A sudden hollow boom sounded from behind them. The church door opened and an icy gust of wind raced along the pews to douse the sea of lit candles. Some blinked out instantly, releasing small tendrils of smoke upwards, whereas others flickered and fought to remain alight. The door behind them swung open again, and another cold draught blew most of the remaining candles out. Only one remained lit. This one appeared in the centre of the extinguished group, burnt down almost to its roots. Both men looked beyond the single light at the face of Christ. From this angle they witnessed – believed – that the Holy Son's eyes were actually focused on the one remaining candle.

Joseph's thumb stayed as it was. He looked first towards the candle, then back to Carter. The detective's attention was riveted to the single flicker of white light. Without looking away, Carter reached out to take Joseph's wrist. He pulled gently, removing Joseph's thumb from the bent flap.

"Maybe we should let Viktor open that," he advised, finally breaking away from the strange connection.

Joseph nodded. "Yeah. Perhaps you're right." Gently, he returned the envelope to his pocket.

The detective placed his hand on Joseph's shoulder. "We should be getting back now."

"Yeah," Joseph agreed. He stood and moved out of the pew. He took a few steps down the aisle before turning back to Carter.

"You ready for what tomorrow brings?"

Carter looked first at the statue of Christ, then back to Joseph. "I swear on my boy's soul I'll do everything in my power to get Jake back."

Their eyes locked together. Both nodded in silent agreement, then Carter joined Joseph ready to make the trip back, ready for what the morning had to offer.

***

The morning came solemnly. There was no blaze of sunshine on the horizon, just a slight lightening of the sky, which turned slowly from black to darkest grey. The thin scattering of snow had cleared, blown away by the harsh February winds. The sun's failure to break through the thick clouds had left the cityscape stark and monochrome.

Like the streets outside, the Department was quiet, sombre, subdued.

Joseph lay with his head on his arms, which were crossed over and resting on Carter's desk, forming a makeshift pillow. The detective sat opposite, his feet propped up on the desk, snoring softly.

The few remaining FBI agents were gathered in Mendoza's office, resting peacefully, apparently unfazed by the magnitude of recent events. It seemed as if child abduction and cop killings were commonplace in their daily routine.

As if on a timer, set to awake everyone at the stroke of seven, the phone rang at that exact time.

Joseph bolted upwards and Carter nearly fell out of his seat. One of the FBI agents quickly left the Captain's office to rush over and take his place behind the electronic equipment.

Joseph made his way hastily towards the phone. He picked it up and pressed the handset to his ear.

"Yes?"

"Big bear?"

"Yes."

"Nine o'clock at Union Station – main foyer, and come alone."

The phone line died instantly.

Joseph simply placed the handset back, not looking at the agent, already knowing that the call had been too short for them to trace.

Carter asked, "Okay – what now?"

"New York Union Station – main foyer – nine o'clock."

Carter turned to the clock. "Gives us two hours to plan."

"He said come alone," Joseph added.

Carter just nodded, his mind already moving into overdrive. "They always say 'come alone'."

"So what do we do?"

"Exactly as they say. You go alone – or make them think you have."

"How do we do that?" Joseph asked.

The detective's head tilted somewhat, a slight grin playing across his face. "Union Station at nine o'clock."

Joseph looked back blankly. "And?"

"And, the place will be busier than a parade on the 4th of

July. We could hide the entire Department among the commuters and nobody would be any the wiser."

"Oh…" Joseph said.

"Yeah – oh. Our killer just made his first big mistake. He's not going to try anything in such a busy place."

"So why pick it then?"

The detective shrugged.

Joseph had expected to be ordered to meet in the most remote of places, not somewhere you could hide a platoon of FBI agents and detectives. He looked towards the detective's face and found excitement there. Just for a second, Joseph felt anger and hatred towards Carter. How dare he gain pleasure from this terrible event. In the next instant, though, Joseph recognised that it was the pursuit of justice that drove the detective.

"We'd better go and wake Tyler," Carter said. "We've got a lot to plan before nine."

Chapter Forty-Four

Nothing felt real: Not the usual heavy morning traffic or the sound of rubber over asphalt, engines purring or revving noisily, or the hoot and holler of horns and hotheads. The detective's Sedan moved slowly through the flow, sandwiched in tightly moving channels of chrome and paint.

"What time do you make it?" Joseph asked from the passenger side.

"Eight-thirty," Carter replied. "Relax, Joseph, we'll make it with time to spare."

"And then what?"

"We get Jake back – no matter what."

Joseph's attention returned to the outside world. The colourless streets and avenues, along with this grizzled detective, made Joseph feel as if he'd been sucked into a bad Film Noir. With him as the hapless victim and Carter as the gritty no-nonsense cop. He shook his head, trying to focus his thoughts away from the bizarre images that his tired, overstretched mind seemed intent on conjuring up.

Taking a deep breath, he cleared his head and then asked, "What if the FBI agents are seen, or you, for that matter?"

Carter pushed his way into the lane to his right, then left the highway and headed towards Union Station. Once he'd negotiated his way along the turnpike and onto 5th Avenue, he answered Joseph's question.

"They won't. Why would they? Nobody knows they've even been assigned to the case."

"Assigned?" Joseph quizzed. To him, the agents had taken

a decidedly backseat role in all of this. They'd hovered around the Department, looking interested and concerned, but had only really shown any excitement or commitment once the final call had come through. Perhaps, thought Joseph, that that was a good sign. Maybe the team were of the highest calibre, trained only to react when most appropriate.

What had Edward Jones said? *They have their own agenda...*

With the exception of Agent Vitos, now that he thought about it, even if they lined up before him with suits and ties straight, and shades tucked neatly into breast pockets, Joseph wouldn't have been able to identify them. No, they had not only been aloof but also enigmatic.

"Look," Carter said. "They're professionals – good men. They wouldn't allow any mistakes to jeopardise Jake's safety."

"What about *my* mistakes?" Joseph asked, needing counsel now that the encounter was imminent.

"You won't make any. All you got to do is show up, do as you're told, and we'll do the rest."

"This is all too convenient, too simple, meeting at the station. Why?"

"Safety in numbers," Carter replied. "This Yurius may just want to hand Jake back and then slip away in the crowd."

"Hardly. He could simply drop him off anywhere, call it in, and then keep out of view."

Carter turned towards New York Union Station, the flow of traffic thickening again, as passengers were dropped off outside the main foyer, ready to begin their journey.

"Joseph, this Yurius is not going to try anything on with so many witnesses around. For now, we must take strength from the fact that Jake is okay, and we still have the element of surprise. He has no idea we have his identity – remember?"

"Yeah..."

"Okay – let's stay positive."

"Yeah..." Joseph repeated, hoping to God that the next few hours wouldn't end in tragedy.

Carter pulled the Sedan up at kerbside. "Okay – this is as far as I dare go."

Joseph looked at the detective, his eyes full of need. "What happens if he wants to go elsewhere?"

"Then go. Don't ask questions, don't look too aware, and don't challenge him – no matter what he says."

"Meaning?"

"Meaning act like the distraught parent, desperate to get your child back and willing to do whatever it takes."

"Shouldn't be too difficult," Joseph replied, feeling exactly that. He dug inside his pocket, pulling out the letter that Edward Jones had given him. "What the hell is in here?"

Carter looked at it with suspicion. "Don't pin all your hopes on that. Stay alert, be ready for anything."

"Okay."

The detective held out his hand. "Good luck, Joseph."

Joseph took it and replied, "You think God – or this 'something' – will be watching out for us today?"

The detective nodded. "Yeah – I do."

Joseph opened the door. The wind clawed its way inside the Sedan, instantly freezing both men. With awkwardness, Joseph climbed outside. He stooped to bring himself level with the passenger opening. "You got my back, Thomas?"

"You bet."

Joseph slammed the door shut and turned away from the parked Sedan. And, as he made the short trip to the station entrance, he felt like the loneliest man on the planet.

***

Carter watched as Joseph disappeared into the steady throng of people. Eventually, even Joseph's tall figure was taken by the bustling crowd. The detective clicked on his two-way radio. It came to life with a sharp crackle.

"Tyler – this is Carter, you copy?"

A metallic voice came through the static. "Yeah – reading you loud and clear. Over."

"Good. He's coming your way. Over."

A short pause followed. Then, "I've got him in sight. Nobody's making a move on him yet. Over."

"Stay frosty. Over."

"Copy that. Over."

Carter dropped the radio into his inside pocket. He turned the sound up higher and listened to the unsettling chatter that filled the airwaves with white noise.

Now, all he could do was wait.

***

Joseph entered the busy terminal. His eyes turned to the large clock that hung from the arched ceiling.

8:49 a.m.

His heart beat a little faster. Was he too early? Was the killer watching him now and wondering why he'd arrived already? He tried not to focus on any one face in particular, already deciding that he would act surprised by the face that did eventually challenge him. Equally, he tried not to look too out of place, which would inevitably draw suspicion. He had no desire for anyone to recognise him or even acknowledge his existence.

He decided to wander over to one of the benches in the centre of the foyer. Only one seat was unoccupied. He took it, positioning himself between two businessmen, both engrossed in the financial section of the *New York Times*.

The clock now read 8:52 a.m.

Joseph folded his arms and then closed his eyes, understanding that he had no other option but to wait it out.

***

The sidewalk was full of pedestrians, flowing around the parked Sedan like a stream running about a stone. Carter tried to remain focused on the map spread out on his lap. Still, the wish to observe forced him to use every ounce of will to keep his attention on the map. He kept his head down, hoping that his presence would not alert any curious eyes that may be out there, watching and waiting.

***

The second hand ran towards the hour. Joseph watched as it climbed past 9, moved towards 10, then on to 11. The last five seconds felt like an age. Eventually the second hand disappeared behind the long arm of the clock.

9 a.m.

Nothing happened. No Russian hit-men jumped out of the crowd. No alarms went off to cause mass panic, allowing the killer a clear path to Joseph. No nearby telephones rang with orders to jump on the next train available, ready to take him to an undisclosed location.

Nothing.

Panic hit Joseph instantly.

Why hadn't Yurius shown?

Where was his son?

The businessman to his left coughed slightly, forcing Joseph to look toward him. They made eye contact. Joseph's breath caught in his chest. Had Yurius sent another in his place? The guy looked worried; possibly by the battered, bruised and desperate-looking black man who sat beside him. He closed his newspaper quickly, made a show of checking his wristwatch, realising that time had slipped by him, and then stood, before disappearing into the crowd. Joseph tried to follow the guy's progress, but a multitude of similarly tailored suits camouflaged his movements almost instantly.

He took a deep breath and forced his heart to steady. He reached up to wipe away the cold sweat that had broken out

251

along his forehead. Thirty-three seconds had ticked by since he last looked.

The remaining businessman, sitting to his right, looked towards Joseph and then quickly turned his attention away. Understanding that his body language was drawing unwanted attention, Joseph picked up the discarded newspaper and opened it in an attempt to look normal, composed. He rested it against his thigh, the words swimming before his eyes, his mind unable to steady itself long enough for him to read anything of significance.

Then, suddenly, a bold headline came into focus.

Joseph squinted, forcing the words to take shape. He blinked once, twice, not fully comprehending what they said. He read the headline again, then for a third time. "Oh, dear God…" he breathed, understanding coming to him in a flash. He jumped to unsteady feet, the newspaper slipping from his fingers. Now, he spun full circle, looking for a familiar face – an agent, or undercover detective. Nobody. Just strangers in a strange world: a world that had just been knocked out of kilter and tipped towards absolute madness.

***

Carter's radio crackled to life. Tyler's voice filled the interior of the small Sedan. "This is Detective Tyler. Something's happening. Ruebins is on the move. Over."

Carter hit the communications switch. "He made contact with anyone? Over."

"No. Not that I can see. Over."

"Wait. I-I think he's…" – the reception faltered and Tyler's voice became a squeal of static.

"Tyler?" the detective called. "Tyler. You copy? Over."

Just the hiss of airwaves.

"Tyler?" Carter was momentarily frozen by indecision. What should he do? His orders had been to remain here, ready to pursue any fleeing vehicles. If he left now and

Joseph was taken elsewhere, then the chase would prove more difficult.

"Tyler?" he barked again.

The radio just hissed with contempt.

"What the hell," he said, reaching out to open his door. His hand froze. Someone in the crowd had just gone by. Clean and tidy, and whistling a tuneless melody, as if he cared not about the world around him.

***

Presley Perkins strutted boldly down Broadway, oblivious to the man whose child he had so recently murdered.

Chapter Forty-Five

The crowd seemed to contract around Joseph. He became dizzy, and for one terrible moment thought he was about to suffer a third attack. He staggered forward slightly. The commuters nearest to him unconsciously stepped away, primeval instincts putting them out of reach of trouble, before minds full of present-day thoughts sent them on their way.

Joseph filled his lungs to capacity, breathing in deeply, waiting for the bout of dizziness to pass. It did, and the walls of the foyer retracted back into place.

Now, he took a minute to examine his surroundings in more detail. Directly before him stood a small information desk, circular in shape so that it could be approached from every angle. Two young ladies, both wearing heavy makeup, their faces tanned to a bright orange even in this cold month, stood in the centre of the commuters, offering a wealth of information.

Joseph turned his attention away from the helpdesk and towards a newsstand that was wedged into one corner of the foyer. The stand was barely larger than a puppet booth, something he'd seen as a child. Two employees were playing out the roles of Punch and Judy. One, a woman, was busying herself with selling her assortment of candy and editorials; the other, a man, stood rigid, his eyes pinned to Joseph. Instantly, Joseph realised just how out-of-place the guy looked.

Joseph tried to focus on the guy's face. He was clean-shaven, handsome and muscular – and way too big to be stuffed behind the counter.

The tiny kiosk was meant for just one person, not two.

Was he one of the FBI agents?

The guy held Joseph's gaze for a second longer and then made a show of straightening out a row of magazines that were already neatly arranged.

A small coffee house pulled Joseph's attention away from the kiosk. Steel tables and chairs were occupied by commuters, either engrossed in morning newspapers or chatting animatedly to friends or colleagues. Joseph flipped from one face to the next. Most were wearing identical business suits: matching dark blue jackets and pants, or straight skirts, which stopped just below the knees, and an assortment of different coloured ties, some sombre – blues, blacks, greys – others bright reds and greens, which gave those who wore them puffed out chests, like those of exotic birds.

Only one guy stood out. He wore casual slacks and a baseball cap. Nothing unusual in that, but he held a financial supplement in his hands, and the rest of the newspaper could not be seen – nor was there a cup of coffee or other choice of beverage before him.

Another agent?

Joseph spun full circle, seeing faces that could be either innocent or full of intent. He looked again at the large clock. 9:02 a.m. Had the killer spotted something that had unnerved him? Just as Joseph was about to head towards the entrance, a figure caught the corner of his eye. The figure cut through the crowd and headed directly towards him. Joseph tensed, his instincts telling him that this was it – the defining moment.

Joseph was joined by his nemesis. Now two people shared the open space that had formed around them.

"Big Bear…" Yurius greeted, his lips stretching out over bright white teeth in a smile.

Joseph turned towards Jake's kidnapper. "Where's my

son?" he demanded.

"Safe," Yurius replied. "Come."

Yurius turned his back on Joseph, casually, confidently, and started to make his way towards the entrance. Joseph followed obediently, doing as Carter had instructed. As he trailed behind, he felt – sensed – that someone had taken up position behind him. He dared not look that way, in fear of seeing another face – another gun-wielding maniac who wouldn't rest until Joseph had been erased.

He did chance a look to his left and right, to see if either the café occupant or the newsagent had made a move to follow. Both stayed where they were.

Get up! screamed Joseph silently.

Neither paid any attention.

Yurius stopped just a few yards inside the lobby. "Wait here," he ordered, glancing over his shoulder. He left Joseph standing alone. The sensation of being watched almost pulled him around. Somehow, he managed to remain focused on the busy sidewalk just beyond his position.

A steady stream of commuters continued to mill through the entrance, some hurrying to catch trains, others saddled with backpacks that looked fit to burst, ready to start early vacations. Just a few appeared as if brought here by the flow of people, caught on the moving wave of flesh, with no real destination in mind.

One such character caught Joseph's eye. He was a large fellow, ruddy-faced, who wore tight-fitting sweat pants and jacket. A small sports bag hung by a strap from his shoulder. He seemed pleased with himself, a large colourful smile playing across his face.

The guy headed straight for Joseph. Joseph looked at him expectantly. Was this another accomplice? The guy nodded in his direction.

Joseph nodded back, only to realise at the last moment that the guy had actually been acknowledging someone standing directly behind him. The guy brushed past him, his sports bag nudging Joseph's elbow as he did so.

Joseph heard a single sentence come from behind, and then the general clamour drowned out the conversation.

"I got Viktor's money..." the guy said.

***

Carter felt trapped, unable to breathe. Indecision, loyalty and inner turmoil fought against each other. Should he get out and follow Perkins? His need for revenge demanded it. Get out now and cut Perkins down, no matter what the consequences were. Loyalty towards his profession and Joseph Ruebins screamed for him to stay put and see what the kidnapper had to offer. Nevertheless, this loyalty was a double-edged sword. The devotion to his son, Billy, cried out for him to avenge his death. Carter's understanding of what was right and wrong thrashed it out in the pit of his stomach.

Why was Perkins here, of all places?

Was he finally ready to flee the city?

Carter needed to know. He couldn't just let Perkins get away scot free, never to pay the price for his terrible actions. Without thinking, Carter opened the door and then stepped out into the windswept street. Absentmindedly, he patted his jacket, feeling the small revolver that rested there. Then, ignoring the voice of Tyler, now clear and present, he started to make his way over to the busy entrance.

***

Joseph became rooted to the spot. The sudden arrival of this newcomer had thrown off what senses he had remaining. Immobility had struck him down.

Just as he was about to turn, Yurius reappeared. The kidnapper spoke in Russian to the guy behind Joseph. A similar reply came. Yurius nodded, and then focused his attention on Joseph.

257

"Follow me," he ordered, and again retreated through the entrance.

Joseph duly followed the order. He sidestepped an elderly couple and then, unexpectedly, came face-to-face with Detective Carter.

"What..?" Joseph gawped. "What's going on?"

Carter seemed to blank Joseph completely. He failed to make eye contact; instead, his attention was riveted to something else. Like a man caught in the spell of sleepwalking, Carter moved beyond Joseph and continued to draw away.

Joseph reached out, ready to take Carter's arm, but Yurius had already disappeared from sight. With no other option, he let the detective pass by and quickly stepped out onto the sidewalk.

The Russian was just yards away, talking casually into a cellular. He raised a hand to stop Joseph short. Words that Joseph had no comprehension of fell from the Russian's lips. They seemed to go on for an eternity, which in reality lasted for no more than a minute.

Desperate now, Joseph took a single step closer. He was halted by the thunderous blast of gunfire.

Yurius stopped talking. A wave of people rolled out of the lobby, screaming and fear stretching their faces into ghastly masks of terror. More gunfire sounded, amplified by the resonance of the foyer.

The killer's confidence appeared to evaporate instantly. He cursed in his own language and then took off down West 14th Street.

"Yurius!" Joseph cried.

The man didn't stop.

Summoning every ounce of his strength, Joseph gave chase.

Chapter Forty-Six

Presley Perkins smiled to himself. The train station appeared to have more people in it than The Rangers Stadium. People branched off in many different directions, disappearing into tunnels and stairways, eagerly going about their business. He couldn't think of a safer place to hand over Viktor's money and collect his bus ticket and falsified documents.

For a second he questioned his choice of transport. Now that he was here, should he have asked for train tickets instead? For one, the journey time would be cut by more than half. No, Presley thought, the trains running into Mexico underwent far more stringent checks on passports and papers, whereas a bus ride would be considered a simple daytrip, a tourist sampling what this neighbouring country had to offer. He'd still be expected to reveal his passport, but with the promise of return, border control would be less rigorous.

Anyway, Presley thought, the checkpoints were more to keep the Hispanics out, rather than stopping Americans going the other way.

He moved deeper into the crowd. Then he spotted one of Viktor's men: the Georgian, Pyotr Krylov.

Krylov waved Presley over. He passed a towering black man, someone Presley thought he recognised from somewhere, but in the next instant he reached the Georgian.

"I got Viktor's money," he announced.

The sports bag on Presley's shoulder drew Krylov's attention. "All of it?"

"Yeah – the whole shebang."

Krylov reached inside his jacket. "I have your papers here," he said, withdrawing a small brown envelope.

Perkins looked at the package with something close to desperation. "They all there?"

"Yes. Passport, driving licence and ticket to Mexico."

Presley grinned slyly. "No need for the return – hey?"

The sly grin was mirrored on the Russian's face. Little did Presley Perkins know that a tip-off to border control would see him dragged from the bus and taken into custody. A simple and relatively small sum of money had bought this guarantee, and a second amount, paid to one of Viktor's Mexican contacts, would see that Perkins never left the holding pen alive.

"Drop the bag," Krylov ordered, now staring back coldly.

Presley did as he was told. He placed the bag at the Georgian's feet. Krylov dropped to one knee. He unzipped the bag and opened it out. A bundle of green bills filled the bottom. He closed it and then stood.

Presley licked his lips. "The envelope?" he asked.

The Russian made as if to give Presley the small package but, at the last moment, he tossed it into a nearby bin.

A hysterical whine burst from Presley's lips. He dived into the bin, scattering litter in all directions, digging to find his one chance at freedom. The envelope appeared amongst a pile of empty food cartons. He snatched it up, holding it protectively against his chest. He noticed then that Krylov and the bag of cash had simply disappeared.

No matter. He had what he'd come for.

His antics had attracted a small measure of attention. Most people looked quickly away as he turned from one face to the next. Only one held his gaze, and this person's eyes were full of hatred.

"No…" Presley breathed.

Detective Thomas Carter stared back.

A terrible moment of déjà vu passed. Perkins and Carter had squared off like this recently. Only now, William

Carter's father had all the advantage. His weapon was drawn, held steady at his side.

"No…" Perkins said again, in total disbelief.

Carter tapped the weapon against his thigh, making sure its presence was well noted. Presley's eyes widened slightly when he recognised which weapon the detective held.

"No… No… No…" he chanted foolishly. "This can't be."

The detective took a step closer, making sure his words could be heard clearly over the general noise.

"You're coming with me – now."

"No," Presley said, taking a step back.

"You've two choices," Carter said. "You can either live or die."

***

Pyotr Krylov snatched the bag and then turned his back on Perkins. He heard a whine of desperation and grinned maliciously: Perkins seemed to be in a rush to reach his journey's end – a crude shank in the ribs, no doubt.

The Russian threw the bag over his shoulder and quickly headed for the exit. He'd taken only a few steps when two figures appeared to flank him on either side. He halted then, wondering if there had indeed been a cop presence within the station. A long examination earlier had revealed nothing. Now, though, his calculating brain quickly processed a sudden change within the internal layout.

The café front appeared to have one chair empty, while the newsstand was occupied by just the woman. Krylov chanced a glance to either side. No mistaking it, the guy from the café and the one previously busying himself with magazines had taken up position on either side of him.

FBI?

Thinking quickly, Krylov made a show of exasperation, as if he'd just remembered leaving something behind. He spun on his heels and headed back the way he had just come.

Momentarily confused, the two pursuers appeared to lose sight of their target.

Krylov was making his way towards one of the platforms. He reached the first step to one and looked up to check if the path was clear. Most of the human traffic was heading in the same direction as he was, hurriedly climbing the steps towards an arriving train. In opposition, two men, broad shouldered and broad faced, were descending quickly towards him.

Krylov stopped with his foot an inch from the second step. Both men had weapons drawn. Compact pistols were pressed tightly at the hip, hidden from the unsuspecting eye, but not to a man of Krylov's disposition.

This was not standard FBI procedure.

The Russian felt a spasm of fear. What did these guys want? They were coming fast now. Krylov held their gaze for a moment longer, and then twisted around, ready to head back the other way. The two men that had originally flanked him had closed off his escape. Krylov looked from one to the other. Both had cold expressions on their faces. One, a handsome individual of impressive size, held Krylov's stare with vehement attachment.

Krylov caught his breath. He knew this guy. Yes, the slight scar that ran from his nose to the side of his upper lip was unmistakable: a telltale sign of a corrective procedure for a harelip.

Although the two were at a distance, the guy with the scar spoke loud enough to be heard.

Krylov's blood turned cold. This was not a linguistically trained FBI agent speaking to him in his native tongue. No, the words had been spoken with a distinctly native Slavic enunciation. The guy was of Muscovite ancestry through and through.

Pyotr Krylov understood without question that these men were here for just one thing: his blood. His hand moved towards the weapon at his side. The guy with the scar mirrored his movements as he too went for his weapon.

A fifth figure appeared, directly between Krylov and the armed men. She was of slight build with cropped brown hair. Her gun was already drawn and aimed towards the Russian's head. Krylov took his eyes off the two men for an instant, to gauge the woman's intentions. When he looked back over her shoulder an instant later, the two men had gone, simply disappearing in the throng of moving commuters.

***

"Freeze!" Tyler ordered, her weapon drawn.

Krylov did just that.

"Put the bag down, and turn around," Tyler instructed.

A string of foreign words came from the Russian's mouth.

It was enough to knock Tyler out of her rhythm. Did this guy understand English? She pointed to the bag. "Down," she said, now pointing to the floor.

The guy made a show of lowering the bag to the floor, twisting slightly to one side, as if it weighed much more than expected.

Tyler missed the man's intention. He used his bent frame to conceal his free hand. It was then she became aware of his objective.

Too late.

The guy's weapon appeared – a large oily-looking monstrosity – with a long barrel and elongated handgrip. It took just a millisecond for Tyler to see that the firearm had been modified to hold a larger clip of ammunition – possibly converted to be fully automatic, too.

Her inexperience and the fear of injury to nearby commuters made Tyler freeze for just the briefest of moments. It was more than enough.

The gun continued to rise.

A brilliant flash of gunfire blinded her and, in the next second, she felt herself crash heavily to the ground – her breath knocked out of her and her chest agonisingly tight.

Tyler found someone lying on top of her. She gasped, in an attempt to fill her lungs. She struggled awkwardly, and the unexpected face of the gun-bearer came into view. His mouth was open, eyes staring straight ahead, and a thin trickle of blood dripped from one ear. She pushed against him, pulling herself free. In the next instant, Detective Carter was by her side.

"You okay?" Carter asked, holding out his hand.

Tyler placed her hand to her chest. No warm sensation of running blood, or the numbness of a body in shock. She allowed Carter to drag her to her feet.

A small revolver hung at the detective's side, a wisp of gunsmoke snaking slowly from its barrel. "Close call."

Tyler turned to the body at her feet. Now that she was standing she could see the gunshot wound – a small hole just to the right of his earlobe – which leaked surprisingly little blood. A thick pool of crimson was rapidly spreading from the other side of his head. The bullet had travelled clean through, killing him instantly.

What remained of the crowd had now pushed themselves back against the foyer walls, cowering away from the bloody violence, leaving just the two detectives in an open arena.

"What are you doing here?" Tyler asked.

Carter looked pained.

"What is it?"

"My son's killer, he's here," he said.

"What? Where?"

"Here."

Tyler spun full circle. Nobody moved. She searched each face available, finding none that fit the description of William Carter's killer.

"I don't see him," she said.

"He's gone, in the confusion."

"Wait," Tyler said, now uncertain. "Where the hell is Joseph?"

Carter's mouth opened, but no words formed.

"Where is he?"

"I–I'm not sure," he admitted, shaking his head.

A little voice spoke, just to the side of them. The detectives turned to the speaker. A toddler, a blond-haired girl with pigtails, holding onto a teddy bear, had stepped forward, away from the cowering commuters. The child's mother rushed forward, quickly scooping her up, and the small teddy bear fell from her grasp. The mother looked terrified, and the child reached out in an attempt to retrieve the stuffed toy.

Tyler flashed the mother her shield. "I'm a detective," she said simply, and then turned to the child to ask, "What did you say, honey?"

"Mr. Tickles," the girl said.

"What?"

"Mr. Tickles," the child said again, jabbing her short arms towards the floor.

Tyler reached down to grab the bear. She handed it over. "What did you say, honey?" she asked again.

"The big black giant and the fat man," said the girl.

The woman gasped in shock and embarrassment at her child's political incorrectness.

"Ella – don't speak so rudely," she chastised.

Tyler ignored the woman. This was the type of witness that all cops preferred: Tell it straight. "Which black giant and fat man?"

Ella used her stubby arm to point first to the foyer's entrance and then towards one of the passageways, which led to a nearby platform.

"The black giant went that way," she said, pointing back to the foyer. "And Mr. Tickles saw the fat man go that way," she finished, using the bear's arm to indicate Platform 7.

Carter almost fell over himself to get past Tyler. The young detective stopped him short.

"No," she said, seeing his murderous intentions. "Go get

Joseph and Jake. I'll deal with Perkins."

Carter hesitated for just a moment and then nodded. What the hell had he been thinking? He leaned forwards, patting the toddler's head, and then took off in the opposite direction.

Tyler quickly stepped back to the dead Russian, took his discarded weapon, and then raced towards Platform 7.

Chapter Forty-Seven

Icy patches made Joseph almost lose his footing. Slipping and sliding, he kept up the chase. The dangerous conditions were also thwarting the Russian's escape. Joseph watched as Yurius fell to his knees. He clawed his way up and then cut across the street, heading quickly for one of the adjoining alleyways.

Joseph stepped off the sidewalk, almost falling under the wheels of a truck. The blare of a horn stopped him short, just as flesh and chrome were about to meet. The truck whizzed by in a blur.

Hurriedly, Joseph crossed to the opposite sidewalk. A few pedestrians stood back out of his way, unwilling to either engage or obstruct this frantic-looking man. The clatter of a trashcan lid falling to the floor reverberated towards him. Joseph took off in pursuit.

The alleyway narrowed quickly to become a tight funnel of brickwork. The open trashcan forced Joseph to step carefully. It slowed him down. He pushed the thing to one side and scooted around it. Clearly, Yurius had simply vaulted over it, catching the lid as he went.

Joseph stumbled his way towards the end of the alleyway. An abandoned parking lot opened out before him. Just one car was parked there, and it was this vehicle that the kidnapper made his way towards.

"Yurius!" Joseph bellowed. "I know who you are! Where to find you!" This went against everything Carter had told him. Nothing mattered more now than getting Jake back, and this unexpected announcement halted the Russian's escape.

Yurius stopped abruptly.

Joseph entered the parking lot. "Where's my son?" he demanded.

Yurius stood square-on, his hand slipping into his jacket.

Joseph stopped.

Only fifteen yards divided them.

Yurius grinned, his perfect white teeth beaming. His hand appeared, and it held the silenced weapon.

Joseph stood his ground.

"Big Bear fell for trick. Now foot in trap," Yurius said. The weapon rose to Joseph's chest. "You loose end that needs snipping."

"Where's my son?" Joseph asked, unfaltering, even this close to mortal danger. He took two steps closer and, surprisingly, Yurius took two back.

"You stay there," Yurius ordered.

"What's up, Yurius. You scared?" Joseph asked, taking a few more steps.

The Russian grinned again. "Not by dead man." His hand rose and the weapon levelled at Joseph's head.

Joseph stopped.

Yurius seemed to regain his confidence. Just a few yards separated them. The trunk of the car – an old Ford – lay within Yurius's reach. Using his free hand, he dug into his pants pocket. A set of keys jingled in the wind. A high-pitched *bleep, bleep* sounded and the Ford's indicator lights flashed together for a second or two.

"Lots of car thieves," Yurius mocked, taking his finger off the alarm button. He half sidestepped and twisted at the same time, leaving the firearm out straight.

"What are you doing?" Joseph asked.

"I have gift," the Russian said. The key slid into the lock, and the trunk popped open by a couple of inches.

Joseph felt sick. What lay inside? His son, no doubt. But dead or alive? "Open it," he demanded.

The contents of the trunk were concealed.

"Open it!" Joseph yelled, needing to know what the Russian had done.

Yurius slipped his fingers underneath the trunk lid. He paused for a moment, almost pushing Joseph to breaking point. Then, with a flick of his wrist, he revealed what lay inside.

Joseph's knees buckled.

Jake lay motionless. He didn't turn to look up, or shield his eyes from the sudden glare. His hands and feet weren't tied together, nor was he blindfolded or gagged.

He just lay there limp and lifeless.

"Oh… no…" Joseph cried, tears filling his eyes instantly. He took a faltering step closer, the weapon only a few feet from his head. He turned to Yurius and his agony turned to instant hatred. He rushed the kidnapper then, all thoughts of his own safety forgotten. Yurius sidestepped, evading the awkward, lumbering attack. The butt of the gun struck across Joseph's temple. The boxer fell to the ground, the world turning dark for just a moment.

"My boy…" Joseph wept. "What have you done?"

The Russian waved the keys around, back and forth, as if trying to get the attention of a disobedient dog. "I am not monster," he said.

"What..?"

"Yurius is not monster."

Joseph managed to get one knee underneath him. The world tilted and a bout of nausea made him gag. "What?" he asked again, swallowing heavily, holding back bile.

The Russian swapped the gun to his other hand. He half perched on the trunk opening, forcing the car to drop slightly. Then he forced his free arm under Jake's limp body.

"Careful," Joseph said. He held out his arm, hand spread wide, offering caution, needing to believe Jake was still alive.

Yurius lifted Jake clear. The boy's head rolled listlessly.

"Oh – God, no," Joseph breathed.

Yurius placed Jake on the ground, not far from Joseph's

feet. The Russian stepped back, allowing Joseph to drag himself to his boy.

He snatched Jake up. The boy felt warm and supple, and Joseph cried out in relief.

Was Jake still alive?

Tears cut two pathways down Joseph's cheeks. "Jake," he said, holding him tight. The hollow boom of the trunk shutting forced him to look towards Yurius.

The Russian gestured with the gun. "Come, Big Bear – you know price for boy's return." The hammer of the gun clicked back, and the dark eye of the barrel bore into Joseph.

Chapter Forty-Eight

On this side of the train station things continued as normal. The brutal event that had just happened in the main foyer had not, as yet, had any effect here. Most passengers stood about idly waiting. Some busied themselves with the morning papers, while others tapped their feet to tunes that came from oversized earphones. A couple of small groups chatted animatedly – fuelled by large doses of caffeine. Just a few commuters glanced towards the connecting tunnel, somehow aware that things were afoot, their primeval instincts more attuned towards trouble.

Presley Perkins barrelled through the steady flow of passengers, receiving a torrent of abuse as he went.

"Watch where you're going, fat ass!"

Another cursed in Spanish – a long string of profanities – that thankfully saved the ears of a young white girl, who was holding onto her mother's hand.

Presley pressed on. A thick sheen of sweat had broken out over his face. He reached up to wipe this stinging irritation from both eyes.

"Perkins!" someone yelled.

The voice was too high-pitched to be Carter's. Spinning back, Presley saw a woman rush towards him. He paused, wondering who the hell she could be. Her look of hostility made him understand that she was after his blood.

He pushed his way through the crowd of waiting passengers. Most stepped away from this agitated stranger.

"Stand back," the woman was shouting now, waving

people out of her way.

Presley scanned left and right. Both offered escape routes, but to nowhere in particular. The right stretched out towards a tunnel, and the left gave way to a crisscross of tracks and signal boxes. The fear of the dark pushed Presley to his left. He raced to the end of the platform, now alone, and checked for another exit.

He found nothing. No second tunnel, ramp, or barrier to scale, which would lead him to safety.

He thought about crossing the lines to the other platform, but after checking behind him, he concluded the woman would simply do the same and catch him on that side instead. With no other option, he started towards the signal boxes and network of tracks.

He stumbled along, his attention pinned to where his feet landed. A set of tracks to his right started to hiss. He took a fleeting look upward, expecting to see the arrival of a train, but the route ahead was clear. With a backwards glance, he checked the pathway behind him.

The roar of a diesel engine filled his ears. The jarring noise and appearance of the freighter made him stumble. Hot, oily breath burnt at the side of his face. His feet slipped on the bed of stones and, for one terrible moment, he thought he was about to be crushed. In the next second the train hurtled by, drawing up a wind current that snatched at Presley's sweat pants and threatened to pull him under. He battled to remain upright, slipping and sliding as he went. In a blur of bright chrome the last carriage whipped by, which left Presley gagging for a cleaner breath.

The woman shouted something from behind, but the roar of the passing train drowned out her words. It mattered not; Presley wouldn't have heeded them anyway. He carried on deeper into the maze of ironwork and sleepers. The stones underneath his feet were becoming fewer and fewer, now replaced by a continual stretch of train lines.

Here, the hiss of the lines sounded like a nest of snakes.

All about him the metalwork vibrated. Up ahead, he saw the towering front of an Amtrak passenger train. The distinctive colours of red, white and blue broke through the grey morning. Presley hopped onto the tracks to his right. The deafening blare of a horn scared him half to death. From behind came another engine, this one covered in dirt and grime, pulling a thousand tons of cargo and moving at just half the speed of the oncoming passenger train. He quickly stepped back into the first set of lines.

The cargo train rolled lazily by like a bloated serpent. Presley's left leg moved over to the next set of tracks. Before he had the chance to place his foot down, a bullet ricocheted just inches from his position. His foot stayed on this side of the tracks and, in the next second, a third train roared by – an express that must have been going at nearly 80 mph, which almost took his leg with it.

The noise from both trains, coming from either side, was deafening. Now, Presley found himself trapped in a forward moving corridor, with no way out. He stumbled and almost fell to his knees. This blur of movement was nauseating. His senses were overloading with both visual and audio input. He clamped his hands over his ears in an attempt to gather his wits.

He stopped, turned and looked back the other way. The woman was still coming, like him trapped between these moving masses of metal. She was staying close to the slow cargo freighter, putting as much distance as possible between her and the fast-moving express train.

She was yelling to him, pointing at him. He stood confused for a second before realising she was actually pointing to something beyond. He spun around to find the oncoming passenger train only three hundred yards away.

"Oh Jesus…" he moaned.

He tried to pick up his pace. It was no use. Even the slow cargo freighter was moving too fast for him to outrun. He tried to grab onto one of the carriages, but his fingers slipped.

He tried again. His fingers found purchase but he couldn't pull his ample frame up alongside.

Glancing up, he saw the passenger train was now just two hundred yards away, and coming fast.

He whined hysterically.

He had to go back.

His heels dug into the stones as he turned tail and quickly headed in the opposite direction. He tucked his head down and pushed himself to go as fast as he could. A voice came to him then, faint and indistinguishable. He looked up and was amazed to see the woman standing firm, with her arm out straight and weapon on view. She clearly wanted him to stop and give himself up.

Fuck that you crazy bitch, he thought. He reached into his jacket and drew the Derringer. And then, without really aiming, he simply fired the pistol. He heard a crack, even over the roaring trains, and was astonished when she fell to the ground, her weapon lost and her hands clutching at her thigh.

With his pathway cleared, he redoubled his efforts. He was closing on her fast. Yet the train behind him was gaining ground with every second. He chanced a look over his shoulder. His bladder opened. The passenger train was only fifty yards away.

He was never going to make it.

He almost clattered into a metal post, sidestepping it at the last moment, before grasping what it was he'd just passed.

A lane changer.

With a panic-stricken cry, he reached behind him, aiming with the Derringer. He fired his last shot, in an attempt to activate the lever. In his short life he'd only fired a weapon four times before, each time hitting his target. He had the Midas touch – right? How could he miss?

He didn't.

The bullet hit the lever dead centre. However, the mechanism was designed to work in a vertical direction, not horizontal, and with a brief shower of sparks, the handle maintained its position and the tracks stayed fixed in the same configuration.

In the next second the passenger train hit Presley full on. For just the briefest of moments, less than a millisecond really, he was pinned to the front of the engine, his arms and legs splayed out in a star-jump configuration, before his entire body exploded in a bright red shower of gore.

***

Detective Tyler watched in horror as Presley Perkins vanished from existence. The train bore down on her. Then, mercifully, with only a second to spare, the last carriage of the cargo freighter passed. She launched herself into the next tracks. The passenger train zipped by, leaving behind it a crimson cloud.

Tyler rolled onto her back and watched as the Amtrak Superliner cut its way through the station, before disappearing into the tunnel on the opposite side.

She scanned quickly around. For now, the network of tracks was empty. The cargo freighter and express train had both rolled out of sight. She held her hand against the leg injury, feeling hot blood leaking from between her fingers. She climbed awkwardly to her feet and hurriedly hobbled back towards the platform and the startled passengers who stood there.

Chapter Forty-Nine

Yurius stood over Joseph. The weapon levelled at his head. Joseph began to rise, climbing up slowly, making sure his body stayed between the Russian and his son. A deep well of anger – pure hatred – boiled to the surface.

What had this man done to his family? The agony they'd endured, both at Jake's taking and Eugene's loss. And for what? Nothing. Yurius's identity was already compromised. By now, almost every law enforcement agency on the planet would know who and what he was.

Joseph started to shake then. His hands formed into two solid fists and the muscles of his jaw clenched tightly. Rage was quickly taking over: a red mist started to form at the corners of his eyes. It was something he'd never experienced before – such a torment of emotion. This resentment felt alien to him. Still, Joseph remained the master of this dark feeling, as it boiled away in the pit of his stomach – just waiting to be released.

Yurius misunderstood Joseph's shaking as a symptom of fear. He smiled now, confident again in his authority.

Joseph reached carefully into his pocket.

"Hold it," Yurius ordered.

"I have something for you," Joseph replied.

The weapon drew closer, the cold metal almost touching Joseph's brow. "Too late for you," Yurius said.

Joseph maintained eye contact. His hand appeared holding the crumpled letter that Edward Jones had given him. "This is from an old friend of Viktor's."

The use of his brother's name forced Yurius to take a step back. Now, his eyes flicked to the letter, just briefly, before finding Joseph again.

Joseph brought the letter up for Yurius to see. "Edward Jones sends his regards."

Yurius's eyes widened. Then they quickly formed into tight, questioning slits. "What is this?"

"Take it," Joseph said. The letter had had some impact on the Russian, proving that Edward Jones' comment about it being his saviour could be true.

"Take it," Joseph said again, thrusting the letter outwards. Like a vampire in terror of a crucifix, Yurius reared back, bringing his free hand up in front of him, palm out, in a defensive gesture.

The Russian's confidence began to crumble in front of Joseph. His self-assured posture evaporated, leaving behind it an anxious, unsure mess. Yurius's hand began to reach out, intent on taking the letter. At the last moment it returned to his side.

"No more games," he said, trying to gather his wits. His arm tensed, and the weapon found its mark once again.

Joseph understood that this was it – his time of reckoning. Yurius had not taken the bait by reaching out for the letter, allowing Joseph to make a grab for the gun or throw a punch. Now he found himself staring down the barrel. He started to slip, first one way and then the next. His head bobbed back and forth. This made Yurius almost laugh out loud.

"Big Bear thinks he can dodge bullet?" he mocked.

Joseph just continued to slip from side to side.

It worked.

Yurius started to follow Joseph's movements, mirroring them, the weapon trying to follow his progress. Like a dancing Cobra, Joseph bobbed and weaved. He continued to slip and slide. Yurius allowed the gun to fall, moving from head height down towards his chest.

Then, with a flash, the barrel ignited with gunfire. Joseph

felt himself hit with the force of a truck. He was thrown back and the air exploded from his lungs. Another round slammed into him, forcing him through the air. He landed heavily. The oxygen in his lungs exited in a violent burst.

He heard a voice cry out from a faraway distance: Carter's, maybe?

His eyes fluttered and then something appeared above him. It blocked out the weak light of the sun.

Yurius fired again and the darkness around Joseph Ruebins flooded in, covering him in a flood of liquid shadows.

***

Carter skidded to a halt. Which way now? He had his police shield out on view, folded outwards and hanging from his breast pocket. It gave him immediate credibility, and nearby pedestrians were pointing directions out to him, help being offered without his asking for it; the savvy commuters understanding that two men chasing each other was not your average morning's activity – not even for New York City.

A businesswoman came towards him. "They went that way," she said, raising her arm and using her briefcase to point towards a narrow alleyway.

"Thanks," Carter replied, quickly heading into the tight maze of brickwork.

He stumbled along, breathing heavily, almost falling over a trashcan that lay in his way. The brick passageway opened out to reveal a parking lot. There was just one vehicle in the lot, and two men stood close to it.

Carter watched in horror as the Russian fired his weapon. The blast reverberated around the parking area. Joseph's head rocked back and he back-pedalled, with his arms spinning full circle. Another shot threw him back and this time he lost his footing. The Russian fired again, stepping over Joseph and firing at point-blank range. Joseph jolted

278

violently as the bullet ripped into him.

"NOOO!" Carter yelled.

The Russian looked up. He fired without pause – two shots almost finding their mark, even from this distance.

Carter dropped to one knee.

The killer leaned forwards to snatch something out of Joseph's hand. He fired another shot at the detective from this position, and then made towards the car.

Carter managed to get two shots off before the driver's door slammed shut.

With a screech of rubber the Ford took off.

Carter tried to memorise the number-plate. The car disappeared within a matter of seconds. Silence fell and the two figures lay still. He edged closer. Did he want to see what lay there? No, absolutely not. Still, his professionalism guided him towards the two bodies. Legs that seemed to be wading against running water took him closer.

Joseph Ruebins lay rigid, arms and legs splayed out at odd angles. His son lay curled up in a foetal position. Both looked like sculptures, as if they'd been chiselled from the rock beneath Carter's feet.

The detective concentrated on the boy. The condition of the boy was unknown. He passed Joseph, for now, forcing himself to look away.

Hot bile rose in his throat. He gulped it back, understanding that this was likely to become another crime scene, another bloodbath, and not a place for him to contaminate.

Treading carefully, subconsciously looking for spent casings or other evidence, he made his way towards Jake.

"Jake?" Carter whispered quietly, not wanting to disturb the dead.

Nothing. Not a sound. He stepped closer. The boy's face came into view. Jake looked as if he were sleeping soundly.

Dead peaceful.

Chapter Fifty

Joseph found himself once again in the empty void, where silence ruled absolute. He tried to look around, but the darkness was everywhere. He waited, half expecting the two rifts to open up, spewing forth the musical lines, notes and symbols. Nothing happened. No bright tears in the seamless dark blanket, no clash of guitars – nothing.

He panicked then.

Was this it?

The end!

Although no air could possibly be found in such a barren place, Joseph felt himself gasping for breath. His lungs hitched as he tried to force oxygen into them. A thought burst into his mind: The old man, Edward Jones' father, lying at his side, desperately trying to draw a breath. Had Henry Jones come here to rest? Joseph hoped not. This was nowhere to be. What of the perpetual light that was supposed to shine down on God's dearly departed children?

Fear consumed him then – blind terror, which twisted his heart into tight knots.

Was Jake here, lonely and lost?

God no!

Joseph forced himself to look around again. He imagined himself turning his head, first to look one way, and then the other. Now, he could just about make out the vaguest suggestion of outlines.

Something with hard edges lay to his right. A square-shaped 'something' that had slightly more density about it hovered there. A doorway, Joseph noted. No – wait, not a doorway, but a garage shutter. The darkness gave way to detail, which cut slivers of light into the void.

What was this?

A grating noise filled the air. The shutter moved slightly. The squeal of metal rubbing against metal came again, and a flare of blinding light filled the gap at the bottom. Fingers appeared then, small digits, which wrapped themselves around the bottom of the shutter.

The light grew by another few inches, and then stopped suddenly. A small head appeared.

Jake.

"Dad," Jake called. "Hurry..!"

Joseph took a step closer, now in possession of a solid state and a platform to walk upon. As he drew closer the shutter began to take on more definition. The metal panels that formed the doorway became more solid, glinting with a metallic sheen. The shutter was now fixed within a building and, as Joseph came even closer, the garage swelled out into a full-sized house.

His house, he realised, instantly.

"Jake," he called.

"Dad," Jake replied. His little hand appeared, and he used it to wave his father over to him. "Hurry," he said again.

"What is it?" Joseph asked, bending low to see Jake's worried looking face.

"Mom," Jake said.

"What?"

"Hurry, mom needs you."

"Where is she?"

"Upstairs. The thing is trying to take her…"

"Thing?"

"The bad thing," Jake said, tears appearing at both corners of his eyes.

Joseph reached out to take Jake's hand. "What bad

thing?"

Jake swallowed deeply. "Mom's trapped and the dark thing wants her."

Joseph had no idea what his son was saying, but the boy's panic was obvious. He took a quick step back, surveying the house. He understood then that this wasn't an exact replica of his home; no doors or windows could be seen on either of the two levels.

"Stand back," he ordered.

Jake's head disappeared out of view.

Joseph wrapped his thick fingers underneath the shutter's edge. He took a deep breath, now able to fill his lungs, and then heaved with all his might. A sharp squeal of protest filled his ears. He tried again, but the shutter remained tight.

He looked up to see if something blocked the shutter at the top, and found that the metalwork had a distinctive crease running down the front.

He remembered then how this had come to be. The basketball game that he and Jake had been playing only weeks earlier.

His head.

His stupid, thick head had bent it out of shape.

A noise came to him then, a desperate shout for help.

"Marianna!" he called.

Her voice came again, desperate and scared.

Joseph dropped lower, bringing himself almost to floor level. He pushed himself into the small gap the shutter had to offer. Beyond the doorway, darkness had now filled every inch of space.

"Jake?" he called, fearful that the 'thing' had taken him too.

"Dad," Jake said, reappearing at the gap. Fear was still visible in his face, but less so now that his father was nearby.

"Hurry, Dad," Jake said.

Joseph concentrated on working his fingers underneath the shutter. He tensed and then heaved with all his might.

The squeal of metal came again, and the barrier held firm.

Jake brought his head as close to Joseph's as he could. "MAN OF STEEL."

"What..?" Joseph asked.

"Remember – Dad. You're the MAN OF STEEL."

Joseph looked deep into Jake's eyes. He found such a mixture of emotion there that its power almost knocked him to the ground. Pride was in the boy's eyes, a deep understanding that Joseph had never seen or thought his son was capable of. Joseph almost burst into tears then, understanding that this admiration was aimed at him. Jake not only loved his father, but also revered him. Fear was evident too. Jake reached out and touched his father's arm. A sudden surge of panic filled Joseph to his core. Whatever had Jake spooked had now been transferred to Joseph. Finally, grim determination and belief shone from the young boy's eyes. At that moment, Joseph knew, without doubt, that his son would grow to be a man who valued integrity and morality in equal measure. They were qualities that Joseph wanted to see for himself – wanted to experience his son's rise into adulthood with his own eyes.

Joseph nodded. "MAN OF STEEL."

"Yes, Dad. MAN OF STEEL."

Joseph looked away from his son, concentrating on the barrier between him and Marianna. He took a huge breath and then attacked the shutter with everything he had. The thing was jammed tight, forcing Joseph to find strength he'd thought had long abandoned him. His arms bulged with effort and a great roar burst from his lips.

The shutter moved an inch.

Joseph bent his back, pulling with all his might. Another inch was gained. Marianna's plea was clear, coming through the gap loud and distinct.

"Don't leave me, Joseph," she was pleading.

Joseph forced the barrier to rise a foot higher. Now, he was able to place both shoulders underneath the shutter's edge. He felt the sharpness of the metal cutting into the muscles around his shoulders and neck. No matter – he ignored the agony and redoubled his efforts. He planted his arms firm and then began to push upwards, as if doing a push-up. As the shutter rose, the light inside the garage began to grow, and with each inch gained it intensified. Joseph began to make out individual items.

The winter tools that he and Jake had used to shovel away snow were piled untidily in the centre of the floor. Hand tools that Joseph had never used, and probably never would, hung shiny and new from pegs that displayed each one in a careful arrangement of size and shape. Their modest Sedan was parked to one side, rust taking hold around the wheel-arches and patches of paintwork scraped down to the metal – a symptom of Joseph's bad parking. A medicine ball, brown and lumpy, lay in one corner, looking like a ripe pumpkin, shadows casting a macabre face across its surface. Another ball had bounced underneath a worktable: Jake's basketball.

Joseph acknowledged then that these things – objects that had no real value – were the simple components of his life: the things that bound his family as one. Their car, unspectacular in its appearance, had taken them to many places of enjoyment: the zoo, picnics in summer, ball games and a thousand other places that made up the jigsaw of their life – their time spent together.

Then, in the next second, something dark uncoiled from Joseph's gut. Rage thrashed its way free. Joseph swelled with hatred and anger: how dare someone – something, anything, *threaten his family! He pushed against the shutter with a force unmatched.*

"MAN OF STEEL!" he roared.

A single high-pitched squeal sounded, and then the shutter gave way, clamouring noisily against the roof of the garage.

In the next second Joseph was up and running. He barrelled into the garage and barged his way through the connecting doorway. His living room came into view.

Everything looked as it should have – no twisting of realities in this alternate universe. Joseph raced across the room to reach the base of the stairs. Darkness filled the landing above.

"Joseph..!" Marianna screamed.

He hit the stairs three at a time, reaching the landing in just four long strides. Instinct guided him directly to their bedroom. There, he found the door shut tight. He wasted no time trying to open it conventionally. Instead, he reared back before kicking it open with his boot. The door flew off its hinges and disappeared into darkness. Joseph stepped inside.

Marianna was laid out on the bed. Something terrifying hung above her. A dark monstrosity, with a huge body and long tendrils for arms, hooked barbs at their ends, was suspended above her. Joseph watched as she tried to slip from the bed. With the snap of a bullwhip, one of the arms lashed out. She twisted away and the hook missed her by mere inches.

"Marianna!" Joseph cried out.

She turned towards him, her eyes full of fear. The 'thing' scuttled around, using its hooked arms to manoeuvre. The hideous face of Yurius fixed on Joseph, peering down on him with blood-red eyes. The body split at the centre, as a gaping mouth opened to reveal rows of razor-sharp teeth.

Joseph took a faltering step back. The 'thing' grinned, and the gesture was both terrifying and ghastly.

"Big Bear..." the 'thing' said, in a rasping wet hiss.

Joseph regained his composure. "Get away from her, you son-of-a-bitch!"

Yurius's mouth opened even wider and a white, ulcerated tongue rolled out. The tip of the organ flicked towards him. Sickened, Joseph ducked out of the way. He maintained his momentum and reached the centre of the room.

"Joseph," Marianna said.

"I'm here," he announced, climbing up beside her.

The thing had turned back towards them. Now so close,

Joseph could smell the putrid stench of death coming from the thing's open maw. The cavity opened wider, and Joseph caught a glimpse of something rotten within. Henry Jones, his face bloated and white, hung at the back of the thing's throat.

The old man's eyes were open, white like dead fish eyes, and they were staring towards him. Joseph squeezed his eyelids shut.

"Hold on," Joseph ordered. He felt Marianna's arms cut into him. Joseph waited for an opening. The hooks swept from one side of the room to the other. Occasionally, they caught against the walls or ceiling, and as they did, the very fabric of existence ripped open to reveal inky-black darkness beyond.

Joseph saw his chance.

The flailing tentacles split to find purchase in the ceiling. Barbs dug deep, and a twisting of worms fell from the resultant tears.

With Marianna clinging to his back, Joseph leapt to his feet. He catapulted over the writhing worms, his boots squelching down on a few, and dashed towards the open doorway.

A barb lashed out to catch Joseph's shoulder. He gritted his teeth and pushed on. His next step took him outside. Now on the landing, he moved towards the stairs. But the hook held him back. He twisted his head and found the barb buried deep into the flesh of his right shoulder. He couldn't feel any pain, and so dragged both him and Marianna away from the bedroom. His skin split to reveal an open wound. He yanked harder, and the hook pulled clear in a tearing of flesh.

Free now, he bounded towards the stairs. From behind came a wail of anger and resentment. Joseph ducked his head down in an attempt to shield his ears from the terrible moaning. He took the stairs blindly, leaping down them in just three strides, and in the next second he arrived back in the living room.

He froze.

Jake was over by the door that connected the main house to the garage. Behind him, with a lethal blade in hand, stood the young police officer, Gore. A river of blood ran freely from the wound in Gore's neck. Blood gushed out over his uniform to gather in a thick pool around his boots. One of Gore's hands had Jake by a handful of hair, while the other held the serrated blade at the young boy's throat.

Gore's eyes were like Henry Jones' covered by milky films. They focused on Joseph. "Big Bear..." Gore rasped, in a parody of the Russian killer. Joseph just stood there, immobilised by fear. The blade at Jake's throat glinted with intent. Suddenly, from above them, came a mighty crash of thunder. The plaster split and a tentacle burst from a hole. Gore's mouth opened in a silent scream.

The barbed tentacle wrapped itself around the officer's neck, squeezing as tightly as an Anaconda. Gore's milky-white eyes bulged outwards. The blade slipped from his fingers and then he was pulled from his feet and swept up towards the open ceiling. Joseph reached out to snag Jake before he was taken along with the officer. The boy lost a handful of his scalp, Gore's bleached fingers holding onto a dark tuft of hair. Not waiting to see what terrible fate befell Gore, Joseph tucked his son under one arm and barged into the garage. With Marianna on his back and Jake under his arm, Joseph hit the shutter head-on, his shoulder ramming it with a deafening clatter.

And, in the next second, he was back in the light.

***

Carter hammered against Joseph's chest again, his fist now numb from his repeated attempts. Below his fist, Joseph lay grey and motionless. Carter leaned over to breathe into Joseph's mouth, filling his lungs, forcing his chest to rise.

"C'mon – goddamn you!" he cursed.

Joseph's shirt had been ripped away to expose his chest. Three angry bruises had turned his dark skin to deepest black. Two were spreading out around his abdomen, growing with every minute; the third, directly over his heart, black and circular, like an extra nipple. Tossed to one side lay the bullet-proof vest that he'd been wearing – something Detective Tyler had insisted he use.

The third bullet – the one that Yurius had fired whilst standing over Joseph – had stopped his heart dead. Carter understood this without question. He could find no pulse. No wisp of breath. He hammered Joseph's chest again in an attempt to restart his heart. Joseph lay there, limp and lifeless.

"C'mon Joseph – work with me," Carter said.

The detective returned to Joseph's mouth. He filled his lungs again, and then hit him with his fist directly over the breastbone.

A gasp came from Joseph. Then a clicking noise sounded from somewhere at the back of his throat. His eyes opened and he looked around with terror before the face above came into focus.

"Jake?" he croaked. "Did I get him out?"

Carter looked puzzled for a second. Of course, he thought then. Out of the car – the trunk – that's what he meant.

"Yes, Joseph, you got him out."

Joseph's eyes swam under a film of tears. "Is he alive?"

Carter took Joseph's hand and said, "Yes, Joseph, he's alive…"

Chapter Fifty-One

Joseph was back in the hospital room. This time, though, he was here as a concerned visitor – not the patient. Jake occupied the bed, his small face poking out from above the sheet. Sitting opposite him was Marianna. She looked away from Jake and fixed Joseph with her deep brown eyes.

"I love you," she said, softly. Fresh tears slipped down her cheeks.

"Hey," Joseph soothed. He reached over Jake to take her hand. "We're all safe now. Jake's fine, and I'm gonna be okay."

She nodded. Earlier, one of the other detectives had brought her here, and they'd arrived outside the main foyer in time to meet the ambulance. Both Joseph and Carter had stepped out; concern etched into their features and they had helped lower the gantry before rushing Jake inside.

After a couple of basic tests Doctor Greenwood had explained that a sedative had been used on Jake, a simple anaesthetic that would soon work itself out of the boy's bloodstream. Joseph and Marianna had collapsed into each others arms, weeping with relief.

Now, they were simply waiting it out.

The door to the room opened slightly and Detective Carter popped his head inside.

"Joseph, can I have a word?" he asked quietly.

Marianna looked back concerned.

Carter's hand rose. "Nothing to worry about," he added quickly.

Joseph stood. He bent over Jake to kiss his forehead. Then

he allowed his fingers to brush gently over Marianna's cheek. "I'll be back shortly."

Marianna smiled. "Don't be long."

"I won't." He turned away from them and slipped outside.

In the hallway, Carter's face went from concern to elation instantly. His eyes were on fire, burning with excitement. "Got a copy!" he declared, holding up the *New York Times*.

"Front cover!" Joseph said.

Carter spun full circle looking for a suitable place to rest the paper, finally settling on the chair that the uniformed officer had used, and spread it out over his lap. In the right-hand corner of the first page, an article started with the headline: *Russian Mafia Supergrass Found Slaughtered!*

Carter took a moment to read the paragraph of text. The article continued on page 5, but the detective simply folded the paper in half before placing it at his feet.

"I'll be damned," he said, shaking his head. "This is impossible."

"It's there in black and white," Joseph replied.

"I know – but … still."

They stared at each other, both hoping the other could offer an explanation – anything that would shine some light on the baffling development that had transpired. The real Edward Jones had been murdered the day earlier, leaving both Joseph and Carter unable to guess who the guy posing as Jones really was.

Carter looked towards both ends of the corridor. A pair of armed cops could be seen at each.

He said, "I don't know what to believe. First Henry Jones, then you and Jake, plus Presley Perkins, and now the FBI..?"

"FBI?"

Carter looked concerned. "They had us all duped – that's for sure. Thing is, they all checked out. Captain Mendoza ran their IDs personally. All involved were either registered FBI or FSB agents – and all actively working in the field."

"Can't the real Bureau arrest them?" Joseph asked.

Carter smiled ruefully. "They're all dead."

"What?" Joseph gawped.

"They were using IDs taken from dead agents – recently dead agents. A simple click of a button and it would be easy to reactivate an agent, giving credibility to those masquerading as one."

"Who would have access to such a thing?"

"Someone seriously connected," Carter responded.

Joseph shook his head. "What kind of motives must someone have to risk taking such a chance?"

"Strong, powerful ones," Carter replied.

Joseph grunted a short concurrence. "What about the letter?"

The detective shrugged. "I guess that's for Viktor to worry about. Not us."

"Yeah – I guess you're right." Joseph felt uneasy still, unsure if it was right to feel safe now, or remain on guard. He huffed slightly, almost in defeat, deciding that he would have to rely on those around him to protect both him and his family. "Tyler? How's she doing?" he asked finally.

"She's fine. Took one in the leg – it's just a scratch really. Doc says she'll be up and about in no time at all."

"And you?" Joseph asked.

"Me?"

"Yeah – how are you holding up?"

Carter shuffled awkwardly for a second, looking down at his feet, uncomfortable at being on the end of Joseph's curiosity.

"I'm fine," he mumbled finally.

"C'mon Detective, level with me."

The detective offered him a weary sigh. "Guess justice was served – one way or another."

"So what are you gonna do now?" Joseph asked, understanding that Carter's life had been on hold for the last three months.

"Get busy living, I guess," Carter said. "Perkins got his

just deserts. Maybe now I can start grieving Billy's loss. Take some time off, even."

Joseph reached out to lay his hand on Carter's shoulder. "My door is always open. You want to talk some – you come over anytime. I got plenty of time on my hands, now that I'm retired. Could use the company, too."

Carter nodded with gratitude. "Thanks. I will."

"Hey," Joseph began, "we ain't out of the water just yet."

"Viktor and Yurius?"

"Yeah."

The detective's face clouded over. "Yeah – we still need to tread with caution. At least until the real FEDs have brought them in."

"You think they got Edward Jones' letter?" Joseph asked.

"Edward Jones?"

"Whoever *he* may have been?" Joseph said.

"Possibly…" Carter replied.

"You think they'll like what they find inside?"

"Possibly not." Carter concluded.

They stood silent for a moment, wondering what ramifications the mysterious letter may have on the Russian criminal kingpin and his hitman brother. Finally, Joseph took the detective's hand. He shook it gently. "Thank you, Thomas. For everything."

Carter was momentarily lost for words. Then, with a slight nod, he said, "For everything a reason – I guess."

Joseph smiled slightly. He couldn't argue that nothing good had come from this, even with the terrible loss of his old friend and coach, Profit. Two killers had been taken off the streets today, with two more to follow shortly, in Viktor and Yurius – if they had not already met their fates. And now, although Carter had many months of sadness still ahead of him, he could finally begin the grieving process, and then, just maybe, rejoin the rest of the living.

"For everything a reason," Joseph repeated, finally understanding.

The detective nodded, and then slipped past Joseph, ready to continue with his investigation, eager to bring an end to this whole affair.

Joseph watched him go. As the detective rounded the corner, the starched lab coat of Doctor Greenwood replaced him. The physician looked excited and was taking long strides to reach room 2b. He was carrying a thin folder underneath his arm. He looked up to see Joseph waiting for him.

Greenwood broke into a pleased smile. "Mr. Ruebins, I have great news!" He held up the folder and said, "Got your results back from the MRI scan…"

Chapter Fifty-Two

Viktor checked the time again. He fidgeted awkwardly, now becoming worried about the morning's events. Yurius's call had been abruptly cut off, and Pyotr Krylov had not called to tell him what had happened. The bank of TV screens at his side flashed hypnotically, the sound down to its lowest, and mute faces talked – conspired – together in silent whispers. Even Nikolay could not be found at his normal place of work. Viktor had the whole place to himself. And he didn't like it one bit.

A loud hammering from the rear of the building jolted him almost out of his skin. He jumped to his feet, turning towards the noise, and then back to the corridor that led to the main doorway.

"Nikolay..!" he called, checking to see if the old doorman was around.

No reply came.

The *thump, thump* for attention came again.

Viktor pulled the pistol from his waistband. The weapon was identical to Dirty Harry's – a gleaming .44 Magnum – and tipped downwards slightly, due to Viktor's inability to hold it correctly.

"*Nikolay...*" he called again, but in a forced whisper this time. Now, he was fearful of revealing his presence.

The old Russian was nowhere to be seen. Viktor checked the time. 9:45 a.m. He wasn't expecting any deliveries, and it was too early for his working girls to arrive. The thumping continued, and Viktor's heart beat harder with every rap.

He moved towards the rear, his Magnum weighing heavily in his hand. He stopped at the doorway. A thin shaft of light, like a laser beam, shone from the eyehole. Viktor moved forward to look outside. He stopped. What if someone was standing outside just waiting for the eyehole to blink out? Ready to fire into the door at point-blank range. He hesitated then.

"Viktor!" someone called.

Yurius, the Russian boss realised.

"Let me in," Yurius demanded.

Viktor swapped the Magnum to his other hand, then reached out to slide the heavy-duty deadbolt free. He pulled the door open to find his brother standing before him. Yurius looked uncharacteristically shaken.

"What?" Viktor asked.

Yurius pushed his way inside. He headed quickly into the main room. Viktor slammed the door shut, fixed the bolt back in place, and then followed his brother.

Yurius was pacing up and down. He turned, opened his mouth to speak, shook his head, and then sat heavily on the sofa.

Viktor walked around to stand before his brother. "What happened? I haven't heard from Krylov, yet. Where is he?"

Yurius sighed. "He didn't make it."

"Make what?"

"You know – *dead.*"

"What?"

"Not coming back alive."

Viktor seemed as if he was going to pass out. His shoulders dropped and he looked deflated. "How..?"

"He took one in the head," Yurius explained.

Viktor just gawped back. "Uh?"

The younger brother stood. "He's dead – dead as a dodo."

"What happened?" Viktor asked, swapping places with his brother. Now, Viktor sat on the sofa, leaning forwards, his face expectant.

"Everything went to hell. Heard it on the police scanner. They killed Krylov and then chased down Perkins on the train tracks. Guy definitely got a one-way ticket out of here."

"What of Ruebins – you tied up loose end?"

For the first time since his arrival, Yurius broke into a slight grin. He nodded, and said, "Put three into him, last one at point-blank range into his heart."

"So this business is finished then? Both Ruebins and Perkins are out of the picture. Okay, losing Krylov is unfortunate, but we can handle that. So what has you so spooked, Yurius?"

Yurius stood still. Fear had taken up residence on his features. "This," he said, withdrawing the letter.

"What is that?" Viktor quizzed.

"I do not know."

Viktor stood again. The letter looked like any other. Simple envelope, brown and sealed, and its thickness hinted at just a single sheet inside. "Where did that come from?"

"Ruebins."

Viktor's hand stopped short, his fingers just a few inches from taking the letter. "Ruebins?" He looked toward his brother for an explanation.

Yurius didn't have one. He stepped a little closer and pushed the envelope into Viktor's hand. The Russian boss took the offering, cautiously, and then seated himself back down.

"What could this be?" he asked himself, turning the letter over. There was no address, name, postal stamp, or other distinguishable markings written anywhere on its surface. "You think they're trying to plant evidence?" he asked, turning his attention away from the letter.

Again, Yurius shrugged. "Strange, if you ask me. I was just about to kill him, and he pulled that from his pocket and started telling me to take it."

"It would be entrapment if they tried to plant something,"

Viktor stated.

"Open it."

Viktor nodded. Just a simple letter, right? What harm could a letter do anyway? He pushed his thumb underneath one corner and then ran it along the length of the envelope. The flap came away in a tattered and torn mess.

Viktor peered inside. A single sheet of folded paper was tucked inside, blank white and offering no hint of its purpose. Viktor paused. Should he go get a pair of gloves or tweezers, or something to help him extract the letter? Yurius drew nearer, expectant, and the Russian boss felt his brother's eagerness. Viktor took a breath and then simply pulled the sheet of paper free.

He turned it over in his hand to examine each side: Blank both front and back.

"Open it," Yurius pushed.

Viktor nodded. He pulled the sheet open using delicate fingers. No text or pictures came into view. Just a small amount of white powder had gathered within the fold that split the sheet into two halves.

Cocaine.

"Is this a joke?" Viktor quizzed, looking towards his brother.

Yurius shook his head. "That's what Big Bear gave me. Insisted I take it."

A frown creased Viktor's brow. Were the authorities seriously trying to plant evidence? What good would that do? Curious now, he licked the tip of his finger and dabbed at the small pile of powder. The tip of his finger came away with a speck of residue fixed to it. Yurius leaned closer. His brother licked tentatively at the white substance. Viktor's face scrunched tightly in a show of disgust. He shook his head and then sneezed violently, blowing the powder off the paper, turning it into a cloud of white dust.

Yurius caught most of it in his lungs. He expected the smell and taste of ammonia, clear indication of cocaine powder, but his chest went tight and the back of his throat contracted instantly. He retched and his eyes filled with tears.

Viktor sneezed again and, as he drew a deep breath, he too inhaled the dispersing cloud. He had just enough time to register pain, before his body went into spasms.

The strychnine, the most deadly toxin known to man, filled his lungs and was then instantly absorbed into the bloodstream. It took just seconds for the poison to reach his brain, where the toxin shut down all the nerve signals to his muscles. His arms and legs turned rigid, back arching off the sofa, and his face turned into a ghastly mask of agony. Jaw muscles clenched together in a cast-iron grin.

The Russian's brother fell to the floor, his body twisting itself into a horrible contortion, his back bent all the way until his head touched the heels of his shoes. A desperate clucking noise left his throat.

Viktor began to choke. He tried to fill his lungs with air, but they refused to obey his command. Instead, he slipped sideways off the sofa to join his brother on the floor. There, they bucked and thrashed, until the strychnine stopped all respiratory input, leaving them brain dead within minutes of each other. The strychnine fell gently to the floor like a light fluttering of winter snow.

In an hour or so, an anonymous call would notify the authorities of the two bodies, warning of the potential dangers. And, before the two brothers had grown cold, a team of experts wearing biosuits would enter to find the pair locked together in rigid embrace.

Chapter Fifty-Three

Cold wind snapped at ankles. The hems of pant legs flapped about like the fluttering of flags. A group of bent figures made their way towards the stationary aircraft. The small private airfield was deserted except for this small group and the LearJet. The first member reached the short flight of steps that led to the cabin. He pulled himself inside as the rest gathered around the foot of the steps. The passenger reappeared a moment later. With a wave of his hand he beckoned for the rest to board.

Like their comrade, the next three to enter all wore dark blue suits. And even though the sky was clouded over, dark sunglasses hid their eyes. The fifth member to board was dressed in simple casual clothes, his head bowed submissively to the harsh winds that tore across the airstrip. He pulled himself to the top of the stairs before turning to look back. He stood poised for a second, looking out at the panoramic view. He took a few moments, contemplating recent events, scanning the grey horizon. Finally, he nodded to the two who remained, before disappearing inside. They ascended the steps, paused momentarily to look about them, and then reeled in the short retractable steps.

The whir of engine noise began. Within seconds it had grown to a deafening roar. The aircraft rolled onto the blacktop. More power was added to the twin engines, the roar growing quickly towards an ear-piercing scream. Now, as if freed from a catapult, the jet raced away, tearing down the runway. The plane took to the skies, quickly cutting towards the heavy clouds above. In a matter of seconds the jet had disappeared, ready to deliver its cargo back across the Atlantic Ocean.

Nikolay unbuckled his belt. He turned towards the window and gazed at the thick clouds below him. They rolled by like the white surf of crashing waves. He wiped at his brow and his palm came away with a layer of sweat.

The guy sitting opposite him laughed gently. "Not one for flying, Nikolay?" he said, in a flat American accent. His eyes were soft and filled with compassion and understanding.

The old man grimaced slightly. "It's been a while."

"Too long," replied his companion, smiling.

Nikolay nodded. He'd worked in New York for almost ten years, not once making the return trip home. Yet, in just fourteen hours, he'd feel the soil of his homeland beneath his feet.

The guy opposite leaned forward to pat Nikolay's hand. "It's good to have you back," he said.

The old man nodded again. It would be good to be back. He looked his companion in the eye. "What of Viktor?"

The guy opposite offered a dismissive wave of his hand. "Taken care of. Not to worry, Nikolay. Business is back in order."

"And the FBI and FSB?"

The guy shrugged. "Those not committed to our homeland still pose a threat. But we must remain one step ahead. As always."

"As always…" Nikolay echoed.

They were interrupted by one of the other passengers, who almost filled the aisle with his bulk. The bite of the wind had turned scar tissue, which ran from nose to lip, into a bolt of white lightning. Agent Vitos spoke to Nikolay's companion in a thick Slavic accent. "We will land in Moscow in fourteen hours. You need anything, Boss?"

Nikolay's companion opened his mouth to speak. He paused for a second, as his face underwent a drastic transformation. The gentle demeanour that had been Edward Jones evaporated instantly and the soft, sensitive eyes turned hard. He coughed heavily, as if trying to shift something that was lodged at the back of his throat.

The old man shifted slightly in his seat. This was the real boss he'd left behind over a decade ago: cold and calculating, with the heart of a poisonous snake.

"Nothing needed, Comrade," Sergei Mikhailov said, in his native tongue.

The heavy nodded and then quickly returned to his seat.

Sergei Mikhailov turned his attention outside. He sighed wistfully. He'd had a pleasant and productive trip. He'd been busy, sorting out first the Colombians and then, more importantly, Viktor and his pet rat. Still, he hadn't been overseas for quite some time and the change had done him good. He felt invigorated and was now looking forward to his return home.

Nevertheless, he'd been forced to use every help available. His contact at the Bureau had had to first get him manpower, pulling a few agents from the field and assigning them directly to Sergei. These agents had come willingly, ready to help their homeland, eager to prove that their 'repatriation' had not been wasted.

Luck had played its part, too. They had intercepted Edward Jones' call to his father, and then traced it to the accountant's place of hiding. Now, there would be no trial. The authority's star witness had been silenced once and for all.

Viktor had been Sergei's prime reason for coming. Now, that problem had been resolved, with the added bonus of ridding the world of Viktor's uncontrollable brother, Yurius. It was just a shame Sergei had not got to Viktor before innocents like Henry Jones and Joseph Ruebins had been involved. Still, these innocents had played their part in helping Sergei achieve his objective. And now, thanks to their unwitting intervention, business was back to normal.

Sergei's smile widened slightly as he remembered a song he'd heard the day before. It had been played out over the radio during the return trip from silencing the accountant.

Sergei Mikhailov grinned happily, catching Nikolay's attention. The Russian Mafia boss opened his mouth and sang…

"…Back in the U-S-S-R!"